MONSTERS IN SPAAAACE!

MICHAEL CIESLAK

Dragon's Roost Press

CONTENTS

INTRODUCTION

2019
The 50th anniversary of the Apollo 11 Lunar Mission.
The 40th anniversary of the classic horror film Alien.
One year after the proposal of the US Space Force.
How could we not create a collection of space themed horror?

We've explored loneliness, isolation, and solitude in our first anthology. We Put the Love Back in Lovecraft in our second anthology. We explored the creatures of cryptozoology in our recent pair of anthologies. Now we will go where all good series eventually go...

...to space.

Anyone who knows the history of Dragon's Roost Press knows that our anthologies have given us the opportunity to explore some of our favorite topics. All right, so loneliness and isolation may not be favorites, but *Desolation: 21 Tales for Tails* gave us the opportunity to help our favorite canine rescue organization. We've been long time fans of the Cthulhu mythos. Cryptozoology and cryptids in general have fascinated us since childhood.

So has science fiction and the exploration of space.

The desire to leave the planet and explore the stars has been with us all our lives. It was there before our love of monsters and horror. In fact, our Editor in Chief once seriously entertained the idea of becoming an astronaut (then he learned how much math was involved). Still, that desire to feel weightlessness, to rocket beyond the reaches of Earth's gravity and discover what lay out beyond the black has never left us.

Jason, the Leprechaun, the Cenobites, even the Critters ended up going (back) into space. We decided it was time to give some other monsters that same chance.

Earlier this year we started accepting submissions for an anthology featuring classic monsters with the stories set in space. You hold that anthology in your hands. We have collected 16 stories and one poem that we think you are really going to enjoy.

And by enjoy we mean scare the space suit off of you.

NANA

BY SARAH HANS

You sit with your feet dangling in the black water, kicking at a plastic bottle, when the latest drop crashes to the beach. The delivery ship jets away across the gray sky, and you're up and running like a dozen other kids, leaping over old tires and bounding across mounds of reeking refuse. A fresh drop means unpicked treasures, and whoever gets there first will have first choice.

You scale the mountain of garbage and wade through knee-high detritus searching for a prize. There's no competition among the children, not like there is between adults. You're not after items to trade or build, you're after items to collect. You call to Arin to see the holographic baseball card you found wedged between two glass bottles. It's sticky and one he already has, but duplicates are more exciting than nothing. You bring Rissa an action figure to add to her collection. The legs are missing, but she's delighted. She can always splice it together with a torso and a random head to create a finished hero.

"We're gonna throw stuff down the whirlpool later, if you want to come," Rissa offers.

You shrug. You desperately want to go, but you have responsibilities now that you're old enough to contribute to the household.

"I have to look for books later, for Mother. The whirlpool is for little kids, anyway."

Rissa narrows her eyes at you and then scurries away.

Afternoon humidity sets in and most of the other kids drift away to enjoy their finds. Your energy wanes in the heat, and the pile of fresh trash starts to stink. Your stomach aches, ready for a midday meal. You turn to climb down the pile and something slick slides out from under your foot and you're thrown off balance. You fall, sliding and rolling down the incline, and the trash heap shifts around you. Your heart hammers when you slide to a stop halfway down, awaiting an avalanche, certain that you're about to meet the same end as so many pickers before you, buried beneath a mountain of steaming garbage.

The trash settles and you breathe a sigh of relief. As you scramble to your feet, ready to inch your way carefully home, something catches your eye, something fabric, stained but originally flesh-colored. You grab for it, excitedly at first, and then more cautiously, slowly pulling your treasure from the mound so as not to disturb it again.

The object is a doll. She is made of beige fabric, now stained a filthy gray, the same color as the sludge water that taints everything here. Her eyes were once buttons, but they went missing long ago, leaving behind only two pieces of discolored brown felt. Her mouth is stitched on in a wide smile that, combined with the missing eyes, gives the impression of a grimace. Her hair is little more than a few frayed strands of yarn. She's clothed in a dress that might once have been lavender with tiny purple flowers, and her shoes have been painted on, still glossy and black.

She's exactly the treasure you hoped to find. You clutch her to your chest and rush home, heedless of the dangers in the sliding garbage beneath your bare feet.

You climb the ladder to your house with the doll tucked under your arm. You and your mother live in a house built on stilts to protect it from the dangerous tides that threaten to sweep the whole community away during the monsoon season. Your house is not the largest, but you have no brothers and sisters with whom you must share your tiny bedroom, so there's no one to resent your doll collection. You straighten the new doll's dress and present her to the others, arrayed all over your bedroom. In your collection there are mostly baby dolls and a few fashion dolls, as their plastic shells are the most likely to survive decay. Most are naked, many are missing limbs or eyes, others are merely watchful heads without bodies to support them. But you know all their names, all their personalities, their likes and dislikes, and which dolls get along with which others.

"This is...Nana," you announce, holding up the new doll so each of the others can get a good look. "I expect you all to be on your best behavior." The room is crowded, but you find a spot on the mattress where you can place the newest addition to your collection. Nana grimaces up at you.

The midday meal is shrimp dredged up from the bottom of the ocean, the meat gray and sludge-flavored. Your mother offers you half a piece of fruit from that morning's picking, a rare and fantastic thing, and you savor the delicate sweetness of it, the soft texture, the edge of rot giving it a sour aftertaste.

You return to your room for a rest after the meal, curled up on your mattress stuffed with bits of fabric from the trash heaps, and you dream of Nana. She is whole, with bright button eyes and red yarn hair braided down her back in two neat plaits. She stares and smiles, and you hold her hand, and you skip through a field of wildflowers. You know what a field is because of the books your mother brings home from the heaps, but you've never experienced a wide-open space full of flowers, with a blue sky above you. Everything here on Tethis IV is gray, gray and brown and black and stinking. In your dream, the air is clean and smells sweet, and you hear birdsong in the distance. There are colors here you rarely see, pale pinks and bright yellows. You wake with tears in your eyes for a life you never knew you wanted.

Mother shakes you awake. "It's alright. You're safe," she says, her brow creased with worry.

It's rare for Mother to touch you, and rarer still for her to look at you with concern etched in her features. "It wasn't a bad dream," you say. "Nana and I were playing in a field of flowers. They smelled so good."

She frowns at the doll pressed against your chest. "This is Nana?"

You hold up your prize proudly. "I found her this morning."

Mother recoils, disgusted. "She's even filthier than the last one."

"That's not her fault," you say. "Everything here is filthy."

Mother reacts as if she's been slapped. It is, after all, her fault you both have to live on this awful trash planet. She's the one who was exiled to Tethis IV, alone except for you, without a partner to help her raise you. Her expression hardens again into the mask of indifference she usually wears, and she leaves your bedroom.

You feel guilty for making Mother unhappy, and spend the afternoon picking the new heap for books, Nana tucked under your arm. You find enough texts to fill the largest canvas bag you can carry and bring them home when the monsters start to roil the depths in preparation for evening, driving all the pickers inland.

Mother isn't home. You light the only lantern and sit on the floor, dumping books out around you to explore their pages. Most of the children of Tethis IV can't read, but your mother made sure you could read, and read well. It was, she said, one of life's greatest pleasures, and there were so few pleasures here. Mother's trade in books had, of late, suffered due to the illiteracy of the other exiles. She used to trade books for food, fuel, fabric, and whatever else you needed with ease, because the other exiles were hungry for new titles. Lately, though, demand had dried up. She had a theory it was because many of the exiles who could read had died or had their sentences commuted, and fewer prison ships were landing here each year, their human cargoes diminished.

You only know of what happens beyond your filthy shores thanks to the gossip new exiles bring. Most of it is meaningless and holds little interest for you. Tethis IV is all you've ever known, except for what you've learned in Mother's precious books. Sometimes she lets you read the nicest ones before she trades them. She has kept a few of her favorites on a shelf above the door, a handful of her most treasured texts, and you've read them with her so many times you've memorized the pages.

You prop Nana beside you and flip through the new books, looking for pictures. One is a dictionary, with a few drawings of plants and animals you've never seen. You find a medical text with fascinating anatomy illustrations. There's a small red journal, leather-bound, and very unlike the others. The pages are handwritten, and there are sketches of people and places. The journal falls open to a sketch of Nana, as you saw her in the dream, with buttons for eyes and her hair styled in two neat plaits.

A chill makes you shiver. Out of the corner of your eye, you see Mother at the door. You look up, and the shape of a woman dissolves into shadow. Panic flutters behind your breastbone. You pick up Nana and the journal and go to your room, shutting the door. You feel safe surrounded by the dolls, watching and protecting you. You slip the journal under your mattress and go to sleep with Nana tucked under your chin.

You dream again, this time of playing with Nana in a big, clean house. You're wearing clean, soft clothes, and your hair is freshly washed and curled and full of colorful ribbons. A tall, pale woman clothed in black smiles down at you, but her eyes are sad. She loves you, but death hangs around her like a shroud. She is sad the same way your mother is sad, and you take her hand and tell her you love her, trying to chase away the ghosts that mar her lovely face.

When morning comes, Mother makes you a breakfast of something she calls "grits." From the descriptions you've read in cookbooks, this viscous substance is nothing like grits, but it's made from the only edible plant that grows on Tethis IV, which the exiles cultivate and trade. It tastes sour and has a lumpy, gooey texture. It's not your favorite meal, but it does fill you up and make your stomach feel warm and satisfied. Mother must have found some valuable books, or someone who found books valuable. It has been months since you've enjoyed a breakfast so decadent.

After breakfast, Mother begins sorting the books you found to take them for trade. You retreat to your room to thumb through the journal. You're particularly interested in the pages that talk about the doll. The journal's author also calls her Nana, a fact that makes your hands tremble as you turn the pages. The author writes about her vivid dreams, where she lives in another time, in another place, on Old Earth. She sketches the field of wildflowers and the face of the pale woman in black.

You drop the journal to the floor and kick it away from you at the sight of the woman's face. How did you know the doll was named Nana? How did the author of this journal draw what was in your dreams? Who is the woman in black? You stare down at Nana, unsure what to do. She grimaces up at you, her smile suddenly malevolent. You need space and time to think. You open the door and take her into the main room of the house, placing her on the shelf above the door with your mother's most precious books. Then you hurry out of the house, off to the trash heaps, where you do your best thinking while looking for treasures.

Hours later, you return to the house with a broken chair and part of a coffee pot. Mother is pleased, as she thinks she'll be able to trade them both. There's no fruit for the midday meal, but there is bread. It's gritty and has a bitter flavor because the flour is made from ground-up insects, but it's nutritious.

Nana is no longer above the door. You assume Mother must have gotten rid of her. You find yourself relieved, and then you feel a pang of guilt for feeling relieved. When you go in your room, you find that Nana sits on the bed, and now she has eyes that gleam in the dirty gray light. You scream.

"I thought I'd surprise you," Mother says, her hands fluttering in distress. "I found the buttons this morning. They're real abalone shell."

You nod slowly and twist your face into a smiling shape. "They're beautiful." Your pulse gallops and you hope Mother doesn't notice.

Mother goes out to pick in the afternoon. You tell her you don't feel well and you want to stay in. She has books for you to sort while she's gone, but while you work you can feel Nana's pearlescent eyes watching you. The red journal calls to you where you left it on the floor. Eventually the presence of both is oppressive. You go into your room and pick them up, ready to toss them out the window.

But held in your hands, Nana is just a handmade doll, and the journal is just an old, crumbling book. Why are you so afraid? It seems silly, now, your fear. You sit on your mattress and your doll collection watches as you seat Nana in your lap and open the journal. The author found Nana in something called an "antique shop." The doll has "Nana" stitched on her behind, so that must be her name, and you reason that you must have glimpsed the embroidered tattoo, and that's how you knew what to call her.

Nana and the author became inseparable. The author began to have vivid dreams, and then started seeing the pale woman in black during her waking hours, always out of the corner of her eye. She had a dream about the woman trying to kill her, to drown her.

An old newspaper clipping falls out of the journal. You unfold it carefully and try to read it, but the ink is faded and the paper yellowed, so you can pick out only a few words: infanticide, disappeared, scandal. You'll need to look them up in the dictionary above the door to learn their meanings. There is a photograph, an image that makes your pulse beat hard. It's the face of the woman in the black dress. She isn't wearing black and she looks happier than she did in your dream, but it's the same woman. She holds a child in her lap, a child a little younger than you, with pale curls and bright eyes.

The author decided to return Nana to the antique shop in hopes of ending the frightening dreams. The journal pages after that are full of nonsensical scrawling and a drawing of huge, angry, black eyes.

You tuck the journal back under your mattress and gaze into Nana's shiny button eyes. They're so bright and colorful against the filthy brown of the felt, the stained beige of her fabric skin. They don't look right. You think how pretty they would be sewn onto your own shirt or woven into your hair, how Arin and Rissa would be jealous. And then maybe Nana wouldn't be able to stare at you anymore.

You rip the buttons from her face and spend the afternoon in front of your mother's small mirror, figuring out the best way to tie the buttons into your long, tangled hair. A few times you swear there's a shadow behind you in the mirror, a shadow in the shape of a woman in a black dress, but when you turn, it's gone. The journal calls to you from under the mattress, but you ignore it. You consider burning it so it will leave you alone.

Mother returns with fish, and you help her prepare it for dinner. She doesn't comment on your new adornments, or the fact that Nana is now eyeless and perched once again above the door. Mother is in one of her sullen moods, so you eat the fish in silence. Then she chooses a book from the stacks on the floor and disappears into her bedroom.

You choose a book yourself and stay up as long as you can, reading by lantern light, reluctant to sleep. Eventually your eyes close and you find yourself once again in the big, clean house, wearing soft, clean clothes. The pale woman in the black dress smiles down at you, but tears sparkle in her eyes. Her hands close around your neck, squeezing the breath from you. You try to pry her fingers from your throat but her slender digits are surprisingly strong. She thrusts your head underwater, and when you gasp for air, water fills your lungs, and the last thing you see is the woman standing over you, sobbing, her image distorted by the water.

You wake gasping for air, but something is pressed over your face. You struggle and squirm and the thing pressed over your face jerks back. Mother crouches by your mattress, holding her pillow, which bears the indentation of your face. She shakes her head, as if trying to wake herself. You scramble away from her, into the piles of dolls. You shake and suck down great gulps of air.

"I'm sorry," Mother says softly. "I don't know how I got here." She glances around, as if the room will somehow reveal the source of her sleepwalking. Her eyes light on Nana, and she runs from the room.

You gather up Nana and the red journal and climb down the ladder in the dark. Tethis IV has two moons: tonight Arisia is a pale sliver and her brother Boros, far across the sky, is almost full, providing most of the pale, silvery light. High above the garbage, a few houses provide additional pinpoints of illumination, but it's late. Almost everyone is sleeping.

The beach is silent except for the rushing of the waves and the pounding of your own heart. No one goes out at this time because of the monsters lurking just off the shore. They have long arms and can snatch trash pickers from a hundred feet away, so you creep carefully as far from the shore as you can until you arrive at the inlet caves.

The caves are a place where you and your friends have played many times- or you did, until you became old enough to pick trash and contribute to the livelihoods of your families. The moonlight can't reach inside the caverns, so you quickly find yourself shrouded in darkness. You feel your way along the familiar walls, following the flow of ankle-deep water, breathing the nostalgic aroma of cool earth and stone. You walk slowly, and your muscles start to shake from being tensed for so long. Your teeth chatter.

You feel as if you've been walking for hours when you finally come upon the whirlpool. The whirlpool is the reason the caves stay mostly free of trash. Everything that ends up in the caves gets sucked into the whirlpool and comes up elsewhere in the ocean unless it's strong enough to fight the current or someone has fastened it to the cave walls. Throwing things into the whirlpool is a fun activity for younger children. You remember losing several dolls into the swirling water before you understood they wouldn't come back.

You can't see the whirlpool but you can hear it rushing and feel the salty spray of it against your cheeks. You take a deep breath and heave both Nana and the red journal into the water. You don't hear a splash or anything else that would indicate their disappearance, but you swear you feel unwatched for the first time in days, as if the eyes on the back of your head have finally gone away.

You go home to find Mother sitting in the main room of the house, sobbing, her face red and snot-streaked. Several of your dolls are piled in her lap. When you enter, she jumps to her feet and spills the dolls to the floor, rushing to you with open arms. "I'm so sorry," she wails.

"It's okay," you say, returning her embrace. "It wasn't you. It was Nana. She's gone now. Everything is going to be okay."

As Mother weeps against your shoulder, you actually believe that maybe, just maybe, things really will be okay.

The long days of summer stretch into monsoon season. The rain pounds down, and you and Mother spend most of your time reading and sorting the books you stockpiled during the dry season. For an hour each morning you go to trade and find food and even do a little picking with your friends before the storms start again, but otherwise, you're trapped indoors. The house sways frighteningly on its stilts, sometimes, but they hold for another year.

Truth be told, it's your favorite time of year. Toward the end of the season, you have to reduce your rations, so your stomach hurts. But you and Mother spend a lot of time together and develop a quiet, pleasant rhythm. You absorb the stories in dozens of books, each one opening a world far away from Tethis IV. The storms smell of fresh water and tamp down the stink of the landfill that surrounds you. The gray days run together into one cozy, hazy, endless stretch of time.

Finally, the first day of the new summer season announces itself with clear skies. Birds wheel overhead and you venture out with your friends to hunt them with spears and arrows. The birds aren't particularly good eating, but it's a relief to eat something until your shrunken stomach is full, and tracking them across the trash dunes is a fun exercise after so long cooped up indoors.

You're with Arin and Rissa, tracking a bird to its nest in the hopes of stealing its eggs, when you find yourself at the inlet caves. "Let's go see the whirlpool," Arin suggests, his eyes twinkling.

A feeling of dread simmers in your stomach. "Isn't that for babies?"

Arin shrugs. "I just haven't been down there in a long time."

"I go all the time," Rissa says. "It's nice. I like the sound of it, and the smell. The younger kids don't hang out there like we did, not anymore, not since Duggy fell in."

You all take a few moments to think about the tragedy when Duggy, one of Rissa's cousins, fell into the whirlpool and the parents made the kids promise never to go there again. Naturally, the younger children keep their promises, but your mother never made you promise anything, and Rissa has eight brothers and sisters, so nobody keeps track of her. And Arin takes any parental order as a challenge, every rule as something to be broken.

You can't think of any further objections, so you follow your friends into the caves. Rissa has a flashlight cobbled together out of a bunch of electrical parts and a half-corroded battery. The light is dim but it's better than nothing.

The smell of the caves, the feel of the wet stone against your fingers, the slosh of your feet in the ankle-deep water, all brings you back to the night you disposed of Nana and the red journal. It's been so many months, the whole event seems hazy and unreal, especially since so much of it happened in total blackness. Your throat burns and you have a hard time taking deep breaths in the caves, as if the memory of the pale woman's hands around your neck has physical substance here.

Arin walks in the front, and he lets out an exclamation, the sound of which is nearly drowned out by the rushing of the whirlpool. Rissa splashes up to him, shining the flashlight on whatever he's found, and you follow, but slowly, reluctantly, dread making your feet leaden. You reach them and look down, expecting to see Nana lying there, soaked and filthy but intact.

It's a chunk of plastic with wires sticking out. You breathe a sigh of relief, your vision briefly filling with stars. "This is stupid," you say. "I'm leaving." You turn and head for the entrance, retracing your way in the dark. Behind you, Arin and Rissa's laughter echoes.

You spend your afternoon digging in the freshest trash heap near the water. It already stinks, as there's a lot of food waste, but you find a few oranges that are only half-moldy, and a couple of almost-black bananas. You make your way home excited to present your finds to Mother. She's been much less sullen, these past few months, and surely her spirits will be buoyed by the nice weather.

The house looks like it was hit by a monsoon. The meager furniture is smashed, your dolls thrown about, some of them dismembered. The little mirror is shattered and you cut your feet stepping on the shards of glass before you notice them. The books have been flung about the room and torn to bits, and one looks as if it has scorch marks on it. Mother is nowhere to be found. What could have happened?

You climb down the ladder and go to the neighbor's house to inquire after Mother. Your feet bleed on their rug. They haven't seen your mother, they don't know who ransacked your house, and they offer you bandages for your feet, but you don't have time for bandages. As evening approaches, you limp to the shore, but your mother isn't among the pickers coming in from the beach.

You go home, finally clean your stinging feet, and start setting things right around the house. A few times, you think you see your mother in the doorway, but the shadow is gone when you turn. You arrange the dolls in your room, taking comfort from the familiarity of the activity, brushing their hair and wiping smears of dirt from their cheeks. You fall asleep curled among them, waiting for Mother.

You dream of Mother holding you down, drowning you. Her face is pale and she wears a black dress. She cries and her face is distorted by the water, her tears making the surface ripple. You splash and struggle but she's strong, and your lungs fill with fluid, and darkness overtakes you. Your chest aches and then you feel nothing.

When you gasp to wakefulness, a woman is silhouetted in your doorway. It might be your mother, but it doesn't really look like her, and she's wearing a long dress, unusual clothing for Tethis IV. Something misshapen dangles from her right hand. In her left, something rectangular. She steps into the room and the moonlight briefly limns her form, picking out details: the doll gripped in her right hand, the journal clutched in her left. Her face is pale and twisted, but it is Mother, you think. But it's also...not Mother. Like someone else is wearing Mother's skin.

You crab-walk away from her, backing yourself into the corner, pulling your dolls over you, trying to hide. Her head turns, slowly, gaze fixing on you. She drops the doll and the journal, and then she steps to the wall, scaling it like a lizard you saw once in a book. She climbs across the ceiling until she dangles directly above you. Terror paralyzes you as she leans down over you, somehow still clinging to the ceiling, her face appearing in front of yours, upside-down, her long hair dangling so that it brushes your lap. Her eyes are black and her brows drawn together in a way you've never seen before. She's so angry the rage practically pours off her.

You manage to choke out three words: "Who...are...you?"

She says only one word in reply: "Nana." The voice is not your mother's. It's too low, too rough, like something dredged up from the depths of the black ocean.

"I want my mother," you say.

She laughs, a sound like a door creaking wetly. "Your mother never loved you. She never wanted you. You were an accident, a mistake. You got her exiled here. She hated you before you were even born. She wishes you were dead, so she could leave this place."

Her hands reach for your throat. You sink back into the dolls and she grabs at them instead. She screams in frustration, tossing dolls everywhere, snarling and scrabbling at them. You slide into and under your collection, crawling and wriggling until you emerge on the other side of the room. You run for the door. Your mother hisses and follows you, her knees and hands thumping against the ceiling as she crawls above you.

You snatch the Nana doll and the red journal out of the doorway as you pass through it. The lantern is on the shelf by the door, the matches beside it. You throw the doll and the journal into a basket full of books. You open the lantern and pour the oil over the contents of the basket, your hands shaking so hard you can barely manage the cap. Oil goes everywhere, on the floor, on your clothes. But it lands on the basket, too, on the doll and the journal.

There's a thump behind you. Your heart pounds and your breath comes in great, ragged gasps, inhaling the scent of the oil, the reek of the rotting trash planet. Everything slows as you turn to face your mother.

Mother reaches for your throat again, and this time she has you. She slams you against the wall, crushing your windpipe with her powerful grip. You squirm and kick but she's so strong. Your lungs burn and darkness gnaws at the edges of your vision. Your hands flail and find a book, bringing it up to slap the side of Mother's face with it. She ignores it until you drive the corner of the book into her eye. Shrieking, she releases you to bat the book away.

You push her off you, grabbing for the matches and turning to the basket. Her hands close around your neck from behind but not before you strike a match, not before a small flame flares to life, not before you drop it into the basket.

The oil catches fire instantly. Mother screams with a terrible, other-worldly shriek as the doll burns. She tears at you, trying to get to the basket, but you stand firm, holding her at bay. Suddenly you're the strong one.

The room fills with the smell of burning fabric and something else, something sharp and smoky and evil-smelling. Mother wilts before you, collapsing to the floor. Her shriek becomes a wail, and that fades to a despairing murmur.

You kneel beside her, pulling her into your embrace. "I want my mother."

Her face twists with rage one last time. She coughs. Her eyelids flutter. The rage leaves her body like juice from a rotten fruit, and she sags in your arms. Her breathing slows. She relaxes into something that resembles normal sleep.

You stomp out the fire. Fire on a landfill spreads with incredible speed, and you can't risk starting a conflagration that might kill everyone you know. You carry the remnants of the basket down the ladder. You carry it to the caves in the dark, as you did once before, but now, you walk with confidence. You know this place so well, and you traversed it in darkness once before. You see no reason to be afraid. In the cave, you place the basket and its contents on a ledge and light another match. This time you let the bundle burn down until the fire goes out on its own.

You take what's left, mostly ash, and fling it into the whirlpool. You light a match so you can watch it swirl down into the dark water. Then you begin the long, dark trek back to the house, where you know you'll find your mother.

You wonder, as you walk, whether things will go back to how they were, or whether things will be different. Nana's words haunt you. Was your mother exiled here because of you? Does she hate you? Your heart is heavy with exhaustion and sorrow.

As you approach the house, you see a candle burning in your bedroom window, and the shape of your mother moving around the room. She's rearranging the dolls, trying to put your collection back in place, trying to erase the damage Nana did.

You smile, and you think of how much the little kids will love your dolls when you give them away.

COLD COMFORT

JEN HAEGER

R ed light, orange light, yellow light. Red light, orange light, yellow light. Elton watched the warning light on the temperature gauge blink. There was also an alarm that accompanied the blinking light, however, after a tedious eleven hour search of the underlying wiring followed by a furious thirty seconds of yanking out wires, that alarm was no longer functioning. *Stupid human gauge.* Checking the temperature reading again, he saw that it was holding steady at thirty-seven degrees Fahrenheit, but the cold didn't bother him. Elton paused a moment to scoff at the ridiculous way that America resisted the metric system, as if continuing to make calculations more complicated was one final screw you that this former colony could send to the empire. It wasn't enough for them to gain independence, become a superpower, pull Britain's ass out of the flames of war again and again, and walk on the moon, the Yanks also had to one-up the British in unit systems. Elton chuckled to himself at the thought and his soft laugh echoed eerily around the bridge, bouncing off the shiny metal and smooth, hard plastic edges. All around him illuminated panels waited to be used and plasma screens begged to inform him of every minuscule change that was taking place every millisecond in this amazing feat of human engineering that was now hurling him through the vast oceans of empty space between this sun and the next. He ignored them.

A
t first it had all enthralled him, and he'd spent most of his time watching the Earth wither as the outer planets engorged, but this pastime eventually lost its thrill. Now he passed the portholes without so much as a glance. More mundane thoughts now preoccupied Elton's mind. He licked his lips; it was almost time. Dismissing the overactive temperature warning lights, he amused himself by flicking through the short list of victims...er...donors that he had made for himself: Sheryl, the blond and busty microbiologist; Jimmy, the dark-haired and questionably heterosexual nurse; Susan, the colony supervisor with the mousy brown hair. AB pos, B neg, A neg. These few topped his list. He considered throwing in some O pos just so he didn't leave all of them until later and become bored with a bland diet, but no, for this first meal he was going to make it special. Special and tasty.

Elton was daydreaming about the warm, sweet blood spilling down his throat when Control hailed him for the daily update. He scowled at the interruption to his pleasant reverie and made them wait for thirty seconds before answering in a bored drawl.

"Control this is Cryomonitor Patricks report number..." he swiped a finger across the screen to minimize the profile of Susan and bring up the craft's log, "beta-six-four-two."

Elton rolled his eyes, grateful that he was finally out of video-com range and that the quantadetanglethingy or whatnot that they had tried in vain to explain to him was now engaged.

The familiar and crisp voice of the mission control communications expert came out loud and self-important over the speakers as Elton mused that the man had a more impressive title than he did. He was an expert merely for his ability to speak into a microphone. Elton had already had several long chats with the man. One of the more recent chats involved Elton's unauthorized dismantling of the temperature gauges auditory alarm.

"Copy that Monitor Patricks. What is your status?"

Elton knew that he should stick to protocols, but the further away from Earth the ship got, the less interested he became in maintaining the façade of caring about his official NASA position, so he figured, *screw it.*

"Control, my status is bored, terribly bored."

There was silence on the other end of the com link, then, "Monitor Patricks, come again?"

Elton smiled a wide, Cheshire smile that exposed his elongated canines even though the man on the other end of the com couldn't see him.

"I said I'm bored. It has been three months and not a single thing has changed except the view out of the window. All three-thousand colonists are still frozen and I'm getting hungry."

There was another beat of silence followed by a soft click.

"Monitor Patricks, I have been instructed to inform you that the official time of necessary thaw and replenishment is still fifty-two hours and twenty-six minutes from now."

"Elton."

"I'm sorry?"

Elton adjusted his feet where they were propped up on the communications console.

"We have been talking back and forth for three months now, I think that we can call each other by our first names, don't you...err...?"

This time the silence stretched on for almost a minute and Elton passed the time picturing a roomful of people back on the dirt of the disappearing point of light that was Earth shouting at each other and running back and forth like ants whose hill Elton had just destroyed with the toe of his boot. Dr. Pollak especially would be fuming. He had never trusted Elton and had in fact predicted nearly this exact scenario to anyone who would listen back at NASA. Wise man Dr. Pollak, sadly Elton had just been too charming and his particular set of skills were just too tempting to the rest of the Jade Colony mission team.

"Tim. My name is Tim."

Ah, thought Elton, *they finally contacted a psychologist or other form of head-shrinker to try to calm me and get me back on mission track.*

"Well, I'm very pleased to finally meet you, Tim. Tell me, Tim, do you have a wife?"

"Now listen here, you bloo—!"

Suddenly the com link cut off.

"Tim? Yoo-hoo! I think I lost you there, Friend. Oh, sorry, I mean, do you copy?"

The com link went dead and Elton went back to his perusal of colonist profiles.

T he com link opened again and a new voice emanated from the invisible speakers all around Elton.

"Elton, are you there? Elton, my name is Tanya Meyers."

Elton sat up and brought his legs down from the console. He liked this new voice much better than Tim's voice. Not only was she a woman, but she sounded like an interesting woman, down to the way she pronounced her name Tan-ya instead of the more common Ton-ya.

"You must be the shrink," he said, smirking.

"I do have certain degrees in psychoanalysis. I specialize in vampire psychology."

"Called you in a little late, didn't they Tanya?"

"Perhaps, but you said that you were bored so why don't you humor me?"

Elton considered her proposal, but then decided that he would be much more in the mood for chit chat after a light snack.

"I'm sorry Tanya, while you do sound refreshingly interesting and will indubitably cure me of my boredom to an extent, I'm feeling a might bit peckish so I'll have to get back to you after I've had a bite."

Elton cut the com link before she had a chance to respond.

. . .

C ontrol had been pretty much hailing him constantly since he had cut communication thirty-six hours earlier, but he found a way to mute the indicator, so Elton paid them no mind. He still couldn't get over their ignorance and arrogance. Certainly putting a vampire in charge of the cryopreservation units of colonists on a long term, deep space mission seemed like a fantastic idea. No need to worry about keeping large portions of the ship warm or oxygen rich or wasting precious food resources. Not only that, but there was a sentient being on board to communicate daily with and keep everything running smoothly. AI was O.K., but it certainly didn't beat a thinking entity that didn't need sleep or power to run. Elton didn't even need much protection from radiation, and with proper management of his resources, namely the thousand tasty blood makers in the cryohold, he could survive for centuries or even longer. There was just one tiny problem: the nature of a vampire.

Elton dabbed the blood from his chin and activated the com link on his end.

"Tanya are you there, Love?"

There were several clicks, but silence dominated.

"Oh come now, Tanya, you seemed so eager to speak to me. If you don't answer me, you might hurt my delicate feelings and send me on a binge!"

About another minute ticked by and Elton waited patiently, feeling the blood rejuvenating his cells. He tried to remember if this was what it felt like to eat food, but far too much time had passed since he had been a mortal man.

Finally Tanya's tired and slightly scratchy voice radiated around him.

"I'm here Elton." She cleared her throat. "You haven't done anything rash have you?"

"Depends on what you mean by rash, I am definitely feeling more vigorous. But enough about me, how are you?" Elton tut-tutted. "You sound just terrible."

"I'm not going to lie to you Elton, I've been better."

"Still panicking down there or has the panic subsided and the blame begun?"

"Everyone here blames you I'm afraid, but I told them that they're wrong, that any…being subjected to months without true interaction would have eventually reacted much the same way that you did. What's done is done and we just have to move forward now."

"I take it you know *who* is done, don't you Tanya?"

There was a slight hesitation to her reply. "Control has been monitoring the cryo-chambers, yes."

"Ah, but that only tells you that two of them are empty, not what became of the occupants."

"Do you want to tell me what became of the occupants, Elton?"

"Not particularly, and I doubt you'd really want to hear. Really this whole area of conversation is getting quite droll. What are you wearing?"

"Wha—?" There was a loud click of the com being disconnected from mission control's end.

"Yes, Tanya I read the entire file on space sickness, but I really don't feel like it applies to me. How can I be sick if I'm not even truly alive?"

"Are you trying to get me to express remorse Tanya? Well isn't that just adorable?"

"Control is no longer receiving any telemetric data from Jade One? Now isn't that odd?"

. . .

Elton could not remember anymore what day it was or how long he had been on the ship. Obviously there were computer screens and reports that he could reference, but for quite some time he had sequestered himself in the cavernous cryo-hold. He paced back and forth between the peep-cicles, as he liked to call them, scrutinizing, reading the plastic-coated bios that hung from each pod. It was rather like a very large menu that he tantalized over daily.

Then there was Tanya. He spoke to her often, and in exchange for tidbits of diagnostic ship information she would tell him snippets of her own life. She was single, or at least had been last time he asked, and of Mexican heritage on her mother's side giving her a darker complexion, thick black hair, and deep brown eyes. She had studied psychology at Harvard, but gotten her PhD in vampire psychology at Oxford, where they were a little more open-minded about the subject matter. She had wanted to be a mediator in vampire relations in vampire-oppressive countries such as Spain and Turkey, but had been approached by NASA when this project was first proposed and had turned them down until Elton went off protocol.

When Elton pictured her, he imagined her pretty much in Wonder Woman garb, but with glasses, trying to bind him in her lasso of truth. She hadn't spoken to him recently, in fact he had taken to leaving the com link open just in case she came back and he was preoccupied and didn't notice the blinking blue light of the com. He guessed that he'd upset her last time they'd spoken by asking her if she wanted to hear the screams of his latest meal.

"So, what is the latest women's fashion trend back on good old Earth these days Tanya?"

"Elton, this is going to be our last conversation, so is that really what you want to talk about?"

Tanya's voice sounded odd today, distant and scratchy.

"Whatever do you mean?"

"I think that you may have lost track of time, Elton, but it's been sixteen years and with no progress having been made, NASA has chalked this mission up as a total loss and moved on to other projects, and I'm retiring."

Elton blinked. *Sixteen plus...no. Thirty years since the launch? Impossible!* Yet as he glanced up and down the rows of cryochambers and counted the empty pods, he knew that Tanya was telling the truth. "But, who will I talk to now?"

"No one. NASA is going to sever the communications link."

"But, but they can't do that! There are still living, frozen humans aboard. Don't they care about them? What will their families think?"

Tanya sighed. "Just another tragic, space disaster. This was always a risky mission."

"You can't severe the com link! I'll wake them, they'll want to talk to their families!"

Tanya coughed for several long moments and Elton suddenly remembered her coughing getting more frequent the last few times they had spoken.

"I'm sorry Elton it's over. I just want to ask you one thing before I sign off."

"Anything Tanya, just don't let them shut me out."

"Why?"

"Why...what?"

She was racked by another fit of coughing that echoed grimly through the cryo-hold. "Why didn't you stick to the protocol? You could have been the first vampire ever to set foot on another planet. There were stipulations in place that would've kept you well-fed and comfortable indefinitely on Jade-Three-Seven-Six. You would have been the hero that kept them safe and guided the colonists to their new home. With just a little patience, you could have had it all. Now, even if you stopped feeding and survive until the ship lands, there aren't enough colonists left for a viable settlement. You signed your own death warrant. Why?"

Elton sighed noisily. "More than thirty years as a psychoanalyst studying me and you still don't get it. Vampires weren't made to be astronauts or colonists or heroes. We were made to be killers. The only reason vampires don't kill on Earth anymore is because there are consequences. But here, in this great metal can of vast technology and abundant blood makers, there are no consequences. I am free to follow my nature."

"So NASA made you your own private bloody vampire nirvana?"

"Ain't science grand?"

"You know that you're going to die, right Elton? When the remaining colonists die, you'll die too."

"Impossible. Humans breed like rabbits. I'll be fine."

Tanya sighed heavily and Elton detected a wheeze near the end of her exhalation.

"Goodbye, Elton."

"Tanya, wait!"

The com link clicked and then crackled in an odd way, then all Elton could hear was a whisper of static. Tanya was gone, and for the first time Elton truly felt the vast yawning void of the cosmos around him. Though he still did not actually feel the cold, he shivered. It was over and he was alone. Then a musical chirrup rang out from the pod next to him denoting a successful reanimation. Elton turned, his eyes dilating and his mouth salivating like Pavlov's dog at the chime of a dinner bell.

THIN AIR

JUDE REID

"Something's caught on the aerial."

"Well, that explains why we stopped broadcasting," Soyinka said, her voice tinny in my headset. "All of space to choose from, and it crashes into us. What've you got?"

I fired my thrusters again and moved to take a closer look. White in my suit's beams, the debris had a soft, crumpled texture that made me think of plastic sheeting. We'd found space junk snaked around the Deep Space Relay Station's shell before—these days humanity was careful about what it dumped in atmosphere, but out in deep space it was easier and cheaper, albeit illegal, to jettison your rubbish rather than carry it planetside. Still, this didn't look much like the usual debris.

"Soyinka, I think it's a spacesuit."

"A spacesuit?" I heard her gulp down a mouthful of coffee. "You're kidding me. Who dumps a spacesuit?"

It was almost within arm's reach now. I saw that the suit had caught on one of the struts of the aerial, the thick white material snagged under one elbow. I pulled myself close and gave the hand an experimental squeeze. "Still pressurized," I said.

"Can you get it loose?"

"I'll try."

Everything seemed against me as I tried to work it free—my inflexible gloved hands, the suit's unwieldy bulk, the unforgiving insulation of vacuum as my body temperature rose. In the end, I took hold of the suit's arm in both hands and kicked off from the station's hull as hard as I could, wrenching the suit loose at the cost of a bent piece of aerial. I let the momentum take me out to the end of my tether, the suit almost spiraling out of my grip. The movement spun the spacesuit to face me and I saw my own helmet reflected in the gold-visored faceplate.

"Got it."

There was silence at the other end. Then, Soyinka said in a very quiet voice: "I can see you, Banerjee."

"What do you mean?"

"The suit. I've got signal from its camera. It's one of ours."

I t was difficult enough to squeeze myself through the hatch, but pulling a second suit with me made the task close to impossible. I tried not to think of what its contents might be as I forced the limbs to unnatural angles, sweat running into my eyes and turning my under-suit clammy. The others were there almost as soon as the lock had finished cycling—Soyinka, empty coffee cup still in her hand, and our radio-frequency engineer Park, hair sitting in a shock around her bleary-eyed face.

"Where's the Captain?" I asked Soyinka. She shook her head, unable to meet my eye, and I realized that she was staring past me at the space suit on the ground.

"She's not onboard."

Park crouched down next to the suit, fingers working the neck seals until they released with a hiss and the helmet came free.

The Captain's face was swollen and plethoric, her eyes bloodshot and still half open. Her skin was still warm, though she must have been dead for hours. Park was shaking as she set the helmet down; Soyinka's hands were pressed tight to her mouth, fingers digging in hard enough to turn her skin grey.

"When did she go out?" I asked.

"We can check the airlock records," Park said. "Must have been after the end of last shift."

Soyinka was still standing with her back pressed to the inner door. She looked like she might faint or vomit. "Look," I said, with confidence I didn't feel, "Can you go and check the bridge logs, see how this happened? We'll ..." I paused, choking on the words, "get her out of the suit."

"Here?" Park asked.

I shrugged. "I don't think we have a choice."

We didn't have a formal mortuary on the station. Instead of a proper cold storage compartment we simply had a depressurisible compartment the size of a broom cupboard. I noticed the four body bags with a faint sense of unease, and wondered under what circumstances they expected the last crew member to get inside and obligingly wait to die.

Park zipped the bag shut over the Captain's face.

"Are we doing this, then?" she asked. I nodded, and we stepped outside the compartment, sealed it and opened it to vacuum. The Captain's body would freeze dry within minutes. It would take some careful handling to get her out without sending what amounted to a bag of dust home, but that was a problem for the crew of the relief ship, not for us.

"You want to say something?" I asked, but Park shook her head.

"Nothing to say, is there?" She frowned. "I guess it got to her. All this, I mean."

The body bag looked puffy through the plastic window, its air seeping gradually out through the plasticized material. "Worse ways to go, I suppose."

It wasn't uncommon for people to end their lives in space, of course. I hoped it had been a gentle death; just a last, long voyage into nothing, her own exhaled carbon dioxide guiding her towards confusion, drowsiness, and death among a million shining stars. If she hadn't snagged on the aerial we would never even have found her body. She hadn't seemed distressed or suicidal, just her usual brusque and practical self, but I supposed that was always the way. You never noticed until it was too late.

"We should check on Soyinka," Park said. The bridge was at the opposite end of the relay station, past the crew quarters, hydroponics, and the main engine room, through a slim corridor that divided the two main modules like the midsection of a wasp. They were designed to rotate relative to one another, and even when perfectly aligned, there was always a stomach-turning lurch on stepping from one set of artificial gravity to the other. When we arrived, Soyinka was hunched over her console, engrossed in searching through the station's internal camera footage. Park put a hand on her shoulder, and she flinched.

"Got anything?"

Soyinka shook her head. "Not much. Three seconds of her in the rear corridor at 0500."

"Nothing from inside the airlock?" I asked.

"She must have turned the camera off. Airlock opens at five fifteen, runs a short pre-programmed cycle, closes again. Then nothing."

"Headcam?"

"Disabled."

Park sat down heavily in the Captain's chair. "What do we do now?"

"Follow protocol. Transmit an emergency message. Wait, I suppose."

"Transmitter's still down," Soyinka said. "I don't know if we'll be able to fix it without parts."

"The relief crew should be here in twenty four hours," I said. "If all else fails, we just wait it out."

"And when they're late?" Park said.

The blare of the klaxon over the bridge speakers silenced us all, flashing red lights pulsing in time with the siren's wail.

"Fire onboard," Soyinka said, fingers tapping furiously as she interrogated her console.

"Where?" I asked.

"Hydroponics."

Park and I took off at a run. We'd been through the drill twice a week since we set foot on the station, but nothing compared to the reality of a fire on board. Unchecked, flames could spread through the station in a matter of minutes, consuming precious oxygen and filling the corridors and chambers with smoke. In an emergency like this every compartment could be vented to atmosphere, but when it came to the hydroponics lab it wasn't that easy. The algae in there not only supplied the bulk of our calories, but was bioengineered to scrub carbon dioxide from the air and replace it with breathable oxygen. Vacuum would destroy it almost as surely as the fire.

We grabbed respirators and algae-safe extinguishers as we ran, pulling the thick rubber masks over our heads and activating the filters. Park's dark eyes stared at me out from the oval eyeholes as we opened the laboratory door, and stepped inside.

At first, I couldn't see much wrong. Inside, the room was a tropical jungle, water droplets condensing on the outside of my respirator, a faint haze of smoke hanging in the air. Park went right while I weaved my way to the left, past bubbling pools of green scum that looked no more appetizing there than they did on a plate. I found the fire at the far end of the lab; a modest little conflagration that seemed to have taken hold in a few of the larger water-dwelling plants—contained and perfectly manageable. Relieved, I raised my extinguisher and doused the fire from side to side.

With a plume of hissing steam, the surface of the tank erupted as though some submerged monster was breaching the surface. I felt the heat on my face as tongues of flame licked towards the roof, burning plant matter falling like comets to set up secondary blazes nearby. Black smoke billowed upwards, roiling in great clouds across the ceiling, and within seconds the visibility was down to a few meters. Half blind, my respirator wheezing, I turned and stumbled through the thickening smoke, everything cast in shades of crimson and grey.

"Park!" I shouted, voice muffled by my mask. The flames must have spread to the other side of the lab by now; at the very least the smoke there would be almost as thick there as it was around me. The skin of my forearms and neck was starting to singe, my breath quick and deafeningly loud in my ears as I groped my way through tanks of burning algae back towards the door.

A shadow moved in front of me, and I realized with relief that it was Park, her vague silhouette outlined against the light coming through the laboratory door. There was no sign of her extinguisher, and I guessed that she had realized it was useless rather than making the same mistake that I had. I risked a look back over my shoulder, and saw that the whole laboratory was ablaze, not just the algae and surrounding foliage, but the cladding on the walls and ceiling, materials that were designed not to burn. A gobbet of flame dropped on to my shoulder, and I screamed, reflexively slapping at the fire to stop my clothing catching light, strings of molten plastic coming away with my hand. I struggled to catch my breath, my eyes running with tears inside my respirator. Cradling my charred hand against my chest, I made a final, blind dash in the direction I had last seen Park.

I almost hit the wall before I saw it; sobbing, I fumbled my way along until I found the control panel for the door, activated it, then half-stepped and half-fell into the corridor outside, ripping my respirator off my face and sucking in cold, dry air. Park had left a sooty handprint by the door. The comm unit on the wall was flashing, and as the laboratory door slid shut again I slammed the button.

I didn't wait for Soyinka to answer. "We're out! Vent it!"

"Emergency venting, laboratory module," Soyinka said, and through the door I heard the heavy thumps of metal that meant the emergency hatches were opening.

Something dark and shapeless lurched, slammed into the door inches from me. I stumbled back, tripped over my own feet and sprawled my length down the corridor. As the smoke dissipated inside the lab I started to make out a human form, the face grotesquely elongated, hands hammering at the reinforced glass in hungry desperation. "There's something in there!" My voice was almost drowned out by the rising howl of the venting air. The thing, whatever it was, hurled itself forward into the door again, and for one terrible moment I thought it was strong enough to smash through, but the door held. Its face, if you could call it a face, pressed against the glass, and I caught the briefest glimpse of one wide, dark eye before it slid away to the floor.

Slowly, the rush of escaping air slowed and ceased. The flames and the smoke were gone, but soot still covered the glass, streaked where the thing's face had smeared it.

"Someone was in there," I said. "Someone else."

"That's not possible."

"It's there," I said. "Park, did you see it?"

There was only silence on the other end of the intercom, then Soyinka's voice. "Park's with you."

"No, she was out ahead of me...I thought she joined you on the bridge—"

I looked at the black handprint on the wall, the sooty smears of a trail along the bulkheads. The hand looked larger than Park's, larger than human. I felt something drop in the pit of my stomach.

"Soyinka, repressurize the lab."

"What's the point? The algae's dead. We'd just waste air."

"For God's sake, just do it. I think—" I closed my eyes, trying to concentrate despite the pain spreading up my arm. "Park's still in there."

We watched the blurry camera footage over and over; the door to the lab opening, the figure emerging and pressing one hand to the wall with a slow, deliberate air. There was something about the way it moved that made my skin crawl--slow, heavy and lumbering--the limbs too thick, the head too big as it lumbered out of the camera's field of vision. Then, half a minute later, the door opening again, and my own indistinct silhouette emerging, Park's last desperate moments of life pressed against the transparent door.

"I don't understand," Soyinka said. "How can there be someone else on the station?"

"There isn't. There can't be."

I thought of the handprint on the wall. If it hadn't been made by Park, Soyinka was the only possible alternative. She must have read the thought on my face, and she threw her hands up defensively.

"Banerjee, it wasn't me. I wasn't in there."

"Who else could it have been?"

"Look at it!" She jabbed an accusatory finger at the screen. "The door opens. The–whoever it is—comes out. Then you. Then, five seconds later, the room vents. There's no way I could have made it back to the bridge controls in that time."

We watched the hulking, blurry figure emerging again. The detail was no more distinct that any of the previous viewings, but something about the way the figure moved looked familiar. "It's a spacesuit," I said. "Someone in a spacesuit."

Soyinka blurted out a laugh. "Who's wearing it, then? Park was in the lab. You don't think the Captain's in that, do you? Because last I heard she's freeze-dried."

"There can't be anyone else on the station. There's no way someone could have got on board. And if they'd been here since we arrived, even if somehow they'd managed to hide all this time, even if they'd brought supplies, we'd know if they'd been using air."

She was right. Air was tightly rationed onboard. It was one of the reasons deep space crews tended to be female these days, as we used less oxygen. There was no possible way a fifth person could have gone unnoticed. "What is it, then? A trick of the light? Some previous footage that's ended up in the wrong file?"

"Must be."

I decided not to dwell on what I'd seen in the smoky laboratory. I'd been so sure I'd seen someone leaving ahead of me that I hadn't stopped to consider that Park might still be inside. I rubbed at my eyes.

"How's the oxygen situation?"

"Not great, if I'm honest with you. Assuming the relief shuttle's on time, the secondary generator should see us through. Assuming."

"Can we get a message out to them, tell them to hurry up?"

Soyinka shook her head. "We're still not transmitting. The aerial, remember?"

I checked my chronometer. Less than a day until our relief arrived, now. I wondered how long it had been since I last slept. Pain was making it hard to think.

An explosion, the sound deafening in the confined space, shook the bridge, knocking me to the floor and sending Soyinka sprawling into her workstation.

"What the hell—"

"Something exploded," she said. "Looks like we've got a hull rupture."

"Are we open?"

She shook her head. "I can seal the module. Hang on..."

I watched her anxiously, until she nodded and the looming specter of death receded. Her flight suit was billowing strangely, and it took me a moment to realize that the artificial gravity had failed. By the time I got to my feet there was nothing to hold me to the floor, and the pair of us drifted upwards, weightless.

"The explosion knocked out the gravity generator," Soyinka said. "Hydrogen, I think. Something must have stopped it venting from the hydrolysis system."

"If that's blown, it'll have taken the oxygen generator with it." My hands found the wall, and I started to push myself along it to the door. "Gravity should still be on in the rear module."

"The airlock," Soyinka said. "We can run the emergency oxygen supply into it. Even if that's gone, there should be oxygen candles."

We were both rated for zero G, but even so, pushing ourselves down corridors designed for walking was exhausting. The usual day-cycle lights had been replaced with a red emergency glow, and every dark recess seemed to hold creeping humanoid shadows. I stopped briefly in front of the passage that led to the hydrolysis module, where the blast doors had already dropped, but that wasn't what caught my eye. On the wall, just by the door controls, was a hand print, too large to be human, but dark and unmistakably deliberate.

We crossed the intersection into the rear module, and instantly transitioned back to moving in two dimensions rather than three. I sealed the doors that separated the two modules, and the pair of us sprinted for the airlock. The foot thick metal plating behind me gave me a tremendous sense of security, and I leaned my back against it with relief.

"No matter what happens outside, we've got air in here," I said. "In fact, the whole damn station could go up and we'd probably be fine."

Soyinka didn't answer. Then, she said: "Turn around," with a flat, unfamiliar note in her voice. I did as she said, something telling me that any sudden movement would be a fatal error at this point. She had taken an explosive-powered grapnel from the EVA kit and had it pointed at my chest.

"What are you doing?" I asked, feeling my muscles grow rigid.

"Take a step back please. Right against the wall. Thanks." She ran her free hand across her mouth, a nervous gesture I'd seen her make before.

"Soyinka—"

She shook her head, interrupting me.

"How did you do it?"

I blinked at her. "How did I do what?"

She gestured vaguely around herself. "All of this. Park. The lab. What did you spray the algae with, to make it go up like that? Some sort of flammable lubricant?"

"I didn't do any of it. Put the grapnel down, please—"

She cut me off with a sharp, frustrated sigh. "How did you find out?"

"I've got no idea what you're talking about." I tried to keep my voice calm, aware that I was having limited success at best.

She shook her head ruefully. "The same way as the Captain, I suppose. She worked it out from the receiver logs. Clever." She nodded her head, approving of the Captain's intelligence. "As the other stations went dark, we were processing more and more of the incoming signal."

"Went dark?"

"Shut down. We have people on all of them, you know. It's all been carefully planned, closing down communications between Rhea and Earth."

"Why?"

"Not forever." She smiled indulgently, as if the fact should be obvious. "Just for long enough to get the revolution underway. By the time they even hear about it on Earth it'll be too late. I couldn't risk the Captain telling anyone."

"Is that why you killed her?"

"I didn't want to. But she must have checked the transmission logs. When she saw we hadn't broadcast anything to Earth for days she went out to check the aerial. It wasn't a hardware problem, of course, software's much easier to work with." Soyinka shrugged. "She thought it was Park. I'd done everything through her user account, just in case. So I waited until the captain was getting ready, I said I wanted to help her with the aerial. We shut down the suit cams, in case Park was watching from the bridge. She didn't notice me disabling her thrusters and cutting her main oxygen supply. Then, when we were outside, all I had to do was unhook her tether. She was supposed to be gone forever. I didn't expect you to find her."

"How long was she out there?"

"Hours, I suppose. You were asleep."

"Look. You don't need to do anything you'll regret—please. Relief will be here in a few hours--if you're the only one alive they'll know something's up. I can talk to them…tell them—" A ball of panic was rising in my throat.

"What makes you think they'll want to listen to you?" she said, with a tight smile. "They're not coming from Earth. They're coming from Rhea. All they'll want to know is that I got the job done. Sorry, Banerjee."

She aimed the grapnel. I saw her finger tighten on the trigger, and reflexively turned my face away so I didn't have to see my death coming, but instead of the impact I was expecting I heard first one dull thud, then another. I opened my eyes and saw that the grapnel, still loaded, had clattered to the deck and landed just out of my reach. Something had struck Soyinka from behind, hard enough to drive her to one knee and knock the weapon from her grip. She was shaking her head in bewilderment, clearly wondering what had hit her. It was one of the space suits.

I didn't waste time questioning my good fortune, just scrambled towards the grapnel, then I froze as the suit seemed to move again. This time the movement was slow and deliberate, swelling as though gradually being filled with air. All Soyinka's attention was focused on recovering her lost weapon. She didn't notice the great gold-visored helmet rising like the sun, or the gloved hands reaching for her neck.

"Soyinka!" I shouted, pointing behind her, panic rising in my chest. I don't know why I tried to warn her—she had been trying to kill me, but that fact seemed suddenly insignificant beside the sheer terror that the suit's movement invoked in me. Something of the horror on my face must have registered in her, because she looked over her shoulder. In the helmet, her reflection changed from confusion to fear and then to terror as the suit's hands locked around her throat. With appalling deliberation they began to squeeze her airway closed. She lashed out, trying to break its hold, but its grip was too strong, her kicking legs flailing in the air like a criminal's on the gallows. I scrabbled across the floor, groping blindly for the grapnel gun. My outstretched finger found the trigger guard and I fumbled it into my hand, back pressed to the door. Soyinka's corpse dropped to the deck. The helmet turned to face me.

"Captain," I said. "Captain, don't—"

It took a step toward me. I fired the grapnel, and the barbed end lodged in its shoulder. Neither the impact nor the injury seemed to have any effect on it at all, but it pulled the hook free, tossing it indifferently to the side. I locked my arms around the wall cabling, took a deep breath in, exhaled as far as I could—and pulled the emergency decompression lever.

Air rushed around me in a deafening roar that was silenced a moment later as my eardrums ruptured. Tools and debris clattered off the bulkheads, and I clung with all my strength to the cables. Inside my mouth my tongue was starting to bubble, and I knew I had fifteen seconds at most—less, if the thing reached me.

My vision was blurring. I tried to draw breath, but there was nothing to inhale. The suit had stopped six inches from me, and something was leaking from the rupture in its shoulder—a pale grey shadow, insubstantial as smoke, light as air, and pluming out like cigarette smoke. The gloved hands were scrabbling at the hole as if they could seal it by touch alone, but the damage was done.

The grey plume was out of the suit now, streaming towards the airlock, only a ghostly thread connecting it to the suit which spun and twisted and thinned until it was only a hair's breadth thick. It snapped and the suit collapsed, empty, to the floor. The shadow twisted and writhed as the last of it whirled out of the hatch into the darkness beyond, and then it was gone. I hit the emergency repressurization button, and I don't remember much after that.

Humanity pushes the boundaries of space every year, but our

biology remains a hard limit. It must have been less than ninety seconds before pressure was restored, because if it had been longer than that I'd have been dead. As it was, I was deaf and mostly blind, with every inch of my skin burning where it had been stretched like a balloon. Soyinka's body was gone, along with two of the space suits, the oxygen candles and everything else that been unsecured. The captain's suit lay where it had fallen, empty as a corpse.

The oxygen gauge read twelve percent, and already the air felt thin, like I was at the top of a mountain. It wouldn't keep me alive for long, not even if the relief shuttle arrived as scheduled, but there was one source of oxygen left to me. Its golden visor, blank and inscrutable, reflected only my own face. Shaking and clumsy, I stepped into my suit and closed the seals.

When the shuttle arrived I'd be waiting, one way or another.

ASTRONOSFERATU AND THE INVISIBLE VOID

BRANDON BUTLER

Vlad the Impaler hasn't let me rest for three nights straight. He thinks he's onto something, this scheme of trapping Count Dracula in near-earth orbit. I let him prattle on before hitting him with the obvious. "Vlad," I say, "you're closing in on a thousand years old. You don't know what you're doing up there."

He stops mid-sentence, encased in an environment suit showing its age. It's a drab, hazmat-inspired getup the Circle built for spirits enticed from the other side. The faceplate is lowered beneath his paranormal stare, revealing a thick Slavic warrior's mustache jutting like a translucent spear across his lip. "The creature is no older than I," he insists. He's learned English over the decades, and speaks it pretty well.

"I'm over here," I tell him. This happens all the time. I usually wander around in the buff so there's no way of seeing where I am. Sure, it gets chilly, on my calloused feet especially. But you gotta show off what you got.

Vlad corrects his stance toward my voice. "It is a just plan, Griffin. I could best describe the vampire as a *duşmani ai sângelui* – blood enemy, though I do not intend to pun. I would appreciate support."

"Think it through. How're you getting him up there?"

He grins. I should have known he'd think ahead – Vlad's pretty crafty, for an old guy. He walks through plummeting cascades of dust to a monitor taking up the high, opposite wall. This is one of the rooms we haven't looked after, a cavernous briefing chamber with metal strut chairs and bare windows along one side. It's been three years since it's seen regular use but between the two of us, we've gotten both its monitor and the building siphoning off the power grid. He calls up an advertisement, probably grabbed off the internet back when I had the servers running for four hours last week.

It's a cryo chamber. Single-serving unit. Large enough for one person to be forgotten for a century or two. They sell larger versions for entire groups these days.

"A coffin for the stars," says Vlad.

"He making one?"

"We shall bestow one upon him. Once we enshrine it with grave-yard earth, make the necessary alterations and extend an invitation through the shadowy corners of the world, he shall come. He wants to leave this planet."

"Because of you."

"For many reasons. Regardless, we shall offer him an audience upon Lawrence's orbital platform. He may see it as neutral ground without lingering ties to me. Following his arrival, the trap is sprung."

I sit forward, shaking my head. "You're bringing Larry into this?"

"Why not? I thought you admired him."

I did, that was the problem. Larry's fascinating. I could spend decades studying his anatomy head to toe and still find more peculiarities to dote upon. He's beyond an old timer, well over a hundred years but young as ever, living to see the Circle through whole generations before Dracula and other nasties wiped us out for good.

I should explain – until recently, the Circle had been around forever. Got started way, way back in the late Roman Empire. Formed to stop it from falling, but hell of a lot of good that did. They've hung around in one form or another. Maybe you've heard of their disguises. Templars. Jesuits. A couple Freemason chapters. Different names in different times but it's all the same thing. Once in a while they got too big for their britches and got brought down hard, but on the whole, they always wanted the best for you and me. Never shirked from what was necessary.

But three years ago, the evil they hunted turned on them all at once. You wouldn't have heard anything about it. It wasn't that kind of attack. So now, on Earth, there's just abandoned sites like this and the orbital station Larry took over. If the other Circle chapters are out in the colonies amongst the stars, they haven't returned.

"There's no need to bother Larry," I say. "He gets emotional. That's why he's up there."

Vlad goes still. I know he's about to get dramatic before he takes the helmet off, staring at me with eyes that curdle milky white as they hit the air. Long hair falls over his shoulders like a banshee. "Emotions must be controlled," he says.

I roll my eyes, then get up and show him my ass. The things I do, if they ever saw… look, I know his nuggets of supposed wisdom, he knows I know them, so why the show? He gives one, I'll give right back. Good thing it's a big building. I only need to put up with his antiquated self in small doses. "You surprise me," he says ignorantly into my backside, "I had anticipated Lawrence and yourself favoring revenge."

Turning around, I tell him, "I'm not dead. I don't moan on and on like you. And the vampire didn't bring the Circle down alone, he wasn't even the leader. As for our former colleagues, well, I wasn't overly attached."

"No. That is true. You do not get attached, do you Griffin?"

If he'd seen me, I would have shrugged. But his gaze still gave me the creeps. I wish his suit was more than mostly necessary, so he couldn't take any of it off.

"So. You are unwilling to help."

"I'd rather not," I say.

"But you owe me a debt."

Damn. Was hoping he wouldn't remember. The Circle caught Vlad in Ceausescu's Romania during the seventies but he'd gained their trust and joined their office states-side, which was where they found me. They just thought they'd found another ghost. Sorry, boys; no undead abomination here, just a simple man with simple plans invisible to the eye. What a day *that* had been. The Circle had been about to do me in before he stopped them.

And after all these years, Vlad never asked for anything in return. I stifle a sigh and say, "I owe you."

"Good. I shall make arrangements." He turns to leave.

"Vlad."

He stops, but doesn't turn around.

"Dracula's a vampire. *The* vampire. I know it's personal, but your reputation –"

"His works are a disgrace against God," he says. "He has defamed, dishonored and eviscerated my name."

"Well, come on now... your name? You've had PR problems from way back."

He turns his head. "I drink no blood. I am no cannibal. What I did in life, I did for my people. Let me be damned for my own deeds." He lets that sink in, then flashes another smile. "I have done my reading, Griffin. I know your petty crimes. Do not dwell on these gloomier shades of darkness that recess within the human soul. They are quite beyond you."

W eeks later, and he's bought a cryo chamber and reactivated the old maintenance robots to refit it. I'm responsible for that: I learned programming long before joining the Circle, and showed Vlad enough to be dangerous. So now he's got a few of them running around before their power runs out, which he recharges from the dormant backup generators.

I let him do his thing. When he inevitably gets stuck, I improvise a general design for him, then get out of his way. With any luck he'll forget I'm here.

Not to be. By the beginning of the next month he's talking to Larry and working out the whole thing, throwing my name around. I'm not sure why he needs me. Probably thinks that when you're going up against Dracula, you need all the help you can get.

If so, he's right about that.

He calls me in after a while to review the casket. The sliding glass front has been replaced by polished slate. Dirt has been packed into a breakaway plastic frame around the seams, in case the undead occupant needs it open to the air. Otherwise, it's plush in there. Deep, soft, red velvet lining. "If the whole thing's only a trap, why bother building it?" I ask.

"Authentic bait," he explains, "he shall be vulnerable if I can entice his curiosity."

"Just offer virgins. He likes those."

Vlad shoots me a look. Staring straight at me this time, unamused.

He books us, the cryo-coffin, and an assortment of security and loader-bots onto an automatic flight to the orbital platform. It's just the two of us the whole way and that suits us fine, since the Circle always kept us out of sight from the general public. In my case, an easy task.

"He sounded lonely," says Vlad after we've touched off. I'm wearing my own baggy spacesuit for the journey so he knows exactly where to talk. "Mond… that is not his given surname, is it? I do not know Lawrence well, but what I do know, I do not understand. I have been imprisoned many times. Never willingly."

"He wanted to get away from people. That was important to him."

"But none of us left Earth before the Circle fell. He is surely no more familiar with space than I."

That's the difference between me and Vlad. I've always been curious, and sometime over the centuries, he became that way as well. But he's interested in reasons, in history. Who cares why things are the way they are? It is what it is, move on.

"Have you seen him after a change?" I ask, "or somewhere he's been after one?"

Vlad looks at me, then out a window as blue fades to black. "No," he says. I leave it at that.

As platforms go, it's not large. The Circle fought to keep it discrete and off the grid, ensuring its orbital path didn't make itself a nuisance. The important people of the world must be aware of its existence, but they haven't done anything. Probably afraid to touch it. It's dark upon our approach, two trapezoids like twin hulking steel asteroids bridged by the main body along the middle. And on the front, the old insignia of the flaming wheel. Vlad straightens with pride when he sees it.

We dock without incident and bring the cargo onboard. The lights are dim, the interiors gray, flat and polished. Every external viewport is closed over. The transport detaches as we exit the shuttle bay. We're on our own.

It's quiet. Our footsteps and the whir of the robots carrying the coffin echo throughout the station. Every so often a light will flicker, but stay on. Everything's so empty and clean, way better than the caves he used to lurk around in.

"Hey guys," we hear, and there he is, huddled away in shadow. Larry was never large in this form, and he's wearing a brown leather jacket that's padded to keep him warm. He's pale and greasy, as if waking from a cold sweat. But he's always looked like that, like shit; it's the price he pays. Vlad walks over and they shake hands.

"How's it been?" I ask, "are you holding up?" The old Circle folks hated my idle talk. Said I didn't care. That's not true. I'm honestly curious, like I said.

He barely looks at me, which I guess makes sense, pulling his coat tighter. You'd think he was freezing. "Is that it?"

We walk over to the coffin. Larry shakes his head. "You must want this pretty bad, Vlad."

"I hate the vampire. He hates me. I almost caught and killed him with the Circle's help. And once with an agent of theirs before I joined. The Dutchman."

"I still haven't put the word out. There's time to re-consider."

Vlad's tone becomes polite, impersonal. "I will not."

"Thought you'd say that. All right, I'll get on it. Put it in the foyer like we agreed."

Vlad gets to it and Larry walks off, so I hurry to catch up. "Things look nice," I say. "I thought there'd be more disarray."

He keeps going like he hasn't heard.

"So… has it happened again? Up here? What was it like?"

He wheels on me, eyes frantic. "You got my cure, Griffin? You guaranteed a cure."

I hold my hands up. *This again.* Jesus, this guy can turn on a dime.

"A lot of people did."

"Your promises were the biggest."

What did he want? I was part of the research division, it was my job. Yeah, okay, I poked and prodded, ran experiments. Some of them might have hurt, but I did warn the guy. And things had obviously changed. "I'm sorry Larry, ok? If you haven't noticed, you're not the only one in need of a cure. Get in line."

He doesn't break his rabid gaze, his irises glowing crimson. It's always like this when he's mad, but how can he look right into my eyes like that? "You don't fool me Griffin," he says, "not anymore. You're not looking to cure yourself. You've always been comfortable with exactly who you are."

I watch him go. Yeah, Larry. Nice to see you too.

D*eep rumbling from below. Beakers rattling as commotion rages in the halls. I follow like a moth to flame.*

Dogs, but not real dogs, running below an indoor balcony. Their snouts like pigs, fire leaping from their nostrils. Guards fire as I tear off my latex skin, and the flesh-colored gauze beneath.

Mist blankets the room, dark and thick, passing over bodies as it rises into a column with red, baleful eyes.

I blink and fall off my chair, coming to upon the cool deck floor. How long was I out?

Rising, I turn back to the computer screen. I replay the security clip, watching former station inhabitants fight their futile struggle against encroaching darkness. The stories of the day the Circle fell are all different – hell hounds, zombies, gill men – some even hint at alien activity. You'd think that last one would have shown up on an orbital platform but if the tapes were any indication, it was just a shadow. A bleak, hungry shadow consuming the light and everything alive. Its disembodied nature didn't stop the doomed inhabitants from firing on its black expanse again and again to no avail.

I sit back and wonder how the staff might have fared if Larry had been around that day, at full strength. Like everything else from the attack, the shadow had left without a trace.

The Circle had made its enemies. A lot. We'd thought ourselves defended.

The thought rises in my mind, not for the first time: an inside job. I'm still thinking it when the comm buzzes. *Griffin?* It's Vlad.

"Yeah?"

We've picked up his shuttle on the scanners. He's on his way.

Great. I'd hoped for at least another week.

"Be there in a minute."

It was more like fifteen. The station foyer is two stories high, with ramps stretching out like spider arms running up the sides to higher sections. There's a large viewport running ceiling to floor that Larry's shut like all the others. The cryo coffin is here, in the center, with Vlad and Larry on either side.

"You understand how to proceed?" Vlad asks, as if I've forgotten.

"Yeah, yeah. He comes in, Larry shows him the coffin, then you surprise him. We tackle and stake him while his back is turned." I give Larry a sidelong glance. He'd suggested this plan of attack, and impractical as it was, I agreed. We're using his station, after all. "Still got your rabid strength?" I ask.

"Don't worry about it."

Oh yeah, going up against the world's deadliest vampire and that's his advice? I look towards the robots along the wall. Power supplies are topped up, so we can use them if needed. Plus, I'm out of my suit so not even the vampire can know I'm here. It's probably enough. "Vlad," I say, "if we pull this off, you owe *me*."

The Impaler gives one of his cunning smiles. "Griffin. Do you expect me to believe you agreed out of personal gratitude? When has that ever been a salient attribute of your character?"

I'm not fidgeting as he looks in my direction. I swear I'm not.

"You want to see Dracula again. Figure out a way to study him."

"Vlad, that's…" I try laughing him off, but it sounds weak and tittering. "Do I seem suicidal?"

He looks my absence up and down. "Vaguely, at times."

"You don't need to worry. I'm here to kill him."

"I know. Ultimately, even you are not that foolish. But take heed – the vampire cannot glamor you because he cannot see you, but do not listen to any offer he might make. There is no bargain with him that can be struck, no deal that can be trusted. Content yourself with his remains when the act is done."

I hadn't thought about studying Dracula. Honest. I'd been along for the ride this far. But I'll admit Vlad has me wondering if that hasn't been the reason all along. Sometimes things get so ingrained, they become part of your instinct.

Dracula's shuttle is getting close, headed to the bay on the far side. Vlad leaves and I whisper to Larry, "Hey. We've faced this guy before. No pressure."

Larry doesn't respond. He's not as friendly has he used to be.

I draw a short distance away and wait. And wait. A display on the far end of the room eventually tells us he's docked in shuttle bay two. Then everything falls quiet.

He enters without warning. Alone, thin, a long black cloak hanging to his ankles with hair as dark as you'd imagine growing scant around his temples. Amidst a pallid complexion and pointed ears, his aquiline cheekbones seem otherwise regal. I look at his red eyes. Though I see the resemblance, I wonder how anyone could mistake this thing for Vlad. The Impaler's a warrior, with a stomach for shocking brutality. This dainty monster concealed hungers born of crueler appetites.

He floats into the foyer, stopping before the coffin. Mist pours out beneath his feet. "Mister Mond," he says to Larry, "or so you call your-self. It has been a while."

Larry nods, once.

"When last we met, you tried to kill me. The time before that… you tried to kill me."

"I remember it the other way around," Larry says.

"Yet you seduce with such intriguing offers." Dracula looks down at the casket, eyes widening. "I admit, I find the old methods lacking when confronted with the rigors of space travel. I remain Earthbound as a consequence." He put a hand over the surface.

Larry hoists up his coat, draws a revolver he's slipped beneath his belt.

"Let me see it first."

Dracula looks at the toy and smiles. I think he's about to break into one of those diabolical laughs, but instead digs into his cloak and produces a vial.

"As promised," he says, "your cure."

I take one look at Larry and realize something's up.

"Dracula!" Moments later than I would have preferred, Vlad's cry booms from a second story ramp. He stands straight and tall, carrying a weapon, a dark-edged longsword drawn and pointed at the floor. Captivated through his commanding presence, I begin to understand how men might once have followed him to battle and glory. I slowly circle to one side.

Dracula turns. "Beloved ancestor!" he says, "once more we meet!"

"For the last time," Vlad tells him.

Dracula shakes his head. "There's been so many times, it seems. It is a chore, getting you off my back."

"You've stolen my name. My place in history."

"My posthumous fame is not my fault. Not entirely. And as to your place in history, was it I who impaled thousands from throat to scrotum? Who boiled men, women, and children alive? Was that I?"

A long moment of silence. Vlad doesn't move, staring down from the ramp's open steel landing. "Much of that is untrue," he says.

"But not all," replies Dracula, delight in his voice. Then he waves a hand and his mist crawls over the floor. I look down, start slinking away but its around my ankles before I can get clear, crawling up my body. And then suddenly I'm there, wrapped in grey in front of them all, a human cloud.

Dracula looks at me. "Griffin. The arrogant insect. You must have thought me stupid."

I look around, swallowing, and my pride goes with it. "Figured we had a shot."

Dracula smirks and it turns into a sneer. I'm sensing he likes me least of all. He curls a hand into a fist and strikes the casket, snapping the stone into perfect halves. He doesn't break his gaze with me and when he speaks, says, "You may dispense with Griffin now, Mr. Mond."

I look at Larry. He's pointing the gun at me.

Crap. Ok, here we go.

Behind my back, I snap my fingers.

Four robots hum to life around the chamber. They run full tilt, and it's enough of a distraction for me to start getting the hell out of there. I drop the stakes I'd been carrying, doused in the invisibility salve I'd designed. They'll only weigh me down.

Dracula's busy with the robots. Vlad leaps down and charges him. I'm hightailing it away, with Larry hot on my heels. He fires the gun, wide.

"Fifteen years!" he yells.

No idea what that's about. I get out of the foyer. The mist dissipates from my body but Larry's not far and he's still shooting. The aim seems more accurate than I'd like. I duck down the corridor and he follows.

"Stand still!" he roars, and fires three more times. "I can smell you, you bastard."

Uh oh.

I try fleeing, but Larry knows this place better than I ever will. We're moving constantly in one direction, and by memory I deduce that he's herding me to the docking bay, the empty one Vlad and I first entered from.

Before I can think of some way to avoid it, we're there. I hover by the entrance, eying the control panel. That thing can open up the bay doors right out into space. If I go in there, it's over.

I spy the last of our loader bots, just inside the door.

The corridor runs further along and there's a bend not far away, but I'm through running. I walk a few feet back from the door and stand my ground.

Larry walks up, takes two big sniffs, and smiles. "I knew you were lying," he says, "all this time. Dracula told me, but in a way, I'd known for years." He points the gun and though he's not looking me precisely in the eye, he adjusts the muzzle when I lean to the side. "You had the cure for years. And you kept it from me."

Oh, come on. *Seriously?* Yeah, sure, I developed a formula. It was a guess. But it was the boys in the lab who processed the thing, synthesized it into a proper serum. What, it's my responsibility to tell Larry all my notions and theories? If the Circle were such good guys, why didn't *they* tell him? Not my business.

"Test after test after test, stringing me along, when you already knew." He steps into the doorframe and raises the gun. This time it's right at my head. "Smell you in Hell, Griffin." He says, and pulls the trigger.

Click. No bullets, just like I counted. I snap my fingers again.

Before Larry knows what's happening the loader bot grapples and pulls him into the shuttle bay. He struggles. Even in human form, he's strong. I race to the control panel but it's locked – Larry changed the entire administration of this place, right down to the account passwords.

I grin to myself. I'd been here at least a week. Of course I'd cracked his code.

I punch it in, and the door slides shut. But Larry's no slouch himself, and he's given such a kick to the loader bot's leg that it can't maneuver. He's probably not strong enough to break out of there in human form, but I don't want to risk it. I punch the sequence to open the shuttle bay doors.

They don't start right away. There's a caution alarm, a delay, a whole procedure. Larry grimaces at me through the reinforced window and makes for the emergency locker on the far side, breaking the glass to access the spacesuits and tethers.

He's ready in time. The doors open and he's sucked out with the loader bot, jerking to a stop twenty or thirty feet outside the station. He hangs there, dangling like a helpless puppet. Is he...? Yes, he's definitely flipping me off.

But he's not alone, out in space. The stars twinkle, silent and lovely. The immaculate earth spins below, rotating all its blues, greens and browns.

And the moon watches.

He turns to look, and must realize his peril before I do. He starts freaking out, flailing his limbs, and they're already growing bigger. Suddenly he's grown out of his spacesuit, bursting at the seams along the muscles of the great wolf that he is, shaggy fur and jagged fangs, dangling in the void. His maw bursts out of his helmet as he lifts his head in a final howl only his moon can hear. Then he slumps forward, fur and claws whitening with crystalized fringes.

A long moment passes. Larry Mond was an enthralling specimen. I don't suppose I'll work with his like again. That's sad and I try coming up with an appropriate thought or gesture. But just like me, I can't. What can I say? I am who I am and have always been.

I remember the vampire and head back to the foyer.

The bots are all destroyed. Dracula's got Vlad now, torn up his environment suit. That's it for the old Impaler, I realize, since he needs that to stay anchored and can't go more than a half hour without it covering at least eighty-five percent of his body surface. But enough shreds are left for the vampire to grip him by the throat, baring his needlepoint fangs.

"Squirming toads," he says, "I'll build more coffins from this one, and spread my wings throughout the cosmos. Along with the legend of your final failure."

You got to give him credit, Vlad's face doesn't give a stoic inch.

I let it play out a second more, then call up a panel on the wall. I input Larry's code to open up the main viewport, revealing the glare of a roiling sun.

Dracula slumps immediately and I don't waste time, fetching my stakes from where I remember dropping them. He releases Vlad, and the mist that had been wrapping over me again begins to fade. The sun won't kill him, from what I understand, that's long been a misconception – but it will take nearly everything away. The vampire looks up at the brilliant source of his downfall, then roams his hapless gaze around the foyer.

"Griffin," he says, "you… you little…"

I grab his shoulder and run a stake into his chest as hard as I can. Weaker than a baby he falls back and I get on top, applying my weight, plunging the stake through his chest. He screams and screams, blood gushing up out of the wound before he goes still, dead flesh sizzling beneath my nostrils. I get to my knees. I survey my work, and spot Vlad's longsword abandoned on the floor. I pick it up and, with the barest hesitation, chop off the creature's head with a single, precise blow.

It's quiet for a long moment. Vlad weakly raises his hand. I head over as he looks upon Dracula's remains. "Done at last," he says.

I look with him, blood spattered over my naked form. Yeah, can't refute that.

He turns to me, already dissipating. "Thank you," he says.

"No problem. Debt repaid."

"What an oddity you are, Griffin," he tells me, leaning back to let the inevitable wash over him. He gestures to the station around us. "An absence in the heart of purpose. Does it never bother you to know nothing of honor? Of justice?"

I walk over and look down at him. "It ever bother you?" I ask.

He takes my meaning. He doesn't scowl, simply meets my gaze, though I know he cannot see it, and fades away.

Well. That's over. The console is beeping. I go and have a look, realizing I need to do something about Larry out there in space. That's really not right. I know he hated me, and had his convoluted reasons but… yeah, his body is really going to waste out there.

There's an alert on the console. Missives from the Circle. My eyebrows raise as I look into a secured folder and realize other members are out there, on other worlds. They've been talking with Larry for years, and he's been keeping them at bay. Telling them Earth is lost to the enemy.

That little bugger. Was he our traitor all along? Perhaps not working for Dracula originally, but coordinating with our other enemies? Seems that way. Never thought he'd have it in him.

But why? He was always so eager, especially in the early days, signing up for my examinations.

Huh. I don't get it.

I saunter to the viewport, casting no shadow in the glare of the sun, looking towards Earth. I drum fingers over the glass. The Circle is calling, the masses below are waiting. What to do? I think back to my notions of subliminal, ingrained instincts. With an orbital platform at my disposal and abandoned facilities at my fingertips this is, I realize, a moment to contemplate the bright wonders and gloomier shades of darkness the future might hold.

BELLEROPHON'S GAMBIT

HILLARY LYON

The oblong, silvery object was jettisoned from the bio-hazardous waste disposal portal on the dark side of the cruise ship. The lone crew member, Andrew, watched as it sped away, rotating swiftly, catching the sun behind them in staccato glints. For the first time in days, he relaxed, letting his breath out in one long, stress-deflating sigh. After a while, he closed the storm-shutter on his viewing portal, locked the door to the disposal unit, and walked down the plushly-carpeted corridor to the communications room, where he would send out a pre-recorded S.O.S.

It was only a week ago that this compact, five-star cosmic cruise-ship—*Bellerophon's Gambit*—was fully staffed, with crew members buzzing about their duties, catering to the whims of the affluent passengers, with Captain Murphey shouting directives and the first mate, Greeley, muttering his off-color replies. A week ago, Andrew was the lowly assistant to the sous chef, McBride. He didn't mind; the work was not all that difficult, just boring—even with McBride's long-winded yarns about gathering wild herbs and fungi back on Earth with his grandmother. The best part of this gig was, to Andrew's mind, he was on board a rocket-fueled cruise-ship speeding him on his way to Mars to meet his lovely fiancee, Daphne. She of the long-limbs and golden-eyes, with black hair sparkling like a spiral galaxy—some days he couldn't believe his luck. Sure, she loved him, too—but to make doubly certain she'd stay with him, he was determined to look for more meaningful employment once they docked on Mars; you could hardly support a wife of Daphne's caliber—and hopefully someday, kids—on a potato-peeler's pay.

Then the boys in navigation picked up an unidentified object on their scans: a lonely, blinking red spot on the black fields of their monitors—like a hungry little tick swiftly approaching, heading straight for them. This led to much speculation: Was it an escape pod? A sealed cockpit from a raided, abandoned ship? Random space trash? Further scans determined there *was* a life form aboard, though the signal pulse was weak. Scatter-shot rumors abounded. Animated discussions dominated the well-appointed dining room, thrilling the bejeweled passengers over their puffer-fish sushi and Kobe steak tartar. After much discussion among the officers, the decision was made to draw the object in for closer study. If there was someone, or *something*, barely alive on board, and the scans held that there was, perhaps they could save it.

So the silvery object was snagged by tractor beam, and drawn closer to the ship. More in-depth scans confirmed the initial data. The officers agreed to bring it on board, doubtlessly dreaming of their exaggerated roles in this heroic rescue, of glorified stories about themselves all over the news, their inevitable promotions, and lucrative book deals.

Of course, the thing was left in quarantine for 24 Earth-hours. During this time the sleek case—it resembled a man-sized sarcophagus —was subjected to all manner of disinfecting processes and further scans to determine its contents. The data revealed a humanoid *thing* inside, securely strapped in and swaddled in the fog of a chemically neutral, organically mysterious gas. An alien method of suspended-animation, perhaps?

Word threading among the crew insisted the humanoid was a criminal sentenced to abandonment in space for its heinous off-world crimes. The med staff posited two theories: one, the humanoid perhaps suffered from an incurable illness, maybe a contagious one, and the diseased *thing* was likely meant to be quarantined forever inside the silvered casket. Or, two, at the very least, the sickly resident was set adrift in hopes of a merciful, sleeping death because there was no cure.

Thus, they argued vigorously against opening the case; furthermore, they contended the case should be returned to space, unopened. But the higher-ups knew better than anyone else, as they were constantly reminding everyone within earshot, and they ordered the case be opened when the quarantine period expired.

So the case was opened, with all the officers in self-congratulatory attendance. Unlocking it was surprisingly easy; a twist of a knob here, a push of a button there. The event was recorded by the ship's ever-present video eye; though on playback, after the top of the case slid off, after the gasses dissipated, after the humanoid was unstrapped and then *sat up*, the video feed washed out in a wave of static. The audio feed was no better, though through the crackling static Captain Murphey could be heard shouting:

"Dear God in Heaven! What is that? What is it —"

When the security detail finally jacked open the sealed doors of the quarantine unit, there was so much gore splattered across the interior consoles, so many entrails hung like festive garlands all around the room, so many appendages heaped together in one chaotic pile, that even those stalwart veterans broke down and wept. The humanoid resident of the shining sarcophagus was tightly curled up in a crumpled pile in the corner of the room; when a security guard touched it, tentatively, with his gloved finger, the dead creature crumbled into a pile of glittering, ruby-colored powder.

In cleaning up the quarantine unit-turned-abattoir, the maintenance crew did find that one officer survived; hidden and whimpering softly under that mound of severed limbs, the first mate Greeley. Immediately, he was spirited away to the med unit.

The medical unit was sealed off while Greeley was cleaned up, consoled, examined, medicated, and questioned. Between quaking breaths, he stated emphatically that he remembered nothing about opening the sarcophagus, or about the ensuing massacre. Glancing about nervously with red, tear-swollen eyes, he complained of thirst, headache, and light sensitivity. The medics tranquilized him, then left him to rest awhile, with only one guard, Rowan, on duty. He was heavily sedated; there was no reason the post more than one guard, was there? When they returned four hours later because the sensors tracking Greeley's vitals had become unhooked, triggering an alarm, the guard was gone. Inside, Greeley was found lying face down on the the floor, dead. Turning him over and lifting him back onto the cot, the medics immediately began their examination of the body. They found Greeley to be in a state of total hypovolemia—almost completely exsanguinated. Rumors boiled through the crew like a fever dream. Word had it, when the attending doc began Greeley's autopsy, a luminous, sweet-smelling fog seeped from the first incision, rolled over his gloved hands, then quickly evaporated. The doc and attending med staff stopped the autopsy and right away marched themselves through the decontamination showers. *Better safe than sorry*, they reassured one another.

The medics informed the remaining cruise-ship officers that a deadly, unknown contagion had been released on board, not through the autopsy, but most likely through opening the sarcophagus and thereby freeing its inhabitant. *Which they had warned against*, Chief Medical Officer Herbert angrily reminded them. He further speculated, with some certainty, that the missing security guard, Rowan, was likely now a carrier. The guard was to be captured and quarantined as soon as possible; the Chief Medical Officer further urged that all passengers were to remain sequestered in their cabins, and for once, the higher-ups concurred.

But clever Rowan succeeded in evading capture for days, as he slaughtered—no, *fed*—on fellow crew-members and hapless, curious passengers along the way. Andrew heard the tale of a socially well-connected couple, who were ambushed on their way to the dining hall where they were scheduled for cocktails with the mighty Captain Murphey himself. Their fashionably-clad bodies were found callously crammed into a cleaning-supply closet. The lady still wore her filigreed tiara and chandelier earrings, the man still brandished his antique emerald tie-pin with matching cuff-links; though now these evening clothes and ornaments were but garish accouterments of the newly deceased. Their wealth and standing in no way protected them from being drained of every last drop of blood from their flabby, mousy bodies.

Some people just can't do as they're told, Andrew thought ruefully. He shook his head in disgust. *Especially spoiled cruise-ship passengers; they just had to see for themselves, had to get close to danger. What a thrill! Made the trip worth every penny!* Give them something to brag about in the rather baroque Mermaid Bar of the Hotel Mariner when they landed on Mars. Too bad they never got the opportunity to tell their tales; in less than a week, the insatiable Rowan had almost completely depleted the ship's population of 65, passengers and crew combined.

Out of that 65, only two survived: Andrew and McBride, the cruise-ship's sous chef. They managed to barricade themselves in the central kitchen off the dining hall. Here there was food, water, knives —everything needed for long-term survival. They assumed they could outlast Rowan; surely, he would starve to death now that there were no more passengers or other crew members for consumption. Rowan's disease made him mad; why else would he break, butcher and drain his fellow human beings? Surely, he would end up doing fatal harm to himself. Surely.

They were wrong.

Days bled into weeks; with no one manning the cruise-ship engines, the generators ran down and the emergency power switched on. In the kitchen, lights dimmed until the emergency lights came on, red and glaring. The two survivors resigned themselves to surreal boredom swinging into paranoia and then back again to boredom. Conversation between them dwindled. An old-world, key-wound clock, a gift from McBride's grandmother, ticked minutes into hours above the stove. Lulled by its soothing, hypnotic rhythm, the exhausted men soon nodded off, losing the battle to stay awake. They slumped over like dead men; they dreamed deeply, and as they dreamed, a sweet fog lazily drifted out of an overhead air-vent, furtively covering McBride in its velvety, smothering blanket. He awoke soon after, more irritated and impatient than usual, even for him.

"Shut your mouth-hole for once and listen," he hissed, out of the blue, at Andrew. "Hear that? No? That's 'cause there's nothing to hear."

"What are you getting at?" Andrew asked warily. McBride had quickly grown wild-eyed, and began to grind his teeth. Not a comforting development, Andrew realized. He'd play along with the sous chef while doing his best not to panic.

"There's no screaming, no shattering noises of madness and destruction," McBride giggled hoarsely. "We gotta open the door and check it out." He stood up and began methodically moving objects away from the door—boxes of canned goods stacked on a rolling counter topped with a cutting-board, dozens of full five-gallon water bottles, several fifty pound bags of flour, sugar, and salt—all things they'd used for a barricade. He easily moved them aside, as if they'd been empty. It had taken the two of them, with some effort, to build that barricade in the first place.

He glanced back at Andrew as he worked. "Don't help me, coward," he muttered under his breath. He pulled the door open and snickered. "Get over here, little man, and take a look at this!"

Rowan's limp, empty body lay in the hallway just outside.

McBride looked at Andrew through the corner of his eye, and laughed a mean, low laugh. When he opened his mouth, a wisp of fog escaped, rolling over his thick tongue and drooling out across his chapped lips, down his stubbly chin where it rose and curled, behaving like a snake's tongue, testing the atmosphere, searching for prey.

McBride turned back to Rowan's lifeless form, kicked it indifferently with the toe of his shoe. He squatted down to gleefully poke the dead body with his fat finger. Andrew took a few steps backward, into the kitchen, where he grabbed the first handy weapon, an old-fashioned iron skillet. The skillet the old McBride kept to remind him of his grandmother, who taught him how to cook, as he'd pointed out to Andrew when they'd first hunkered down. Creeping softly back up behind him, Andrew raised the heavy skillet and whacked McBride in the back of the head. Grandma's skillet left a pronounced dent in the back of her grandson's skull.

Andrew was not a particularly strong young man, but fear-fueled adrenaline made him strong enough to drag McBride's unconscious form down the long corridor to the quarantine unit. It made him strong enough to maneuver McBride's body into the open silver sarcophagus. That adrenaline rush made him strong enough to tightly bind the errant sous chef with the straps built into the inside of the casket; better yet, it made him quick enough slide the cover back in place as the alien fog began leaking from McBride's slack mouth.

He wheeled the silver coffin, that was how Andrew thought of the alien sarcophagus now, down another long corridor bathed in red emergency lights, to the waste disposal unit. Along the way, McBride awoke and began shouting and thrashing about inside the shiny coffin; it jostled a wee bit, but not enough to knock it off the trolley, and the hollering was nothing but a murmur to Andrew's ears. Neither was enough to deter him from what he now saw as his *raison d'etre*.

He slid the sleek coffin into the third evacuation portal, the one used for bio-hazardous waste, closed the hatch, and spun the locking wheel. Any material shoved through this portal would be sterilized on its way out. Andrew pressed the flashing green button next to the hatch.

He felt a minor rumble as the coffin rolled towards the exit, he closed his eyes against the blinding, brief flash as it went through purifying process. He heard the swoosh as the exit door opened, and the coffin was forcefully ejected. Upon reopening his eyes, he watched until the silver coffin disappeared into the deepest, blackest space anyone could possibly imagine.

THE MOON FOREST

DIRCK DE LINT

The Forest was so big that on clear nights it was visible from Earth, an emerald among the lesser lights sprinkled across the Moon. Ridiculous, ambitious, stupendous — it lived up to every hyperbole hung on it. Even breath-taking; when he had seen it from close orbit, Adebiyi's amazement stopped the air in his throat . When he stepped out of the transit terminal on the promenade, looking out at it from between the layers of the dome, he understood how misused *awesome* was.

He had come to The Forest for a unique experience. He had expected exhilaration from facing the possibility of death. He had not expected to be oppressed by the sheer scale of the place. What might happen later, inside, seemed insignificant by comparison.

He stood there, marvelling, until there was a tap on his shoulder. A voice behind him said, "Hey," breaking his paralysis.

"First time seeing it, eh?" The woman was about his age, a head shorter and as pale as he was dark. She seemed anxious to make up for that lack of color; her hair was all the oranges of fire, her eyes vivid purple. The contacts, a fad that had run out of steam on Earth about four years earlier, made Adebiyi suppress a smirk; he may have needed rescue like a gawping bumpkin, but he wasn't painfully out of style. He might still have resented the rescue, if her expression had shown anything other than sympathy.

"Yes," he said, "it's really…"

When he proved unable to finish the thought, the woman nodded. "Yeah, it did that to me the first time, too. I'm Veroni Rae. Here for the camp-out?" She nodded at him as she put out her hand, indicating his outdoor gear.

"Yes," he said again. "Adebiyi Adeyemi. You too?"

He spoke with a note of uncertainty. She wore a t-shirt, sweat-pants cut to capri length, and the kind of sandals he used at a public shower. She carried nothing. And yet, she nodded, grinning.

"You bet. Been at every one for the past four years." She turned to walk along the promenade. He fell in beside her, pleased to have a reason not to look at the awful spectacle of The Forest. They headed for a sign reading PARTICIPANTS ONLY.

The traffic on the broad walkway self-sorted into three streams. Closest to the outer wall, most distant from the vast green impossibility below, Adebiyi saw people like himself, obvious first-timers. Mostly young, skewed slightly male, all moving awkwardly in the low gravity despite a ballast of heavy boots, backpacks, and in a few cases, weapons.

On the Forest side the passengers were attenuated Lunans, walking with loping grace, dressed casually as anyone might on a day off work. Between them and the first-timers moved a sparse central band apparently composed of people like Veroni, born under Earth's gravity but well-used to the Moon, almost as sure of themselves as the Lunans. This group varied in its dress, running from the profoundly casual wear of the Moon-folk to kit almost as extensive as his own.

Adebiyi noticed that the more thoroughly equipped people in the middle lane carried absolutely no weapons, or none that he could see. He touched the long knife hanging off his belt, wondering if there were some etiquette he was missing.

Veroni saw his gesture, and said, "Hey, a piece of advice, leave that thing outside."

Adebiyi frowned at her. "How am I supposed to defend myself?"

She laughed. "You don't." When she saw his expression go sour, she held up placating hands. "Seriously. The knives, the spears, all they do is make you *think* you've got a fighting chance. You know why they don't let people bring guns in?"

"Unfair disadvantage?" Adebiyi's frown was softening. She might be pale, and possibly she gender-identified other than the way he hoped, but she seemed to be honest about helping him.

"Nope. It's because back when they did allow them, some dummy would inevitably damage the inner dome. Effective range is a lot farther here than on Earth. Exactly zero people who went in with a gun ever came out." She glanced at the knife again. "You might get away with that, and it might be useful for just plain camping. But don't take it out if you see one of them."

"So I just run?"

"Oh, hell, no," Veroni said, bright violet eyes wide. "Running is what food does. Do not, ever, run."

"But what do I do if they attack me?" They were almost to the gate now, and the way was beginning to clog with well-wishers saying farewells to those heading into The Forest.

"Just don't give them a reason to go after you. No one here is starving, and if you don't look entertaining or dangerous, you'll likely be left alone." She looked him up and down, then beyond him, into the all-Terran side of the corridor. "You should probably find a friend, though. It's better to be part of a group."

"Maybe we could stick together," Adebiyi suggested.

Veroni shook her head as they passed through the barrier, the crowd around them thinned to those who were ready to be locked into The Forest. "That's probably not a good idea," she said. "Maybe talk to her, and *seriously* stay away from those guys."

Adebiyi looked over his shoulder to see who the two nods had indicated. The first was a woman, probably in her fifties. She had traditional Maori tattoos and carried a professional-looking camera around her neck. The second was a trio of men about his age, each with a katana slung on his back. When he turned back, Veroni had joined a group of Lunans passing through reception, almost lost among them but for her fiery hair. He tried to dart toward her, stumbled in the unfamiliar gravity, and very slowly fell to one knee. When he picked himself up, she was past the desks.

"Good luck," she called to him, waving, then pointed, saying, "Gotta hurry!" before disappearing among the taller locals. She had pointed to the closest of several monitors in the reception area showing The Forest from far enough above to take its whole width. Most of the scene was dark, apart from the glow of The Forest's lights, but a slice of brightly-lit regolith on one side showed the advancing dawn.

Adebiyi shuffled to a reception desk, and presently stood before a Lunan wearing loose trousers and a tan shirt with The Forest's logo on it; formal uniform, to judge from the other Lunans he had seen. The man scanned his phone and handed him a bar-coded tag on a coiled loop.

"Keep that with you," he said. "It works as a key on the lockers downstairs, if there's anything you want to leave out here, and it also helps with identification if there's an incident. I hope you enjoy your visit."

Adebiyi thanked him, then began to hurry as best he could for the doors he had seen Veroni go through. The man at the desk called after him.

"Wrong way, man! That's the home team side." He pointed to another set on the far side of the concourse. "You want Visitors."

Beyond the doors was a bank of funiculars, their course running more horizontally than vertically. He was deposited in what looked like the locker room of any better-kept civic field house. The place was already well occupied, tourists standing at the far end of the room in small bunches, chatting or watching more of the ubiquitous monitors. They stood near a bank of a dozen blue-painted doors, little different to look at than any in a mall entry back home.

Adebiyi paused amid the banks of lockers, looking at one which stood open and empty. He had already emptied and stowed his rucksack in the hotel room. Everything he carried was based on recommendations by experienced campers, most of whom had been to The Forest at least once. His hand moved to the handle of his knife. He couldn't remember any of those recommendations speaking one way or another on going armed.

He continued past the empty locker, turning his attention to the monitors.

Each showed a different image. The overhead shot of The Forest which Adebiyi had seen upstairs jumped from the farthest monitor to the nearest. The sunlit area was larger now, the edge of the terminator nearly touching the crater's rim. A countdown was superimposed at the top of the image, under the legend TIME TO SUNRISE. There were only a few minutes left.

On the next screen over, the camera looked at an open grassy area lying outside a set of doors very like the ones in front of him. They were clearly not the same doors, as people strolled through them either singly or in small chatting groups. The lights in The Forest had been dimmed, anticipating the dawn, but it was still bright enough to see that all the people in the scene were naked.

Further down still, the monitor showed slow-scrolling text, black on a yellow background. *Be aware*, it said, *doors are open for 30 minutes only after sunrise. If you do not enter, admission fees are forfeit. No late entry allowed. Doors reopen in 24 hours. You may exit any time after doors have opened. You may not re-enter. No refund will be offered.* It was a reiteration of warnings from The Forest's site, terms one had to acknowledge as read and accepted before purchasing a ticket. Adebiyi had remembered the hesitation they had given him, sitting in his own room. Re-reading here brought an uncomfortable constriction to his throat which swallowing did not shift.

The screens stepped sideways again as the countdown reached one minute. The warning text was replaced by the interior view. Nudists began to look up, not at the camera, and not all at once, but conversations concluded as they all lowered themselves to the leaf-strewn turf. Some lay on their sides, while others crouched, hands between feet, like children watching bugs.

Dawn came. Sunlight fell upon the Moon, and that reflected light diffused through The Forest. On the screen, there was a moment of upsetting fluid plasticity, a half-second of formless transition, then where people had lain or squatted, wolves bounded up. The monitors had no sound, but in the silence which gripped all the tourists staring at the scene it was easy to hear distant howls.

The screens suddenly went acid green overlaid by the message ENTER NOW, strong black characters in the ten big languages of humanity. At the bottom of each, an unlabelled countdown timer chewed the seconds of the promised half-hour.

Some of those inside the doors turned away instantly, abandoning both entry fee and a chance to wander among the werewolves. Adebiyi felt the urge to join them. This was not the first time he had watched the transformation—The Forest live-streamed every month and its entire recorded history was archived—but hearing the carnivorous joy directly, however far across the crater it might had travelled, was something else again.

As he stood, his fellow visitors made up their own minds, belatedly retreating or heading through the doors. He watched the trio Veroni had warned him against noisily working each other up, not knowing their language but understanding the tone well enough. *You're afraid, I'm not afraid, I dare you, you go if you're so hot,* on and on, a testosterone-driven chain reaction. The radiation it produced affected him, language barrier or no, when he felt the gaze of one of them pass over him.

He shouldered his pack. There had not been any screams from outside, after all. He put his head down and pulled the door.

The Forest had been designed as a west European broadleaf environment, a biome which Adebiyi had never been close to in his entire city-bound life and yet it smelled *right*, filled with subtle exhalations of leaves and the fragrant rot of soil. He closed his eyes, drawing deep breaths, pulling the rightness in. The tension of being locked into a space roamed by dangerous predators did not vanish, but it lost its urgency. Two steps inside and the whole cost of the trip, what he had paid already and what he might yet pay, had been worth it.

He took another step or two before the unevenness of the ground made him open his eyes again. He looked around. There were monitors over the doors on his side as well, red under the black characters counting away TIME TO LOCKDOWN. Directly above was the canopy of the trees, strangely distant thanks to the low gravity, all but completely obscuring the distant tracery of the dome. Turning away from the doors, he saw several pathways, lines of least resistance between trees and shrubs leading into the heart of The Forest.

Two of the doors banged open. The three young men, seeming to multiply themselves through boisterous activity, tumbled through, and without a pause to take in their surroundings buffeted each other down one of the paths to Adebiyi's right. As the sound of their passage receded, Adebiyi thought he heard a single howl, high pitched and distant. It seemed to be coming from his left. He stood a few seconds longer, listening to the thrashing and bickering moving further into the trees. Adjusting the straps of his pack, he chose a left-hand path.

It was hours before Adebiyi saw a werewolf. He was making his way along the side of a little creek, his attention divided between the act of walking in lower gravity and the effect of that gravity on the flow of water, when there was a crash in the greenery ahead. A deer bounded in a long arc which took it over the river to land on the path ahead of him.

Behind it came two werewolves, moving in a brisk low-belly scuttle that seemed more feline than canine. They clung to the ground rather than leaping in pursuit. The hindmost of the pair paused, only a handful of paces downhill, turning to glare at Adebiyi, ice blue eyes in pale grey fur. Only a moment, then it resumed the chase, the sounds soon swallowed by the muffling leaves.

Adebiyi sat down on the path. He reached out a hand to collect some water from the stream, spreading it over his hair and forehead. The cool water on his skin was electric. He turned his head, looking toward the exit, now very distant and locked for the better part of a day.

A small thrush trilled above him, its song in his ears giving the same thrill of primal purity as the air in his lungs. He shook his head, turning it away from escape, and saw amused eyes upon him. He uttered a tiny vowel of surprise.

It was not a werewolf, but the Maori woman. She emerged from her cover beside the path. In the darkness beneath the leaves, her facial tattoos had broken up the lines of her face, made her humanity obscure. Adebiyi realized then that the werewolf's eyes had been very human, too. Unlike the werewolf, the woman smiled broadly as she emerged.

"Hey, man," she said, coming toward him, "I got a brilliant shot of you and that wolf. Want a copy?"

Adebiyi did, and a couple of minutes later the file was in his phone. The woman drank from the creek using her hand as a cup before clapping Adebiyi on the back. "You'll have fun telling the folks back home all about that photo," she said, then added with a wink, "if you survive." She vaulted the stream then and slipped off into the undergrowth.

Later, Adebiyi sat under a tree on a small rise overlooking The Forest's central lake. Feeling foolish for having become tired and breathless under the tiny weight of his rucksack, he had stopped there to have an energy bar and a short rest. He felt less foolish after checking the time. The sun's creeping movement gave no sense of time passing, but it had indeed been many hours since he'd passed through the doors, time in which he had trudged many serpentine kilometers to end up in sight of the moon's largest body of liquid water.

He had every right to be tired, hiking aside. The whole voyage over he had been feverishly space-sick. The rituals of the arrival terminal had left him very little time to enjoy his hotel room. Several articles he read before coming had agreed on the point that a visitor to The Forest should sleep when tired, and he would have stretched out on the soft grass but for the companion to that advice; the safest place to sleep was up a tree.

That made sense, yet Adebiyi wondered if it was practical. Like the people born on the moon, the trees were elongated versions of their Earthly cousins. He sat up a little, getting his shoulders higher on the small tree he leaned against, and began scanning for any candidates that might bear his weight and which also offered limbs that he could reach. As he sought, his mind proved how tired it was, beginning an orbit around the question of whether it was his mass or his weight that the tree would be holding. He closed his eyes for a moment, hoping to still the inner clamor.

He awoke with a start, certain from the pressure on his hips that more time than an eye blink had passed.

This mild pain hadn't awoken him. He heard what he suddenly understood was *another* shout, not close but urgent, and he straightened, back away from the tree.

On a spit of land separated from Adebiyi's seat by the broad mouth of a creek, the three men he had made a point of avoiding were calling to one another. They had arranged themselves across the slope, one just shy of the ridge, one a meter or two from the water, the other halfway between. They advanced toward the lake, swords in hand, and they were just close enough for Adebiyi to hear what they said, though he still made nothing of whatever language they spoke. The tone was unmistakeable, the same jolly hectoring they had been at in the locker room, mutual encouragement by derision.

At the end of the spit, seemingly trapped by their advance, was a werewolf. It stood, one long forelimb raised in an expectant posture. It looked up and down at its pursuers, watching their advance, and Adebiyi read no panic in its movements. It seemed, in the way of dogs, to smile.

The skirmish line had slowed, each of them bent low as if they suddenly felt the need to sneak up on their quarry. Each would in turn shout while gesturing with his sword, apparently suggesting better lines of approach to the others.

None of them noticed the three other werewolves stealthily closing in behind them.

Adebiyi began to rise, drawing breath to shout a warning. He might think they were obnoxious, but he did not want to see them killed.

There was a sound from behind him, less a growl than a rumble of throat-clearing. There was a werewolf right beside his nap-tree, close enough to touch, watching him with sapphire eyes, almost certainly the same that noticed him earlier. These were, without question, human eyes, and regardless of the shape of the face, the intelligence behind them undeniable. After a moment of frozen mutual regard, it very deliberately swung its head slowly side to side, an unmistakable command not to interfere.

Adebiyi subsided, adrenalin screeching inside him. The werewolf crept forward to lie more directly beside him, its head now hardly a hand's length from the knife on his belt. They watched together as the creature on the spit suddenly darted around the headland. The upper-most swordsman leapt, a long graceless bound which took him across the ridge. The other two began a blunderous run, still following their quarry's line. The werewolves behind them scuffled forward in the same ground-hugging scamper Adebiyi had seen before.

There was a scream from the far side of the rise, high above a sudden chorus of snarls.

On the near side, the man closest to the water began to sprint, accomplishing no more than to send himself in an inefficient leg-flailing arc out over the water. The one on the slope began hauling himself up gripping the long grass, as if he had learned something from watching the werewolves. In turning, he saw the beast that closed upon him, unable to do more than utter a brief squeal before jaws closed on his neck. The werewolf gave him a strong shake that sent them rolling down the slope together.

The one in the water wheeled his sword in a wide arc, using its momentum to help turn his body, and faced the two werewolves which had come for him. They stopped, feet just in the water, one a solid black, the other an almost stereotype of wolf colouration, grey over cream. Man and animals watched each other for a few frozen seconds, until the red-jawed third joined its fellows. A fourth and fifth sauntered from behind the headland, the last showing a slight limp.

The young man in the water called out, a single syllable Adebiyi took to be the name of one of his companions. He took a step back, sending oily ripples across the still water. The black werewolf took a matching step forward, then exchanged glances on either side. All the werewolves advanced.

The man shouted, leaping backward as he threw his sword at his pursuers. They jumped, up or back, avoiding the weapon as it whirled into the slope, distracted for the moment it took the man to land in water deep enough for swimming. One of them bounded after him, its final leap taking it beyond its depth, and it gave up the chase, paddling back to shore in a completely doggish way.

When it became obvious that the man was making for the distant opposite shore, the werewolves walked without any urgency back into the trees. The one that had splashed out into the lake paused to shake off the water. It looked in Adebiyi's direction and gave a little nod. He started, then understood it was not looking directly at him. He turned his head to watch the blue-eyed werewolf stand, yawn, and depart.

He rose at last, sliding his back up the tree. He tried not to look at the body across the stream as he reached for his pack. When he had it, he pursued his policy of trying to put distance between himself and the swordsmen, the form of his disgust with them entirely changed.

He had slept, briefly, before the hunt jolted his system, but presently fatigue reasserted itself. Adebiyi renewed his search for a tree. He was now convinced that the advice Veroni had given him was sound, and that as long as he didn't offer an interesting challenge to the werewolves he would be safe. Nearly convinced. The fact that he had slept through the approach of one failed to completely reconcile him with lying on the ground, stretched out and undefended. Eventually he spotted the right tree, lower limbs high enough to deter something without thumbs and good shoulder rotation. It proved to have an almost chair-like arrangement of branches near its crown.

He nearly died of it. He woke only after he had tilted completely out of his saddle, inner ear lulled by the light gravity. When he finally felt what was happening, the galvanic spasm of a falling sleeper only served to launch him sideways, too far from the tree for his fingers to catch anything but leaves. When going up, he had been concerned with being high enough to be safe. He had gone very high indeed. Adebiyi had a long time to experience the terror of falling as his downward speed slowly gathered.

He twisted at the last moment, anxious to not land head-first. He succeeded, and his reward was an explosion of pain in his legs as they hit seconds before his head. He lay on his back, breath coming in tiny hissing pants that eventually became a chant of denial. "No, no, no, no…"

When the incantation failed, he pulled himself around to assess his injuries. It was a slow effort, interrupted by sudden paralyses and sharp cries as ill-planned movements put a cymbal-crash into his symphony of pain.

His left foot was pointing an unlikely direction thanks to a new bend between knee and ankle. His right leg seemed more intact, but the fabric of his trousers was drumhead-taut from mid-calf to mid-thigh. He got out his knife, carefully holed the fabric, then tore it to release the pressure on the swelling flesh. He wept as a tiny fraction of his pain waned.

After revelling in this small respite, he began to enact the universal modern emergency plan: call for help. It took another minute of gasping struggle to reach his phone in his left cargo pocket. When it came out in two handfuls, he laughed like an old man. Eventually, he was able to stop.

Adebiyi turned his eyes up toward his perch. His rucksack was just visible, one strap firmly looped around a small branch. He could see the red pull on the zipper sealing the pocket full of food. His canteen was invisible on the far side.

"Might as well be on the moon," he rasped. Then he remembered where he was, setting off another round of giggling. When he had himself settled, he took as deep a breath as he could.

"Help!"

It seemed a fine, loud shout, but he took another breath and tried again, concentrating on his diaphragm rather than the way the pressure of calling out somehow made its way to the ends of the broken bone.

After an estimated minute without response, he tried again. There wasn't even an echo. He was about to allow himself the luxury of despair when he heard rattling in the nearby underbrush.

"Over here," he said, loud but not shouting, entirely unashamed of the quivering relief in his voice.

Just higher than his current eye level, the face of the blue-eyed werewolf appeared through the leaves. Adebiyi hissed rather than screamed as he pushed himself to sit against the tree.

The werewolf approached slowly, head level with its back, ears forward. Curious. Not, it seemed to Adebiyi, cautious. He could hear it sniffing, and he wondered if there was a wound he hadn't found dripping blood to tempt the beast. Surely it could smell the chemistry of pain in his sweat.

His knife lay on the ground. He had moved away from it when the werewolf appeared, but it was still close, surely close enough that he could grab it before the creature could stop him... if only he could do more than bend at the waist. As it was, he would do no more than flop onto his face, losing sight of the thing and presenting the back of his neck to it as he scrabbled in the leaf-litter.

Acting like food.

He chose instead to try to relax into his seat. Looking the werewolf directly in the eyes, he said, "Hello, Blue Eyes."

It stopped, cocking its head. One ear flicked.

"Sorry I don't have anything for you. I'm just," a pause to take a slow breath without grimacing, "hanging out here, enjoying the air." He let out the rest of the breath, trying not to let it shake in rhythm with the throb of his injuries. They were slightly out of sync, knee-shin, knee-shin, demanding attention he did not want to take away from the werewolf.

It sat, head still canted, a huge, shaggy parody of The Faithful Companion. They regarded each other for what seemed to Adebiyi like hours. The urge to check his phone for the time swept through him over and again. The agony of his legs seemed to subside a little until he enflamed it by seeking a more comfortable position, a cycle that recurred more often than he could count. Finally, the werewolf stood, padding out of sight with a single brief backward glance.

For a moment, Adebiyi thought he might somehow have waited out the long, monster-filled day; it seemed to be getting dark. He looked up and saw that the sun was not yet even to the zenith.

"Oh, hell." He looked around, trying to spot the werewolf circling him. He saw no sign of it. Stifling cries, he began to crawl away from the direction it had gone. When he remembered, after the agonized creep that had taken him out of sight of his tree, that the knife still lay where he had dropped it, he barely paused.

It was a combination of new pain and an increased pain in his legs that woke him from sleep he hadn't felt beginning. His last memory was a confused worm's-eye view succession of various plants, when his only thoughts were persistence and a vague hope of not being eaten.

His sight was still dim, the light seeming to pass through a brown filter. He watched for a while, only slowly realizing that the passage of the dun leaves above was a result of his own movement, and that this intermittent lurching corresponded with fresh throbs in his legs and the unfamiliar crushing at the end of his left arm.

He looked along his arm. He saw, without surprise, that there was a werewolf worrying at his hand and wrist. Beyond the creature, near the edge of his ability to see, several doors loomed in a taller cliff, monitors above them showing text too upside down and dim to read. He thought he should try to get away from the thing that was eating him. His weak attempt did no more than make its rhythmic grunt-growl louder for a few seconds.

Adebiyi closed his eyes. He felt a very detached remorse at having come so close to escape, only to be devoured. He sighed final resignation and let unconsciousness engulf him again.

The smell of the air changed suddenly. No longer the glorious natural fragrance of The Forest, it was more commonplace smell of air shared by many people. There were additional elements which he couldn't place. He tried to move, tried to open his eyes, and found he could do neither.

"Welcome back, Mr. Adeyemi," a voice said, deep, feminine and pleasant, not very distant. The professional tone and the way it struck the surrounding walls gave the unfamiliar scents context, making the next words redundant. "You are in a hospital."

"Can't see," he said, his voice creaking.

The voice, which introduced itself as Doctor Gupta, removed tape from Adebiyi's eyelids and let him sip water through a straw while explaining the length of the induced coma he had just finished. He hadn't noticed it at the time, but his fall had been nearly as hard on his head as his legs. He had entered the hospital two weeks ago, and with application, he might complete rehab within a month.

"I am very pleased with your recovery," Gupta said, after a few prods at his legs which made him gasp. "You're young and fit, which helps. Do you feel up to a visitor?"

The non sequitur left Adebiyi momentarily dumbstruck, but he assented. Gupta left, and shortly afterward Veroni walked in. Her hair was now bright green, complimenting the cat-slit contacts she wore. "Remember me?"

"Oh, of course." He tried to sound casual, still attentive to the demands of his young man's ego even if he was too weak to lift a limb.

"Great." She consulted a tablet she had brought with her. "So, what's the last thing you remember?"

"Um." Ego wanted him to embellish. He resisted. "Crawling to the exit. Nearly, anyway. I thought one of the wolves got me."

"Got you?" A sly smile appeared. Adebiyi felt his face go a little warm. "I suppose you could say that. You were headed in exactly the wrong direction, you know."

He frowned at her, an incomprehension that was slowly replaced by a cultivated disbelief. Veroni watched the progress of the emotion, then said, "Here, let me clear things up a little."

She set the tablet down on a chair, cupped a hand under one eye, and with the other slid out one of her lenses with the skill of long practice. When she looked up, that eye was vivid blue.

"I'm the one who got you to the door, chum. You would have died out there on your own."

After a slack-jawed pause, all Adebiyi could think to say was, "Thanks."

"I hope you mean that," she said. "I'm actually here in an official capacity."

"Huh?"

She said nothing for a few seconds, busy with a bottle of fluid she had produced from a pocket, wetting the contact before replacing it. She looked at him and asked, "Is that straight? Nothing looks sillier than getting these things in cock-eyed."

"It's fine."

"Good." She retrieved her tablet and straightened a little. "Anyway, I work for the Immigration Authority. Since I'm sort of responsible for the situation, I decided I should help you with the paperwork."

Adebiyi stared. She blushed, her normal pallor gone pale pink. "I guess I should probably apologize, too," she said. "You really weren't in any shape for informed consent."

"What the hell are you talking about?" Adebiyi asked, agitated enough to hitch himself up a couple of centimeters. The bed reacted to the movement, raising his head until he was semi-sitting.

Veroni shrugged. "Welcome to the team, sport." She pointed at his hand, the one not encumbered with an IV line, which he hadn't really noticed until now was swaddled in bandages. "I really tried to not break the skin, but I also had to hurry. You test positive, so you're not going to be allowed to go back to Earth."

Adebiyi went slack as he understood not just what she said but what that meant. The bed shuffled under him, toyed with the idea of returning him to prone, then was still. He didn't notice. He was taken up with the whole of his future life passing before his eyes. The degree in something he hadn't yet settled on. The marriage to one of three or four girls who seemed to like him. Children, possibly. Trips to visit his friends in glamorous international destinations. All of that potential gone, replaced with life in one of Luna's handful of interchangeable mass-produced cities, all free of history worth mentioning.

Veroni stepped closer. "We could, if you prefer, start making arrangements for a passage to Mars. Those little moons don't do anything for us."

"I don't know," he said, bleak and honest.

"It seems pretty big," she said. "I know. I needed a lot of help with the transition, and I thought I knew what I was doing when I got into it. But I can also tell you this…" She took one more step and laid gentle fingertips on his forearm. "It's an amazing community. Every one of us will support you. As acquired conditions go, it's extremely livable. Especially here. Half the time, you don't even know you've got it."

Adebiyi looked up at her. Verdant hair and inhuman eyes aside, her face radiated honesty and compassion.

"The other half of the time, you get to run around The Forest and do pretty much anything you want."

He thought of the three swordsmen. Could he be part of such a scene? Could he avoid getting involved in one?

A thought followed those, and he was not certain it was his own: What might it taste like?

Adebiyi returned Veroni's smile, and he heard himself say, "Sign me up."

THE SILVER CROWN

MARIAH SOUTHWORTH

"How is it looking in there, Comet? Over."

Haley rolled her eyes at the nickname and crossed her fingers, activating her transmitter ring. "Pretty dead, Swampy," she said. "Give me a second to get the files. Over." She went back to the task at hand, trying to ignore her eerie surroundings.

The crew of the *Vega* had been wreckage scavengers for fourteen years; they'd been doing so legally for almost half that time. Haley herself had been crawling through space ship wreckage since she was sixteen and this was by no means her first time on a ghost ship. The thing was, most of the time "Ghost Ship" was a turn of phrase. She found it distressingly difficult to ignore the silent line of dead bodies behind her.

Haley got the cover off of the computer link up and began searching for an access plug amongst various wire and tubes. She crossed her fingers as she worked. "Explain to me why I had to come down to cold sleep for this?" she asked. "I've crawled through open space before—a busted up bridge doesn't sound too bad. Over."

"Sorry Comet," Swampy said into her ear. "The meteors knocked out the main computer—you're lucky that there are backups down in cold storage, frankly. Over."

"Super," Haley muttered, not uncrossing her fingers.

"What's the matter? Afraid someone down there is going to wake up? Over."

Haley glanced over her shoulder with a shudder. The large, pitch black room curved away from her small halo of light. Lining the inner wall were glass-fronted, oblong pods. Inside the pods…well, Haley hadn't looked yet.

The *S.S. Nebula* had been a colony ship—emphasis on the "had been." The big, juggernaut of a star ship had been on its way to the Andromeda galaxy when something had gone wrong. At long last, the ship had drifted back into habitable space, and the owners had contacted the crew of the *Vega* to retrieve the black box and shipboard files. This put Haley in the bowels of the old ship, a long line of dead, perfectly preserved colonists stretching on and on behind her.

She turned back to the section of wall she had pulled away, pressing her lips over an annoyed comeback for Swampy. No sense in drawing this out. She found what she was looking for and plugged Swampy's data retrieval box in. The little light on its side blinked green.

"Your box better be able to talk to this antique," she told the technician. "This ship is older than I am. Over."

"It's all been taken into account," Swampy said. "It's nice working legit, isn't it? The owners gave me everything I needed to know. Over."

"I guess," Haley said, leaning against the wall and crossing her arms while she waited for Swampy to do his thing. She glowered at the line of pods. "I kind of miss the thrill though. Over."

"Knock on one of the pods if you want a thrill. Over."

Haley rolled her eyes. "Haha." She glanced at the glass of the nearest pod, the light from her suit helmet reflecting back at her. Haley swallowed and looked down at the retrieval box. The light was still green. Haley took a step towards the pod. Then another.

"Son of a whore," Haley hissed, gazing past her light's glare and into the pod itself. She had seen cold-sleepers before. Dead or alive, she had been expecting the usual—a sleeping person, perfectly still, like a wax dummy. She had expected the horror to be in thinking that the dead person *looked* alive.

The thing inside the cold sleep pod could never be mistaken for a live human being. The flesh had shrunk and withered down, pulling taut over the bones. Its once-tight silver jumpsuit hung in empty folds over the skeletal body. The corpse had no nose to speak of, and the eyelids had sunken down into their sockets, the barest, open sliver revealing nothing but slits of blackness. Horribly, the thing's curtain of black hair was still long and glossy, though the skin had turned a leathery, pallid gray. A silvery metal ring encircled the corpse's desiccated forehead like some kind of crown. A part of the cold-sleep interface, Haley assumed.

Haley stared for a full thirty seconds, unable to look away. She crossed her fingers. "Swampy?" she croaked out. "Over."

"Yeah? Over."

"The people in the pods are all…they're all leathery and awful. Like mummies. Over."

"Well yeah, cold sleep isn't going to preserve shit with a complete power failure. Over."

Haley shivered and turned back to her retrieval box. "The meteors did that? Over."

"Guess we'll find out. Over."

Almost as if on cue, the data retrieval light flashed three times and turned red. Haley gratefully unplugged the box. Leaving the cover off of the computer access, she turned and started walking back to her entry point. "Heading back," she said. "Over."

The light from Haley's suit bobbed away, and her footsteps echoed into silence. Just as the dim, distant glow began to fade, the glass fronted door to the pod she had been looking into opened.

E milio sat on the storage counter outside the airlock, legs crossed and grinning as she entered the ship. "So were they all gross or what?" he asked.

Haley took off her helmet and ran a hand through her short-cropped brown hair. She scowled at the ten year old. "What?"

Emilio Vega, the son of their captain, Yadiera Vega, uncrossed his legs and jumped down from the counter. He had his mother's dark complexion and black eyes, but the slight curl to his dark hair was probably his unknown father's fault. Raising an infant on an illegal scavenger ship had been surprisingly easy; it hadn't been until Emilio had hit school age that the crew had finally decided to turn their business legit. There had been a lot of debate on how necessary it was, but legal scavenging had begun to be a popular mainstream business, and it *was* convenient to finally get the kid a real birth certificate.

"Were they gross?" Emilio asked again. "You know, the pod people." He held his arms out stiffly and rolled his eyes back into his head.

"Yes, as a matter of fact, they were," Haley snapped, tossing her helmet to him. It hit him in the stomach, and Emilio just barely managed to catch it. "How'd you know they would be?"

"Tch, bad cold sleep makes mummies. Everyone knows that."

Haley scowled and unhooked her radio earpiece. The transmitter ring she left on—it wouldn't trigger accidentally, not with the other piece in her pocket. "Don't you have homework to do?" she asked.

"No." Emilio plunked her helmet down on the counter. "So are you going to tell me about the mummies?"

"No."

"Aw, come on."

Haley shook her head and started past him. "I've got to report to Swampy and your mother. You've got to try and stay out of trouble for five minutes."

The *Vega* was a comfortable ship. It was by no means a luxury cruiser, but it was big enough to house its four-and-a-half (counting Emilio) person crew without them driving each other totally crazy. So by the time Haley made it to Swampy's bridge, she had taken long enough that he was already distracted with something. Swampy sat at semi-circular control panel, glaring at the five screens that surrounded him and spouting out a long line of curses in some northern Earth language.

Haley glanced at the screens, but didn't bother to try and puzzle out the meaning behind the various charts and readouts. "Problem, Earthling?" Haley asked.

Swampy's turned away from his screens, his straw colored hair falling into his gray eyes. Swampy was short and lithe, with a nose that was too big for his long, thin face. Considering that Captain Yadiera Vega was built like a tank, it wouldn't be long before even Emilio out-massed the little techie from Earth.

"Power drain in the airlock," Swampy said, turning back to his monitors. "After you came in—can't seem to isolate the problem."

"Son of a—" Haley scowled and leaned over Swampy to press the intercom button. "Emilio!" She waited.

"Yes?" Emilio's voice came through the speaker.

"Stay out of the airlock."

"I'm not in the airlock."

Swampy and Haley shared a look. "Sure, just leave the mummies alone, kid," Haley said. "I've got a suit-cam if you really want to see them."

There was a pause and a new voice spoke through the intercom. "Don't show him space mummies, Haley," Captain Vega said.

"Aw, Mom."

"*I* want to see space mummies," Vincent, the final crew member, piped in.

"Oh good lord," Swampy sighed, rolling his eyes. He shooed Haley out of the way and pushed the intercom button. "You're still confined to the med-bay, Vincent." Swampy barked. "Clear the intercom, people." He shook his head and went back to his monitors. "Alright, five life forms are aboard, systems look normal. Airlock is doing what it does best." He leaned his head back in his chair to look up at Haley, who stood directly behind him. "Got my data retriever?"

Haley handed it over, and Swampy flashed her a grin. "We're good to go then," he said, placing the little box on the console. He reached over and pressed the intercom button. "Take off in five minutes."

• • •

"Comet? Hey, Comet? Over."

Haley cracked open one eye, noted the dim, blue glow from the corners of her bunk room signifying that it was still after hours, and rolled over.

"Haley Marquis, pick up your headset," came the tinny, distant voice once more. "Don't make me use the intercom and wake everyone up. Over."

Haley rolled onto her back and sighed. She groped one-handed for the bedside shelf and found her earpiece. She fitted it into her ear and crossed her fingers. "What?" she asked groggily.

"You're supposed to say 'over.' Over."

Haley rubbed her tired eyes. "Stow it, Swampy, we're not on duty."

"Alright, well, I've got bad news," Swampy said. "You know the data retriever?"

"Yeah."

"It's dead."

"What do you mean it's dead?"

"I mean it's completely drained. No power."

"So charge it."

"It's a nuclear battery, Comet. There isn't a way to charge it because it's not supposed to die. Did anything happen to it that I need to know about?"

Haley sat up, nearly smacking her head on the ceiling. The bunk rooms were shaped like pipes, long, narrow and round, with half the space taken up by the bed and under storage. "I would have reported it already," she said, glaring at the too-near ceiling before lying back down. "All I did was go in, find an interface, open it, and plug the box in. You were talking to me for most of that. Could you get anything out of it before it died?"

"Not even a gigabyte," Swampy sighed. "I'm trying to run diagnostics and... Shit."

Haley smiled. "You're supposed to say 'over,' Swampy."

"Oh shut up," Swampy growled. "My diagnostic reader just died." He broke off into a line of guttural, northern-earth curses. Haley listened, unamused, for a few seconds.

"Swampy," she interrupted. "Stay with me."

"Sorry, Comet," he sighed. "I can't stand it when my babies fail me. Alright, I think we've got a computer virus. That would explain the lack of power on the colony ship."

Haley sat bolt upright, smacking her head against the bed ceiling. Now it was her turn to swear.

"Comet?"

"Yeah, here, just hit my head." She swung her feet over the edge of her bed and dropped down. "Please tell me your diagnostic reader wasn't plugged into the mainframe."

"Completely isolated unit, don't worry," Swampy said. "We've just got a dead retriever and a dead reader, nothing else."

"Super," Haley rubbed her forehead with a grimace. "So now what?"

"We go back to the wreck and try again, and I work on cobbling together a virus shield for round two."

"Don't you already have virus shields?"

"Only for the viruses I know about."

"All right, great," Haley sighed. "How much longer does Vincent have to stay in bed?"

"Uh…radiation sickness… he's got at least three more days. Sorry Comet, you've got to go back onto the corpse-wagon by yourself."

"Super," Haley sighed and looked back at her bed. "Can I go back to sleep now?"

"Actually, could you go tell Yadiera? She's not answering her radio."

"Ugh, fine, just let me pull on some pants."

"I mean, you don't have to put pants on if you really don't want to."

"Real mature," Haley said with a snort, pulling open one of the drawers beneath her bed. Swampy didn't reply, which could only be a good thing. She finished getting dressed and left her bunk room.

· · ·

"**A**ctually," Swampy said, sitting at his work table. The main control panel sat behind him, the five monitors showing various angles of space that the ship drifted through. Swampy had overridden the blue, off-hours light, so the room was well-lit. "Could you go tell Yadiera? She's not answering her radio." Swampy drummed his fingers on the dead receiver box sitting on the work table in front of him.

"Ugh, fine," Comet huffed in his ear. "Just let me pull on some pants."

Swampy grinned. "I mean, you don't have to put pants on if you really don't want to."

"Real mature," Comet said with a snort.

Something brushed by Swampy's ear. He waved it away without looking. "I am the most mature," he said. "All I'm saying is that, if anything should be optional in space, it should be pants." He waited, but Comet didn't say anything. "Comet?" he asked. He frowned and un-crossed then re-crossed his fingers. "Comet? Are you there? Over."

Swampy sat back in his chair and pulled out his earpiece. "What, are you dead too now?"

A weight rested on the back of his chair. Swampy froze, remembering, suddenly, that he was in space and not back home on earth, where one could expect insects to brush by one's ear. Swampy let out a hissing breath. "Emilio, I swear to god," he growled, turning around.

Swampy screamed.

Yadiera opened her door dressed in sweatpants and a tank top, black hair tied back in a messy braid. The five-foot-ten Latina-Martian cocked an eyebrow at Haley and bit back a yawn. "This better be important."

"Sorry Captain," Haley said sympathetically. "But you weren't answering your radio."

"That's because I'm not stupid enough to leave it by my bed. If it was a real emergency there's the intercom." She yawned again. "So what's going on?"

Haley gestured over her shoulder. "Swampy needs to see you. We've got to go back to the wreck."

"Great," Yadiera muttered leaning back into her room and pulling a pair of boots out of the shadows. She shoved her feet into them. "Brief me on the way."

"Oh god, oh shit. Lort, for søren…" Swampy meandered between Intergalactic and Danish curses. His breathing came short and painful, and he tried in vain to push the broken work table from his chest. His head throbbed from the blow that had knocked him from his chair.

His attacker moved, and Swampy turned panicked eyes to it again.

Tall and skeletal, with a silver cold-sleep jumpsuit hanging off its desiccated form, the withered corpse cocked its head at Swampy, as if it could see him through the empty, dark sockets sunk into its skull. A curtain of silky black hair fell down over its shoulder.

Swampy moaned wordlessly, wide eyes fixed on the monster. "What the hell, what the actual hell?" he spat out, struggling with the work table. He managed to shift it somewhat as the creature crouched down beside him. Then he finally noticed that the monster had something in its hands. Swampy's eyes fixed on the little metal ring. He recognized it immediately—the interface crown of a cold sleep machine.

Swampy looked at the crown, looked back up at the monster, and felt the bottom of his stomach drop out. "No! Dit røvhul! No!" He thrashed, screaming in pain and fear as one of his ribs popped out of place.

The monster silently placed the crown over his head.

Haley and Yadiera had gotten halfway up the stairs to the upper level when the blue running lights snapped off.

"What the—" Haley gripped the railing and blinked into the blackness. A moment later, two points of deep, sullen red light pulsed to life, one at the bottom of the stairs and one at the top. It was enough to see Yadiera's scowl. "Emergency power," she snapped, all fatigue gone from her face. She pulled a little pin light from her pocket and switched it on, then hurried up the stairs. "The virus must have gotten into the system after all. Damn it, we are *not* getting paid enough for this kind of trouble. Swampy!" she shouted as she reached the upper landing. "Swampy, what did you do?"

Haley hesitated at the upper landing. The door to the bridge stood open—all of the doors opened automatically when the power shut off. She didn't know what made her hesitate at first. Then the Captain strode into the bridge, and Swampy still hadn't said anything or stepped out of the red-lit shadows.

"Yadiera..." Haley started, then yelped as something leapt onto the Captain's back. Haley bolted forward as Yadiera cried out, grappling with the thing clinging to her. With a grunt of effort she flipped the thing over and flung it at the wall. It hit with a sickening smack.

Haley stopped and stared as Swampy slid bonelessly to the ground, his face slack. "Swampy!" she yelled, rushing past the shocked captain.

Swampy rolled over onto his stomach and stiffly started to rise.

"What the hell Swam—" Haley cut off as Swampy jerked his head in her direction. His eyes stared, wide and unblinking, his pupils contracted to the barest of pinpricks. The red emergency lights glinted off a familiar-looking silver band of metal around his forehead.

Haley skidded to a halt and backed up. "Swampy?"

Yadiera gasped from behind her. "Haley!"

Haley spun around. Someone with long black hair had Yadiera by the wrists. The captain's face hung slack with horror as she struggled with the stranger's grip. Haley recoiled at the sight of the stranger's black hair and silver suit, but she didn't know why. The stranger's bony hand inched upwards, touching Yadiera's pin light. The bright white beam flickered once and died.

"Captain!" Haley started forward, only to have Swampy grab her from behind, arms encircling her. "Let go!" Haley snapped. "What the hell is wrong with you?"

With a shout, Yadiera kneed her attacker in the pelvis. The stranger flinched back but maintained its grip on the captain, and Haley finally got a look at their face. It was the corpse from the cold sleep pod. Haley screamed, the sound attracting the monsters attention. It turned, and Yadeira managed to wrench her fist free and sucker punched the corpse in the jaw. The mummy stumbled away, straightened, and turned towards Haley and Swampy.

Haley panicked and swung her elbow backwards, catching Swampy in the ribs. Something shifted under her blow, and he released her without a sound. Haley bolted, dodging past the walking corpse.

"Run!" she shouted unnecessarily as Yadiera sprinted for the door. Haley chased after her, thinking of Swampy only after she made it to the hall. She glanced over her shoulder to see Swampy and the mummy standing side by side, watching her run away. Swampy crouched, staring eyes fixed on her. Haley gasped and ran faster, heart pounding so loud that she almost didn't hear him start to give chase.

"Med-bay!" she shouted after Yadiera. "It has its own power!"

Yadiera didn't waste time answering, just bolted down the stairs, practically falling down them in her haste. Haley had just reached them when Swampy came barreling up, glanced down to the lower floor, and vaulted over the railing.

"Look out!" Haley shouted. Yadiera jumped away as Swampy instantly recovered from his twenty foot fall and lunged for her.

"Get Emilio!" Yadiera yelled, racing off into the darkness with Swampy right behind her.

Haley didn't have time to argue—the monster in the silver suit was lurching down the hallway, it's movements jerky and slower than Swampy's, its eyeless sockets turned to her. Haley ran.

An agonizing five minutes later, Haley had a sleepy and confused Emilio over one shoulder as she hurried down the hallway as silently as possible.

"Haley, I can walk, what the heck?"

"Shush," Haley hissed. The corpse had been easy enough to lose, but she didn't know where Swampy was. Hell, she didn't even know what had happened to Swampy. Mummies and… and possessed best friends didn't happen in real life. It was all so crazy that it had to be a dream, it had to, it had to.

"There better really be a mummy, this better not be a joke," Emilio muttered.

They were almost to the med-bay. Haley set Emilio down and pressed herself against the wall. She carefully peered around the corner. The red emergency lights illuminated an empty hallway. She let out a breath, then worried, suddenly, that Yadiera hadn't made it.

"Hey, Swampy," Emilio hissed. "Did you see the mummy?"

Haley sucked in a breath and whipped around. Swampy stood at the end of the hallway, staring at them.

"Shit!" she snapped, grabbing Emilio's arm and bolting around the corner. She hammered on the med-bay door. "Open up god damn it! Open up!"

She sobbed with relief as the door slip open. She shoved Emilio inside and fell in after him. The door slammed shut, and a second later something struck it. The light inside the room went out, but the door held firm. Power or not, the med-bay door stayed closed. Heart hammering, Haley straightened and looked through the thick glass door panel.

Swampy stared back at her, gray eyes wide and pupils so small they looked like needle marks. He didn't seem to see her—just stared, face slack. Then he turned abruptly and walked away. The light in the room flicked back on.

Haley let out a shaky breath and turned to look around the room.

Yadiera knelt on the floor, arms wrapped tightly around her son, muttering in heavily Martin-accented Spanish. Vincent—tall, dark haired, and olive-skinned, with half-healed radiation burns across his neck and chest—stood off to one side dressed in a white med-bay robe.

Ignoring the one wall taken up by medical supplies, the med-bay was actually very pleasant. It housed two real beds, a well-stocked print and film library, and a self-contained bathing chamber and kitchen. The crew often used it as an extra recreation room when it wasn't needed. The bright, homey surroundings seemed almost insulting after that mad chase through the dark.

"I'm glad you made it," Vincent said. "I was just about ready to knock her out to keep her from going after you," he gestured to Yadiera, his face stony and serious. Haley winced sympathetically at his dead-pan expression. Yadiera must have already told him everything.

"Mom, Mom, I'm alright," Emilio said, peeling himself away from his mother's grasp. He looked from Haley to Vincent. "Why's Swampy acting crazy? Did the mummy eat his brain or something?"

"That's zombies, kiddo," Vincent said flatly, sinking down onto one of the beds. "Not Mummies."

"What's the difference?" Yadiera asked, shuddering as she finally let her son go. "They're both dead bodies and they both don't exist! I don't care which one is on my ship. Oh, hell," she stood up and passed a hand over her eyes.

"Are you *sure* it was a mummy?" Vincent asked, wrinkling his nose. "It could be an alien."

Haley shook her head. "It's from the cold sleep pod. I saw it. I…" she blinked, suddenly remembering something. "Swampy was wearing a crown."

"So?" Vincent asked, frowning.

"So I saw it before," Haley said, turning back to look at the window in the door, half-expecting Swampy to still be there. "The mummy was wearing it in its pod."

Yadiera bit her lip. "It must have been a cold sleep interface."

"The mummy wasn't wearing it though, Swampy was." Haley said.

"So what?" Emilio asked.

"So… I don't know, I don't know." Haley shook her head, shuddering at the memory of the mummy. "How is that thing even walking around?"

"I want to know how it got on the ship." Yadiera scowled and picked herself up from the floor.

Haley clawed her hand through her short hair, trying to think past her fear. "Swampy said there was a power drain in the airlock. I thought Emilio was messing around, but it must have been that thing."

"Just opening the airlock wouldn't have drained the power," Vincent said, shaking his head.

"I thought Emilio did something," Haley repeated, grimacing at the kid. He scowled and stuck his tongue out at her.

"I know, but how did the mummy drain the power?" Vincent pressed.

"That's what the computer virus did," Haley said. Vincent frowned. Haley scowled and gestured to the door. "The wreck—we'd just realized that it was out of power because of a virus."

"So the virus is in the mummy?" Emilio asked.

"What, no," Haley snapped. "That's not what I…" she trailed off, remembering how the pin light had gone out at the corpse's touch, how the med-bay light had switched off when Swampy had touched the door. "That's not possible," she said, glancing up at the light fixture in the center of the ceiling. Well, the light was back on, so it didn't actually have the virus.

"How do you know?" Vincent countered, crossing his arms with a scowl.

"The virus was in the cold sleep machines," Yadiera said slowly, looking at each of them in turn. "The machines put the virus into the people, and then the mummy put the interface on Swampy."

"It's trying to spread itself," Haley hissed, covering her mouth, as if that could keep the horror she felt creeping up her spine inside. "Shit."

"Is Swampy going to be okay?" Emilio asked.

No one said anything.

Haley felt her gut twist.

"So," Vincent said, breaking the silence. "Swampy must have put the virus into the main power frame. Emergency power kicked in though, so we've got life support for… how long?"

"Two weeks," Yadiera said grimly. "No propulsion."

"Right. Okay. Gravity?"

The captain shook her head. "Is staying where it is unless he can get to the unit on the outside of the ship."

"Or get to something that connects to it," Haley said grimly. "It *is* Swampy, after all."

"Is it?" Vincent asked, raising an eyebrow, lips pressed grimly together. "If it was, you'd think it would be able to hack into the emergency power by now."

"Unless we need to be alive for the virus to get us," Emilio added. The adults looked down at him. "What?" he asked, frowning.

"Thanks for that, Kiddo," Vincent sighed. He lay back on the bed.

"If this is a joke, tell me now, okay? Because I am not well enough to deal with this."

No one said anything.

"God damn it," Vincent croaked, his dead-pan cracking. He covered his eyes.

"Vincent," Haley said, starting forward.

"I'm fine," he said, sucking in a shuddering breath. He removed his hands from his face and sat up. "Let's start by getting that crown off of him. Maybe that will be enough."

A few minutes later, the med-bay door opened. Vincent stuck his head out and peered down the hallway. "Coast is clear," he said, hurrying out. He had changed from his robe into a black jumpsuit. Haley followed him out and shut the door. They both had their radios in place, and Haley was grateful that she had thought to grab Emilio's for him.

"Keep us posted," Emilio hissed in her ear. "Over."

Haley crossed her fingers. "Right, over."

There weren't exactly weapons stored in the med-bay, but Haley felt fairly confident with the lengths of plastic pipes that they had unscrewed from one of the bedposts.

She glanced sidelong at Vincent's grim face. "You going to be okay?"

Vincent returned her glance and pressed his lips together. "If *your* husband was possessed by a computer virus, would *you* be okay?"

Haley winced. "Sorry." She was more worried about him still being weak from his illness, but didn't press the point.

The two of them made their way down the hall, eyes jumping from shadow to shadow. They reached the open area where the stairways led up to the upper levels. Haley walked over to where Swampy had landed after jumping over the railing. She half-expected to find the metal floor buckled, but of course it didn't have a mark on it.

"So where is he?" Vincent asked.

Haley shook her head and turned to face him.

A black haired, skeletal form stood behind Vincent, half inside the red glare of the emergency lights.

"Shit!" Haley hissed, jumping backwards as her hand swung up to point.

Vincent whirled around, backpedaling as the monster reached for him. He yelled and swung his pipe, the white plastic connecting with the thing's temple. The mummy's head jerked with the blow, and it stumbled sideways. Haley rushed in, pipe raised, but Vincent pushed her back. "Run!" he commanded.

They took off, barreling past the stairs and down another red-lit hall. The black mouths of the open bunk rooms yawned at them as they ran past.

Haley reminded herself that the corpse was slow—it was Swampy who was fast. All they had to do was outrun it… outrun it and then play hide and seek down the red-lighted halls until they found Swampy. Once they got the crown off, he could fix this. He was the one who could build virus blockers. He could….

Haley glanced over her shoulder, but she didn't see the monster. She skidded to a halt, heart hammering. "Shit," she gasped. "I…" she looked around, insides twisted with dread. She couldn't see Vincent either.

Haley crossed her fingers, hesitated, then said, "Vincent." With individual radio contact established, she repeated his name and waited. Nothing. "Vincent, are you alright?"

Haley uncrossed her fingers and swore. She shouldn't have let him come, not while he was still recovering. She started back down the hallway, pipe raised, eyes darting left and right.

Movement caught her eye and she leapt backwards as Swampy came leaping out of one of the open bunk rooms. Haley shouted and brought her pipe down over the back of his head, knocking him to the floor.

She dropped down beside him, cursing all the while, and yanked the silver crown from his head. Swampy froze.

"Oh thank god," Haley half-sobbed. "Swampy!" She grabbed him by the shoulders and pulled him upright.

Swampy's hands shout out and wrapped around her throat.

. . .

E milio jumped as the lights snapped off inside the med-bay.
"Damn," his mother said from beside him on the bed.
Her flashlight snapped on, illuminating the room. She gave her son a wan smile. "Works now," she said.

"Did they get the emergency power?" Emilio asked nervously.

"Hey!" called a voice from the other side of the door. Emilio turned, but the light from the flashlight didn't reach through the little window.

"It's Haley," said the muffled voice. "My radio broke."

"Thank goodness you're alright," Yadiera sighed, standing up from the bed. The flashlight beam jumped around the room as she moved. "Did you get Swampy?"

"Dead," Haley said flatly. "Virus kills you."

Yadeira flinched, and Emilio covered his mouth with both hands, holding in a gasp. He stared at the door in shock as his mother walked towards it. It couldn't be real. It couldn't. No one he had ever known had died before. Swampy couldn't be dead, not like this. It couldn't be real, couldn't be…

The flashlight shined out the window, but no one stood behind it. Emilio felt the hair on the back of his neck stand up. Why was Haley out of sight? Why wasn't Vincent with her?

"Mom—" Emilio started, but Yadiera had already muscled open the door's manual lock. Haley's hand snaked through the gap and slid the door open. She turned her wide, staring eyes to them and smiled stiffly, the flashlight's beam glinting off the silver crown on her forehead.

"Virus kills you," she said again.

THE RISE OF IËS

ROSE STRICKMAN

"Thank you, Mazim." The old man leaned on the balcony railing and panted, trying to catch his breath after the long climb. "That wasn't easy."

"No trouble at all, Grandsire." Mazim hovered around his master as the night wind blew around them. "Will you be all right, Grandsire?"

The old man smiled wryly at his aide. "I'll be fine, Mazim. Go back downstairs. I'd like to be alone for a while."

Mazim half-hesitated, but an order was an order, no matter how frail the Grandsire seemed. Bowing, he stepped back through the door to the interior of the tower, and the long, winding stairway that led down into the main house.

The old man doubted he would go all the way down, though; Mazim was far too conscientious to leave his frail, ancient master entirely alone. But for now, the Grandsire had privacy.

Sighing, he arranged his aching bones more comfortably against the railing. This would probably be the last time he ever made it up here, and he wanted to make the most of it.

Below him, the lights of the town spread out gleaming. Above, the stars winked, faded to near-insignificance next to the blistering-bright asteroids that surrounded the planet. The first of the moons had not yet risen, but would soon clear the fungus-forest, a brilliant, misshapen lantern.

He was going to miss those three moons, the Grandsire reflected: they'd been his only constant companions for five hundred years.

He slumped back, feeling the ache of impending death, and let himself remember.

"Asha, there's something out there."

Asha, only just starting to fall asleep after another long, exhausting day, groaned. "Of course there is, Miriam. It's an unsettled alien planet, remember? Probably got monsters out the wazoo, just waiting to eat us." It was an unkind thing to say, but Asha really was miserable with tiredness.

In the unutterable darkness of the shelter, Miriam stirred fretfully, body wriggling against Asha's. None of the other survivors stirred from their deep, exhausted slumber. "I'm telling you, I saw something. Last night, when I went out to pee."

Asha, who had been falling asleep again, startled awake. "You did *what?*" She wriggled an arm free to smack her younger sister lightly. "Are you crazy? Don't you remember what happened to Deepak?"

"I know." Miriam's whisper was low and desperate. "I think I might've seen the thing that killed him."

"What?" Morbid curiosity prompted Asha's question. "What did you see?"

"I…" Miriam's voice faltered. "I don't know. I can't describe it. It was out there in the moonlight and it—it *looked* at me, Asha. I could swear it looked at me and recognized me!"

"It can't have," Asha said sensibly. "There's no sentient life on this planet...that we know of," honesty forced her to add. She sighed. "Look, Miriam, just go to sleep. Whatever it is, it won't get inside." They'd built the shelter thick and strong, with salvaged metal from the ship and with native rocks and plant materials. There were *some* advantages to being a crew of techs and engineers washed up on this alien shore, Asha reflected, whatever their deficiencies in wilderness survival skills.

"What if it does?"

"It won't." She groped out to pat Miriam's hair. "Try to sleep. Marcus is going to need you on the beacon he's building."

"There's no point." Miriam's voice was suddenly flat and cold.

"What?"

"That power pack he thought would work? Turns out it's not strong enough. We can't power the beacon enough to signal for help. Not past that asteroid field and the gravitic wells."

"Oh." Asha digested this unpleasant piece of news. "Well, you should try to sleep anyway."

After silence fell, Asha belied her own words by lying awake, staring into the darkness that seemed only a reflection of her inner despair. Marcus's beacon had been their final hope. Their ship had only come to this remote sector by hideous accident with the wormhole, and then, battered by the asteroids and sucked down by the gravitic wells that surrounded this planet, it had crashed to the planet's surface, killing half its crew and passengers, engineers and techs on their way to build a new space station out on Janus IV. That beacon may have been useless anyway, Asha reflected gloomily: there had been little hope that there would be a ship close enough to signal for help.

She wondered how long it would take for them all to die. The planetary atmosphere was breathable, and there was plenty of water in this forested region. But there was little food left, and no way for this bunch of astro-engineers to tell which plants were edible. And already so many of them had died, even aside from the crash fatalities: Janet had cut herself on the sharp edges of a fungal growth the first day and died raving; Rohan had slipped and cracked his head open at the stream; and several people had been poisoned eating what they thought was familiar fungi.

And a few days ago, something had killed Deepak. They'd found his body outside the shelter the next morning, completely drained of blood, neck and sides decorated with neat puncture wounds. The forest had seemed a lot darker since then.

Asha cuddled closer to her sister, now sleeping at last, if fitfully.

Her mind ran through calculations: since Deepak's death, there were only thirty-nine of them left, twenty women and nineteen men. How long would it take them to get through the remaining food…?

This is all my fault, she thought miserably. *I insisted we take that job.* She knew this was unfair on herself—there was no way to know that the wormhole would spit them out here instead of Janus IV—but she couldn't kill the curl of shame inside.

If it wasn't for me, we wouldn't be here.

The next morning, after a meager breakfast, Marcus found the courage to stand up and deliver the bad news.

A dismal silence greeted his words. The survivors, already far thinner than they'd been when they'd first crashed, stared down at their makeshift plates and bowls, eyes filled with despair. Outside, the nightly rain still fell, tapping and pattering at the great stems of the flower-trees, running off the sides of the huge fungi.

"I know it's bad," Marcus said. His face was gray and covered in stubble, but he had a determined expression. "But if we can hold on until help comes—"

"Help isn't coming." Miriam nodded at the shelter door, open to let in light. "And there's something out there. I saw it the other night. Whatever killed Deepak."

"We'll make weapons," Marcus said firmly. "Today, that's what I want us all to do. Asha, Elliot, you get people organized into weapon-making teams. Brainstorm; let's all decide what will work and then build it. Meanwhile, I'll take out a foraging team."

"Are you sure that's smart?" Allen glanced uneasily at the door. "Whatever killed Deepak…"

"We have no choice," Marcus said determinedly. "We have to have food. Maybe we can kill one of those shelled creatures and get some protein." Rattling off a string of names, including Miriam's, Marcus chose those few people who had some background in biology to help him with today's foraging expedition. "Asha, Elliot, you get everyone else organized."

It was good to have something to do, Asha admitted. Being engineers, they argued for most of the morning about what weapons they should build and what designs they should use, before deciding on a catapult, made from the stem of one of the tall plants of the forest, bent back and held tense with a rope, and with a net full of rocks to throw. Asha took over the team building that, while Elliot led everyone else in making spears.

It took them all day, but Asha was pleased with the result. Their catapult held an armful of stones, which could be launched with a single tug of the taut rope holding the stem anchored. Not a moment too soon, either: darkness was advancing from the forest, and the first of the planet's moons had already risen, even as the sun sank down.

Marcus's team was less successful. They didn't manage to hunt down one of the endemic invertebrates, and no one dared experiment with eating any native plants or fungi. They ate a subdued meal from the stores of the ship, and tried not to calculate how much was left. *God help us all,* Asha thought as she lay down next to Miriam, stomach hollow.

She awoke to the sound of singing.

Not the cheeping of the night creatures, trilling and lulling from the forest. This was a wavering, wordless song, floating from outside the shelter, and it definitely came from a human throat.

Asha's first panicked thought was that someone had gone outside, at night, alone. *And they're* singing! *Who could be so stupid?*

It sounded like a man's voice. Who among the men could be outside singing? She didn't recognize the voice, but the tune tugged at her, pulling uncomfortably at some association she couldn't pin down.

Asha hesitated a moment before grasping a spear made from ship-metal and tough fungi, manufactured only this morning and laid beside her bed. Picking her way over the sleeping bodies, she eased open the shelter door and peered out.

She knew she was being stupid, even as she did it. But someone had to investigate, and at least she had a weapon. And, if she was being honest, curiosity pulled her, stronger than caution.

Two of the planet's moons were out, blazing blue-silver light down into the clearing, glittering on the stream that ran along its edge. That, along with the starlight and the gleam of the asteroids, allowed Asha to see clearly the bizarre sight that sat at the edge of the water.

It was a man—but none of the men she'd come to know over the last few weeks. This was a stranger: a *human* stranger, on a planet where no other humans should be. He was naked, his white, flawless skin gleaming in the moonlight, and he had his head tilted back, long thick hair pouring down, as he sang, wordless and lovely and impossible. And—and *familiar.*

Perhaps she made some noise or perhaps he just sensed her—Asha was never sure, afterward—but the man suddenly stopped singing and turned to look at her.

He stared at her, calm and unafraid. His eyes were indeterminately dark in the mezzotint of the moonlight, muscles rippling over his perfect body. His face was smooth and beardless, but his hair swung long and free around his shoulders.

Then he lifted a hand to brush away that hair, and she saw the long, glinting claws.

Letting out a yelp, Asha yanked the door shut and scrabbled to secure the latch. She leaned against the closed door, heart pounding.

Was it just her imagination, or could she hear the man outside laugh, light and amused?

A long time later, when next she dared inch the door open and look, he was gone, as though he'd never been. The stream burbled on alone.

Sweating, Asha groped her way to bed. She had to be hallucinating; she was so hungry and tired, after all. She would go back to bed, and in the morning this would all be a dream—

But then, as she finally found her place and lay down, she suddenly realized what had bothered her so much about that song.

It was a tune Deepak used to hum and whistle, before he was killed.

· · ·

Unsurprisingly, it took Asha a while to fall asleep again. She awoke late the next morning, to find the camp already abuzz.

"Asha!" Miriam swooped upon her as she exited the shelter, stumbling, eyes aching from lack of sleep. "Come quick! We've found signs of a *person!*"

Asha's blood ran cold. "Down by the stream?"

"Yes!" Miriam blinked, startled out of her excitement. "How did you know?"

Asha didn't answer, but strode quickly down to the knot of people on the stream bank.

"Look!" Leila was saying. "Footprints."

"And you can tell where they were sitting," Miriam put in. Having grown up on a frontier farm on Terra VI, she and Asha knew a bit of tracking. "Right there, by the water." She pointed to the exact place where Asha had seen the man.

"The tracks go off into the forest," said Marcus, tracing along the opposite bank. "They're definitely human footprints!"

"It could have been one of us!" Asha said desperately.

A dozen pairs of eyes turned to her in sudden interest, and she realized that her sharp squeak had been a dead giveaway. "Asha?" said Marcus. "Did you see something?"

Asha swallowed. There was no point in lying now. "Last night. A man, here by the stream." Swiftly, she described the encounter.

A ripple ran through the group, but a different kind of ripple than she'd expected. "Yes!" breathed large-boned Brian, eyes shining. "There *are* other people on this planet! We're saved!"

"No!" Asha said, horrified. "Didn't you hear anything I said? This guy was sitting here stark naked, singing in the moonlight, all alone. What sane person would do that in this forest, especially with our shelter right here? And I'm telling you, he had *claws* on his hands!"

"You must have mistaken it," said Marcus. "You *were* only seeing him by moonlight."

"I saw he was naked, at least." Asha pointed at the soft, wet ground. "And look. Those are bare footprints. Who walks through a forest like this barefoot?"

"Well, maybe we can ask him when we find him," said Brian.

"Ask him…?" Asha trailed off in horror. They weren't going to listen to her, she realized. No one, not even Miriam, was going to heed her tale, or allow her to communicate the menace of that encounter. They were too desperate, too eager for any shred of hope.

Already, Marcus was getting the search party organized. "Brian, you come with me and Jacob. Miriam and Leila, you as well; you know about tracking."

At the mention of her sister, Asha pulled from her daze. "No!" Everyone glanced at her, and she lowered her voice. "How do we know this guy is friendly?"

"Don't worry, we'll take weapons," Marcus assured her. "And Brian and Jacob are both big guys. We'll be back before dark."

"But what if there's more of them?"

"Let's hope to God there are," said Marcus, suddenly sober. "Let's hope they know a way off this planet." He looked grimly into Asha's eyes. "I know it's taking a chance, Asha, but we have to do this. We have to find this guy, and anyone he's with, and see if they can help us. It's our only chance."

He was right, Asha realized. She swallowed back any further protests, despite the foreboding growing tight in her stomach.

The search party took a further half hour to get organized, making sure their shoes were sound, selecting makeshift weapons, packing food, and slinging on the crude rain slickers they'd devised. Asha hovered around Miriam.

"Please, Miri." Her throat was tight, and she cleared it before continuing. "Be careful."

"I will." Miriam smiled at her, brighter-eyed and more hopeful than she'd been since the crash. "But just think, Asha, this could be escape!"

Asha just shook her head. "You didn't see that guy last night," she said in a low voice. "He was…like something out of a dream. Or a nightmare. If he…if they…"

"If they try anything, we'll run." Miriam reached out and squeezed her hand. "That guy was walking barefoot through the forest; he can't have gone far. We'll probably find him today. And we can run straight home if we have to."

"Don't get lost in the forest." Asha followed her back to where the search party was congregating. "Mark your trail." She swallowed again against a dry throat. "I love you, Miriam."

"I love you too, Asha." Miriam hugged her tightly. "And we'll come back!" she promised over her shoulder. "With help!"

This raised a ragged cheer from the other survivors as the party set off, following the tracks into the forest.

"When do you think they'll come back?"

At Elliot's question, Asha glanced back at the trees, yet again. The search party had disappeared hours ago, the day was waning, and there was still no sign of them. The camp had buzzed excitedly at first, but had since fallen quiet. No one could resist looking at the forest every few seconds.

Finally, out of sheer desperation, Asha had gotten everyone organized to go back to the ship's crash site and salvage whatever might be left. She'd known there wouldn't be much—they'd already stripped the hull of anything edible or useful—but then Elliot proposed that they set up a signaling mirror on top of the shelter, and now everyone scoured the wreck, looking for anything shiny.

"I don't know, Elliot." Asha found a likely-looking piece of metal and started up their one still-functional saw. "They'll be back before dark, Marcus said." She began to cut.

"Yeah. Yeah, hopefully. Here, let me hold that." Elliot took hold of the metal shard as she sliced it off the hull.

"Thanks, Elliot." She tossed it onto the plastic sheet they planned to use to haul their scraps back to camp. She cast around desperately for anything different to say, to think about. "Say, Elliot, where are you from?"

Elliot grinned. "Terra VI, actually."

"What, really? Me too!" Asha clapped him on the shoulder. "Two frontier brats, huh?"

"Not really. I'm a city boy, me. Or what passes for a city on VI." Elliot grimaced slightly. "I got off planet as soon as I could, to go to school."

"Yeah, us too—me and Miriam. Nothing like growing up on a dirt farm to motivate you to make something of yourself." Asha sighed, gloom settling back on her. "But here we are. Ironic, huh?"

"Yeah. Ironic." Elliot gave a humorless laugh. "But maybe the search party will come back with help."

"God willing." Asha smiled. "But, whatever happens…" She trailed off, unsure how to express it. "Thanks for talking, Elliot. For… having a normal conversation for a minute. Like human beings."

He gave her the ghost of a smile in return.

"Anytime, Asha."

B y the time they'd gotten their shiny haul back to camp, darkness was starting to settle and there was still no sign of the search party.

"We've been watching for hours," Ariel assured them, eyes bright with anxiety. "Nothing!"

Asha controlled her ballooning panic. "Okay, people," she called, raising her voice. "Let's get this stuff inside and have dinner. I think we earned it. And let's set up a watch or something, to keep an eye out for the searchers."

The group trailed in, tugging the sheet after them, glancing back at the darkening trees.

The searchers didn't return while they were putting away their haul. They didn't return while they got the watch shifts organized. They didn't return while they gathered together rationed scraps for dinner. By then darkness had fallen completely, the asteroids unveiling against the field of stars.

Asha put up a good front, smiling and encouraging conversation, but beside her determinedly quotidian thoughts danced an idea, a growing possibility, too horrible to face. *Miriam.*

At last, she had to excuse herself. Stepping out the door, she took a deep breath. The night air was still crisp and dry; the rain wouldn't come until later. Starlight bathed the clearing, as moonlight had the night before. She tried to see the place where the stranger had been sitting and singing, but it was all in shadow.

"Miriam." Her sister's name slid out, small and miserable.

"Don't worry." Asha nearly jumped out of her skin as she whirled to see Elliot, sitting on the ground outside the shelter. Her face burned: she'd forgotten about the watch. "They'll come back," said Elliot. "I'm sure of it."

She knew he was sure of no such thing, but she was all the more grateful for his lies. "Thanks, Elliot." She took a deep breath, surveying the forest. "I just hope they're okay."

"Yeah." Elliot leaned back, letting out a long breath. "Me too."

Asha dropped down beside him. "Let me take this watch."

He shook his head. "We'll watch together."

Asha took a deep breath and let it out again. "Okay."

They sat together, while the planet darkened around them and the stars opened their eyes.

Asha dreamed.

The stranger stepped out of the forest, the same man from last night. But this time he wasn't alone. Three other men walked with him, as pale, as dark-eyed, as graceful. And they led with them—in the dream, Asha's heart clenched—Leila and Miriam. Both women wove and swayed, faces fixed with dreamy grins, not even seeming to notice the huge centipede-creatures that swarmed around the group—

Asha's eyes flew open, and she lurched to her feet as she took in the scene before her, almost exactly as it had been in her dream. But now Elliot was here, writhing on the ground, eyes huge, mouth muffled, bound around with the long, serpentine body of one of the chitinous giant centipedes, its carapace gleaming in the moonlight, eyes bright with a sentient greed—

"Quiet." The pale man's voice was soft, but it stopped Asha in her tracks, even as she lunged for the catapult and opened her mouth to scream an alarm. "Quiet, or he dies."

With a huge effort, Asha swallowed back her shriek. Turning very slowly, she faced the pale man.

He was fully clothed this time, she saw dazedly, though they fit him badly. They were—oh, God—they were Marcus's clothes. And, while the fourth man was naked, two of the other strangers wore clothes that had belonged to Brian and Jacob. But Marcus, Brian and Jacob were nowhere in sight…

"My apologies for our arriving at such an hour," said the pale man. His voice was calm, courteous and oddly accented. "This new flesh of ours, I fear, does not deal well with the sun; its light burns us like corrosive acid." He shrugged, a bizarrely human gesture. "We've always favored the night, though, so it's not too inconvenient for us."

He gestured, and another man held up a lamp made of some phosphorescent plant bulb, illuminating the scene clearly: four salt-white men, three of them clothed, holding among them…

Miriam gave Asha a slow smile. "Hi, Asha," she slurred. Giggling dreamily, she slumped against one of the strangers, eyes half-closed. In the bulb-light, Asha could clearly see where her sister's clothes had been ripped, and the puncture wounds on her neck, breasts and arms.

"*Miriam!*" Asha lunged again, but the leader stepped in front of her.

"None of that, Asha Smith," he said. "Don't worry for your sister; the venom should wear off in a few hours, and she will make a complete recovery."

Behind her, Elliot still writhed and grunted. Asha made herself take a deep breath and concentrate, as she did when making a repair in zero gravity on the outside of a space station.

"Who are you?" she asked levelly. "And how do you know my name?"

"You may call me Azar," said the leader. "And I know your name from his memories. I have them all now, you see."

"Whose memories?" Resolutely, she blocked Elliot's desperate grunts.

"Deepak's." Azar tapped his forehead with a glittering claw. She could see his coloring more clearly now, though his eyes were still in shadow: face utterly white, eyebrows dark but his long hair red as apples. The others were all redheads too, she noted distantly, and as pale as he.

"I have all of Deepak's memories," Azar said calmly. "I absorbed them all, you see, when I drank him down—though it took a few nights for all his knowledge to fully settle in my consciousness." He smiled slightly.

Asha thought of the song he'd been wordlessly singing last night: Deepak's favorite song. Her stomach clenched. "So you…you killed…?"

"I'm afraid so," Azar admitted. "It's the only way for us to transform, you see."

"Transform into what?"

His smile widened. "Into *you*, of course."

Asha looked at the giant centipede-things, wriggling and swarming around the human-looking men, brushing against her sister's legs, crushing the native flora of this planet as they hissed and chittered. She felt sick.

"Yes." Azar correctly interpreted her glance. "That is our original form, to which I and these three my brothers cannot return, now that we have drunk human blood and absorbed human consciousness. These—" he gestured at the invertebrates "—are my brothers who have not yet drunk. There are only twenty of us left now."

Like a vision, the scene arose before Asha's eyes: the search party, following Azar's tracks back to whatever dark hideout he and his "brothers" inhabited. Azar, appearing, beckoning them forward from the shadows beyond the reach of sunlight, greeting them in the human manner, mouth full of false reassurances. Leading them in. And only then did the others reveal themselves, leaping upon the men, sinking those spines into them, writhing around Miriam and Leila's legs when they tried to run—

"What did you do to my sister?" Her voice was high and strangled. "To Leila?"

Azar grinned. His tongue touched his two long, translucent fangs, glimmering in the bulb-light.

"We are not quite like you, even after transformation," he said musingly. "These fangs…they have some amazing properties, it would appear. Their venom seems to make a bite very…pleasurable for the victim."

Leila hummed tunelessly, draping herself on one of the other humanoids, smiling, smiling. Asha swallowed bile. "Please, let them go. Let all of them go!" Elliot whimpered in agreement, still trapped in the alien's coils.

"I'm afraid that's not possible," Azar said, still maddeningly calm. "It would hamper our negotiations."

"Negotiations?" Asha cried incredulously. "What makes you think we're willing to *negotiate?*"

"Because you're in much the same position as we are," Azar said. "Yes," he said to Asha's startled look. "We too are aliens on Iës, as we have named this planet. We hail from a race and a civilization far beyond humanity's current reach, and for all we know, we are the last of our kind. Our empire fell, you see, to internal strife and external war, and my brothers and I were a single shattered splinter from our army, our vessel cast deep into space by superior weaponry. We were sucked in by this planet's gravitic wells, battered by its asteroids, and flung down to its surface to survive as best we could." He smiled grimly. "Most of us did not."

"So now…" Asha groped for comprehension. "Now you want…to escape?"

He shook his head. It seemed he had the full range of human gestures, absorbed from Deepak's mind. "There is no escape from Iës— and nowhere for us to return to, even if we did. For long years we have wandered Iës, learning its ways and looking for a sentient species whose bodies and minds we could copy, according to our own species' ability. One that would allow us to survive. But we found no one— until you." He smiled again at Asha. "Escape may be impossible, but I believe we may come to a mutually beneficial arrangement, my brothers and I, and you and your sisters."

"My…sisters?" Asha looked at the ground. The centipedes had all disappeared, unnoticed, at some point during the discussion, leaving the ground bare.

Asha realized that she knew where they had gone. "What—what about the *men?*"

"Alas," Azar said gently, "they're in our way. And we need their blood."

A scream cracked out from the shelter.

Asha turned to run inside, but Azar leaped forward again, light as a shadow. She struggled fruitlessly against his iron strength as he restrained her arms and held her back. More frenzied shrieks rent the night from within the shelter, and the last of the centipede-creatures wriggled in through the hole it had made in the roof—

Elliot screamed.

Asha watched, helpless in Azar's grip, as the alien deployed its long sharp spines from its carapace, puncturing Elliot's clothes and the flesh beneath. He struggled, kicking and sobbing with desperate terror, but Asha could see his blood pumping up through the translucent spines, and Elliot's struggles grew ever slower and weaker as the alien gorged itself on him.

Elliot went still, eyes blank with death, and the alien fell off him, to lie on the ground, rigid and unmoving. For a moment, all was still.

Then a great crack split its carapace, and its shell fell open in halves. Asha cried out, recoiling in Azar's embrace, as a pair of arms, *human* arms, whiter than salt, pushed aside the dead shell with clawed hands, and the almost-man sat up, blinking in the light, torso shaking with convulsive shivers, hair falling in a red curtain around his shoulders.

Two of his brothers, those already in human form, came forward to help him to his feet and step out of his old carapace. He moved slowly, clumsily, as though he didn't quite know how to use this body yet. But he would learn, Asha realized with a sick sensation., Already she could see Elliot's memories, his knowledge, settling into the brain behind that almost-human face.

There came frantic pounding from within the shelter, and the sound of the women screaming for help and escape. Asha kicked back, and Azar grunted as her foot connected with his shin. "Let them go! *Let them go, you bastard!*"

Azar turned her in his arms to face him, wrists locked in one hand, and she stared into his face from inches away. His eyes, she saw for the first time, had red irises, as red as his hair. As red as blood.

"My brothers will have blocked the door." His fangs gleamed, so close. "And I doubt your sisters will struggle long, once they've been bitten." Asha jerked back at this, cursing, and he held her still more firmly. "This doesn't have to be unpleasant, Asha. As I said, we've lived on Iës for years, and know much of its ways. We can help you survive —can *ensure* that you survive. Who knows? Perhaps a new civilization will rise, for our children, and our children's children. The new rulers of Iës." A faint smile crossed that lovely, monstrous face. "We can breed with you, now that we've transformed."

"Of course you can," she snarled. "Disgusting *pigs*!"

He unwrapped an arm, letting her spring away from him, but didn't let go of her wrists, holding her tethered. "We all act according to our natures, Asha Smith," he said with just a hint of a snarl. "We all do what we must. Would *you* choose any differently, if our situations were reversed?" He drew her close again, ignoring her shudder. "Join with us," he whispered, "and you will survive, and perhaps your children too. Spurn us, plot against us, kill us—and I'm sure you could do all three—and Iës will devour you all."

In the shelter, the women's terrified screams had died away, to be replaced by cries of an entirely different nature. Asha could picture what must be happening in there now, beside the dead bodies of the men. She looked beyond Azar, to Leila and Miriam. They might both be pregnant already, she realized horribly. They'd been with their captors all day, after all, pumped full of aphrodisiac venom.

She looked at Elliot's body. Elliot, who had been her friend, and perhaps something more, but who was gone now, along with all the men, half their party. She gazed beyond, at the forest full of blackness and hungry eyes, and the night sky jeweled with lethal asteroids, from which no rescue would ever come.

Slowly, she turned back to Azar. His eyes glittered like ruby stars in the night.

"What is your decision, Asha Smith?" he said quietly.

· · ·

He still remembered her face, the Grandsire reflected, on that other night, five hundred years distant from that *first* night. So bright, so beautiful, so enraged. But even now, he had no regrets for what he and his brothers had done. *Needs must, when the Devil drives,* he recalled the Old Earth saying, dredged up from Deepak's memories. He chuckled slightly.

He was the last of that original cohort, the last of those born off Iës. His brothers had lasted centuries longer than the human women, but, one by one, they'd all succumbed, to age or disease, violence or accident. Of all of them, only Azar was left, and he would not last much longer. Soon, he must take leave of Iës at last, and go to face Asha.

There had been women after her, of course, but she alone remained in his heart. And so he had no doubt that they would encounter one another again, beyond that final gate.

What would he tell her, when next they met again?

For a start, that he'd kept his promise to her. Their children had lived, and built a world for their own children to inherit, and their descendants had spread and created the civilization of Iës. In five hundred years, Azar had watched the children's children's children move out, discover the world, build towns and then cities, create a culture, live their lives—all from that one night of murder and terror.

But he would not apologize to Asha for what he and his brothers had done. For Azar had no regrets, and he'd never once lied to Asha Smith, the one woman he'd ever considered his wife.

There came a tap from the tower door, and Mazim poked his head out, claws glittering on the hand holding the door. "Grandsire? Are you well?" His red eyes were anxious, his skin whiter than salt. Even now, the men of Iës could not withstand the sun, though the women could. And none of Azar's male descendants ever moved past wanting human blood…

"I'm fine, Mazim." Azar waved him off. "Leave me. I want to see the moons rise."

He did not look around as Mazim closed the door. He stayed at the balcony railing, and watched the first moon slowly sail up from the pitch-black forest. *Beautiful*, he thought, eyelids growing heavy. Already he could feel his heart beginning to falter.

Then: *Asha.*

And then the first of the moons looked down, pitilessly, on the lifeless balcony, while, far below, a thousand lives went on.

SPIDER IN A SPACE HELMET

BUZZ DIXON

there's a spider in your space helmet
who gives a fuck who you are or what you're doing in space or how the
damn spider got there

you

space

helmet

spider

little black widow (little? ha! the size of a pea -- that's a fucking
elephant in the spider world!)
scurrying around in your helmet
crawling through your hair
dancing on your cheek
dragging a thin thin thin strand of webbing across your nostrils
there! you see it -- him -- *her* on the inside of your faceplate
silhouetted against the big bright blue & white globe beneath you
now you slide into darkness
no light from below just stars, stars so thick you could walk on them
you see the little eight legged monster

scuttling across a wide sea of stars
less than two inches from your face

no plot in this story
no character
no science
no sense
just that damn spider
crawling down
free floating now
legs spread out
tickling your eyelashes
don't blink
don't you dare
think of two tiny venomous fangs sinking into your eyeball
don't
you
dare
blink
don't you dare

now this is the point where the story is supposed to resolve itself with a
snap twist ending
old school sci fi mags would make this the moment the hero (that's
you!) cleverly figures out a way to purge the spider from your helmet
new wave sci fi would take a grimmer tack; now would be the moment
the spider bites and you die a long slow lingering death stranded in
space

                                        I'm not letting you off easy

I'm not that kinda guy
I'm going to leave you now
all alone
in space
with that spider
in your helmet

pleasant dreams

HAIRY JACK

HAILEY PIPER

Cheers rang through colony ship *U.F. Providence*'s A-level when, millions of miles from Earth, Cherish Fernsbury was found guilty of witchcraft.

The crowd numbered three dozen. They and their cheering washed around Zana Guillain as they hauled Cherish from the A-level meeting room. Zana came because it was a communal hearing, and she was technically part of this community. She hadn't expected Paul Sutter's raving, Captain Adrian Miro's silence, or the ultimate verdict.

She hadn't expected the morose shock on Cherish's face.

As they hauled her toward a gleaming white corridor, she reached out for the captain's help, but he was a statue. Instead she brushed Zana's hand.

"Don't let her touch your skin," Paul hissed. He shoved Cherish away, and her pale, bone-thin hand slipped through Zana's fingers. Paul and his witch-hunters wore white spacesuit gloves over their shirt sleeves. To handle a witch.

Zana stared at her hand. Four fingers, a thumb, the creases that street wanderer Mama Margot once called "fate lines." Zana couldn't remember her fate, only that it felt magical when Mama Margot's gnarled fingertip stroked her skin. No boils or warts blemished her hand now.

"Wait." She was too soft-spoken, and Paul was too much in his own head to hear.

Michael Sloan broke briefly from the group. "It's okay. They'll hold her until we can string up her animal, too." He gave Zana's arm a reassuring pat. "Don't worry, you won't miss the execution." Stringing up was a relic from ancient history. Their metaphorical hangman's rope was the airlock.

But if they were waiting to catch the animal, then there was time.

Zana wasn't alone when the witch-hunters left. Adrian remained, breathing too hard to be silent. She stared at him until he noticed and raised a helpless hand.

"What can I do? I'm one man. If they won't listen, I have no authority."

He commanded the bridge, but would he hold a colony ship hostage over one woman? No, he would keep the ship jumping through star systems until they reached Atta.

"We're outside United Federation laws here. That's what we wanted, a pilgrim ship of sorts. Everyone signed up for this."

Not everyone. Zana came looking for literal greener pastures than Earth. She still hoped to find them. Maybe at Atta, this barbarism would be punished proper, but too late for Cherish. *U.F. Providence* was in the hands of the few.

"Even Cherish came aboard to practice religion freely."

"Then why hurt her?" Zana was surprised she could speak at all.

"They're irrational. You won't win them over with reason."

"As with witches in Salem."

"I'm no history teacher, but if I recall, there were no witches in Salem."

"There's no such thing as witches." Likely Zana and Adrian were the only two people on this ship who knew that. "If I find the animal, I can use their irrationality against them."

Adrian wiped at his blue captain's coat. "I won't stop you." He looked like he wanted to tell her not to get her hopes up, but he walked away without another word.

Zana never pictured herself as someone who got involved. Even the religious specifications of the colony hadn't bothered her until the first whispers of witches. People found dark ages whenever they chose to make them, and the colonists found their darkness millions of miles from Sol. This might have happened on the other ships bound for Atta. Cabin fever in space, violence, mutiny. Perhaps she was witnessing why half the ships never reached the colony.

She left A-level's meeting room through the narrow corridor where Paul and his zealots dragged Cherish.

Dehydrated foodstuff and oxygen equipment packed the walls. There was no space to spare, even on a colony ship ferrying over two thousand sleeping souls from Earth. Zana hadn't seen its outside in months. At boarding, months ago, *U.F. Providence* reminded her of the beached cruise ships she spent her childhood scavenging on the bleeding coast. They were ancient, forever overgrown with carnivorous algae that turned the coastal air red and toxic. She was lucky to have a broom put in her hand and then a meager paycheck, luckier to later be handed a free ticket to Atta. Even a holy pilgrimage needed someone to scrub the toilets.

The corridor reached an intersection. Ahead lay the A-level port-side maintenance airlock. Scuff marks blemished the floor where its door slid up and down. Through its window was a compact chamber, where another door let out into infinite emptiness.

They would execute Cherish here.

Zana pictured her inside, at first banging on the door with her bony hands for sympathy and then, resigned to her fate, seated at the chamber's center. In a split-second, she would be freed of artificial gravity and life support. She would float into the void. The ship would activate the next faster-than-light jump, and then it would be like Cherish never existed. They wouldn't even give her the decency of a lifeboat shuttle.

That made Zana laugh and cringe. These marvels of human ingenuity—the CycloDrive engine's artificial gravity, renewed air and water molecules via TerraTech, and Juggernaut FTL's power to slip through ancient pathways once carved by comets. All these technological miracles, and they were about to execute a woman for witchcraft.

Might as well beat her to death with clubs carved from mastodon bones.

People never changed.

A muffled, throaty bark snapped Zana from the airlock window. The animal's musty stink hit before she knew what she was looking at.

Down another empty corridor stood the black dog everyone had seen the past few days. Large and shaggy, he had a long snout and folding ears. He gave another muffled bark.

Zana snapped the multi-tool off her belt. It had a pen, a flashlight, other things, among them a blade for cutting tape and plastic. Each passenger had one, even Cherish before Paul confiscated it. Zana wasn't sure she could hurt a dog, but against the life of another human being, she might try. She stepped into the dog's corridor.

He waited until she walked halfway from the airlock and then bolted into the room behind him and around a corner.

Zana charged after him. A food cylinder clattered on the floor in front of her, scattering freeze-dried potato and mushroom pellets. The dog waited at the end, his shaggy tail wagging, taunting. She kicked past the spilled foodstuff. He darted down another corridor, where someone shouted and something heavy hit the floor. She followed the noises.

He wasn't in the next room or the corridor beyond, but he had led her to Paul. He stood outside A-level storage, while another man whose name Zana didn't know helped Michael limp to a wall-mounted bench. She started toward the next corridor, but Paul called her over.

"What's your business here? You can see the witch when we execute her."

Zana belted her multi-tool. She didn't want these men to get the wrong idea. "Have you seen a dog?"

Paul crossed his arms. "Skulking around, thinking we're idle. Michael ran after. Sprained his ankle."

Michael raised his left pant leg. The ankle looked fine, but he rubbed it anyway. "Disappeared the second I looked that way."

"You should have stayed put. He'll lead us astray, fade into nothing, and come back to free his unguarded mistress. It's no natural animal. Tales of scavenger dogs date to our forefathers, omens of misfortune and death, like crows with fur. Black Shuck is one, Hairy Jack—"

"Jersey Devil," Michael added.

"Well, not quite, but he has his place at the Devil's table, where beasts sup as men while men crawl on the ground as beasts. She would do his work and make us crawl this way." Paul was talking to Zana now, too, a sermon for all of three listeners. "The dog drains our luck and gifts it to her. It's no coincidence that when she's around we have accidents, malfunctions, nightmares. She'll navigate our ship into uncharted horrors."

Michael cringed. "She's sat on my chest in the dark. I wanted to get up, but she wouldn't let me." The unnamed man nodded.

"If she's so powerful, why's she a prisoner?" Zana asked.

Paul looked taken aback. Had no one asked that question? "She's isolated in space. Nowhere to go."

"And we've taken precautions." Michael held up a spacesuit glove.

The unnamed man's lips cracked open. "Faith."

Paul and Michael murmured agreement. "And we think she's put her power inside that animal," Paul said. "A trick to look powerless to the soft-hearted. That's why we have men searching. Even when she's gone, the dog might tempt another. Neither can join us in Atta. Steel your heart, Ms. Guillain, or she'll steal it."

How long had it taken him to cook that up? He talked like this was a game. Fine then, Zana could play if winning meant saving a woman's life. "Couldn't the dog alone be the trouble? It might've bewitched her." However a dog could do that. Puppy eyes? Laying his head on her lap?

"Calm down. She's just a witch. You think witches don't want to leave Earth, same as the saved?"

"I think a dog that carries witch powers might cast a spell on a woman like Cherish. I'd rather break a spell than execute her."

"You'll find the dog? But you're a janitor."

Zana marched away toward the unexplored corridor, where a ladder descended to B-level. "Then I'll clean up your mess" popped into her head when she reached the bottom. If only she'd thought it up in Paul's face.

Better than what she wanted to say, what she muttered to herself as she searched B-level. "You're evil." It was crystal clear. They weren't drugged, mentally ill, or even ignorant except on purpose. They were evil men whose brains let them check every moralizing box necessary that let them murder a woman in cold blood.

Catching the dog would uncheck some boxes. That was the only spell to break.

Zana's search continued to C-level, where machine noise filled the heart of *U.F. Providence*. TerraTech life support pumped air and water through the ship. Not far away churned CycloDrive's gravity and Juggernaut's FTL engines.

Zana passed a cramped room, where two off-duty engineers played cards on a digital tabletop inside. The black dog waited at the end of the nearby hall. He stood at knee height on A-level, but here he grew every time Zana blinked. It was not the size of animal that should be able to disappear without a trace, not something that should have boarded the ship unnoticed. He must have been smuggled.

Zana drew her multi-tool again, her thumb ready to pop the blade. Every footstep was cautious. Paul was right; the dog did make people crawl, in his way. She neared the corridor's halfway point.

"Here, Shuck. No, not Shuck? How about Jack? Here, Jack."

The dog's left ear ticked as if pecked by a fly. He looked the size of a young mule, and then a cow.

Zana froze. If he stood his ground, she would actually get near him, and then what? Stab a thing like that?

He turned from her and lumbered around a corner.

She started breathing again, hadn't realized she'd stopped. Before his tail slipped out of sight, she charged. One misstep and her multi-tool slid through her fingers and clacked on the floor. Its blade scratched her palm. Wincing, she grabbed it and reached the corridor's end.

No surprise, Hairy Jack was already gone. Witch or no witch, the dog was a chameleon, hair so dark that if he hid against a viewport, he might blend with the blackness of space. No one would catch him unless he wanted to be caught.

"What's that banging?" A bearded, middle-aged man popped his head through a door to Zana's right. His badge marked him as chief engineer.

"Looking for a dog," Zana said. It sounded ludicrous. Every pet was in deep sleep with the rest of the passengers on D-level and E-level. "Never mind."

"No, I know what you mean." The chief scratched his hairy chin. "Captain knows it, too. Bite you?"

Zana glanced at her hand. Blood gelled between closed fingers. "No, that was me. Clumsy."

"Should've figured." The chief beckoned. She followed him to a break room where he opened a first-aid kit. "Anytime it passes, our stuff goes fritzy. Bad luck when it crosses your path."

Bandages piled into Zana's clean hand. She wiped at her lacerated palm until the blood was a faded smear. The multi-tool's cut ran along one fate line. What would Mama Margot have said of that? Zana wrapped white cloth around her hand. "Weren't black cats bad luck?"

"Birds, cats, dogs. Can be black anything." The chief coughed. "Any sort of animal, that is. It's not right, the way it looks at people like it's waiting for something bad to happen. When you wait for bad things, they come. Last time, the air stuttered on D-level."

Zana supposed engineers had their own superstitions apart from Paul and his witch-hunters. Down among the clunking machinery, the chief's fears seemed more cogent. These engines kept people alive. They could bring death, too, especially when an omen of misfortune trotted their halls on four legs.

Across from the break room there stood a door that warned unauthorized personnel to stay out. The way Hairy Jack slipped in and out of sight, it seemed a door like that would be no trouble. Yet he couldn't slip past Paul and his men. Did their faith hold the line or was the dog less spectral than he seemed?

"Can you shut off air to any corridor or room?"

The chief shrugged in a way that meant yes. "Doors seal it, sure." His eyes filled with understanding. "Oh. Well, sure. I'm on Com-6. You can speak to me from any wall pad."

Zana thanked him and returned to C-level's corridors. She passed another restricted door and slipped down three halls before she spotted the dog again.

He leaned his forelegs at the floor, arched his back, and then stood up and wagged his tail. His eyes were two little stars reflecting the overhead lights. He was an ugly thing, his lower jaw misaligned with the rest of his head, his matted hair mucky like he had been rolling in Earth's worthless soil. A rambunctious animal like him would love green Atta.

He wanted to play, like Paul and his zealots. The dog's game was not of murder, but the chase.

Zana squeezed her multi-tool and retreated two steps. Hairy Jack's head leaned in. She had his interest. But if she played his game, he would chase her. He could catch her. Then what?

Cherish's morose face filled her head, that mouth black and hopeless as space outside, as the dog.

Zana darted out of the corridor and across the hall. She paused only to listen. Yes, Jack was following. His were quiet steps for a dog his size, but Zana heard four paws thump closer. She took off again. To her left, a door snapped shut, open, shut again, clearly malfunctioning. Through the living quarters, she heard one engineer shout about a "damn table" and guessed the card game had flickered out at the dog's passing.

At the next corridor, she squeezed against the wall to one side of the door and chucked her multi-tool as hard as she could. It hit the floor several paces down and slid until it clacked against a wall.

Hairy Jack barreled past her. He'd grown elephantine, yet somehow slipped through each narrow opening. His stink filled the air, musty and dirty. He was every mangy dog that escaped the urban unit at the wasteland's edge where Zana grew up and then returned a week later only to be chased off. His jaunt slowed at the thrown multi-tool, where he glanced side to side, looking for her. He wasn't the only one who could vanish.

She slipped around the doorway and pressed one clean finger to the wall pad. "Chief? Hall C-13."

The door slid shut. Through its window, she watched another door drop where the dog's nose poked at her multi-tool. He didn't notice that his game was over.

Almost over. He stumbled back from the multi-tool. His mouth hung open, that misshapen jaw disappearing in shaggy black hair, and began to hack. Zana turned away from the window and covered her ears. She thought this would be quick but wished it would be quicker.

After a few minutes, the chief unsealed the corridor. There was only a quiet stretch of floor to cross, where a prone dog lay beside the multi-tool. He would've only come up to Zana's knee if he could stand. He'd been inflated with fearsomeness and now it had died.

She prodded him with her foot. No movement. Her fingers searched inside his knotted fur for breath or heartbeat and found only soft, still flesh. There was nothing spectral to him, no legendary Hairy Jack. A dead animal, that was all.

She belted her multi-tool and wormed her arms under the body. He was lighter than he looked, built more of hair than tissue and bone. How could she have ever been afraid of an animal so frail? Paul might've blamed God for having him kill the poor creature, but Zana couldn't be Paul. She had done this to keep him from doing worse.

He, Michael, and the other man still lingered outside A-level storage when she returned. A half-dozen witch-hunters had joined them. She knew their names and faces, but didn't feel like greeting them. She looked only at Paul.

He was beaming. "You found him. What did you do?" His smile grew when Zana explained the trap.

"Strung him up," Michael said, resting his leg on the wall bench.

Zana hefted the dog's body. "There's no need to hurt Cherish now."

The men glanced at each other and then at Paul. He closed his eyes. The smile stayed. "Ms. Guillain, she's a witch. What transpired between her and the dog is God's business. We only work his will. Whatever her power, we mustn't suffer a witch to live."

Zana's fingers curled inside the dog's thick fur. Even with the symbol of their superstition dead, they weren't going to let Cherish go. "Evil."

Paul raised an eyebrow. "Pardon?"

"I want to see her. I want to show her it's dead. After that, do what you want."

Michael started. "It's not what we want exactly—"

Paul raised a hand. "Please don't take this as ingratitude. As I said, you'll see her at the execution. Why not rest until then? You've earned it." He reached for the dog's body.

Zana held tight. The dog's musty stink coated her shirt. "I killed him. Alone. You're going to doubt me? Why do you want him so bad?"

Paul recoiled. All of them did, even Michael in his seat. They were so irrational that she could fix her words and point the finger at any of them, name him witch. But she couldn't be Paul.

"I will see her." Zana approached the storage room. No one stopped her. The door slid up to the ceiling and closed behind.

Cherish knelt on the floor. She hadn't been praying, only dozing. She looked ill-suited for travel even before being taken prisoner. Her clothes hung loose on her bony frame, and auburn hair tumbled around her gaunt face. That face would haunt Zana long after Cherish slipped out the airlock, the dog's body being her only companion. Paul and his witch-hunters would forget. The colony would be none the wiser.

Zana would remember. She couldn't help it. She knelt, still clinging to the dog. "I'm sorry. I tried."

Cherish reached beside Zana's face and tucked a red curl behind her ear. "No, dear. You did exactly what I needed. Open up, Jack." Bony hands explored the dog's hairy head and snout. Cherish pressed two thumbs against the corners of his mouth, and his jaw slopped open as it had when he was desperate for air. She dug past tongue and teeth, into his throat, and yanked out a wet, emerald-colored bauble. Jaws snapped shut behind her fingers.

Zana stared into her sunken eyes. "I don't understand."

"You don't need to understand." Cherish popped the bauble between her lips. It made a bulge at her neck as it descended her throat. "Put him on the floor and hand me your multi-tool."

Zana did as she was told.

"But I wanted to save you."

"And you have. You brought my Jack back to me. The chief engineer doesn't hate me, might've been fine, but you have a soft heart. You're perfect." Cherish dug the multi-tool blade into the dog's fur. There was no blood underneath, only deeper hairy layers, as if Jack was built only of shaggy blackness.

"Paul was right?"

"Paul talks too much. He's bound to say something true now and then."

Zana flexed her hand where Cherish's desperate fingers had stroked hours ago. "But there's no such thing as witches."

Cherish's thin lips curled into her cheeks. "They only wish I was something so nice as a witch. They wish I served so kind a creature as their Devil." She threw the dog's hide around her shoulders like a shawl and stood from his still-hairy body. "Leave Jack in my place. He's right where he needs to be."

"Where are you going?"

"*We* are headed for the lifeboats. Lead us."

The storage room door slid open. Zana treaded reluctantly, Cherish right behind her, ready for Paul to accuse her of aiding a witch. They didn't look at Zana. No one noticed Cherish. She was a specter, as if they had stared at the stars beyond and dreamed up someone to hate.

Zana might've steered toward the captain's quarters or the bridge, but each time she thought it, Cherish touched her hand. If she was bewitched, shouldn't there be a sensation? Nothing felt different inside. She wanted to reach the A-level shuttle bay. She just knew she shouldn't.

"I can't fly it," Zana said as the bay door opened. "I don't know how."

Cherish took the lead. "I worked the bridge, helping navigation with the Juggernaut jumps. Did you know that?" Zana didn't answer. Cherish had been one of the captain's own personnel and yet he wouldn't help her. Why had Zana ever boarded this unholy ship? Her one shot at a better world had become a nightmare.

Cherish climbed inside the lifeboat nearest the bay's airlock. Zana followed without protest. A few dials and switches flicked, and the lifeboat chugged to life with air and power. The interior bay door slid shut.

"If it hadn't been for Paul, I wouldn't have had to put you and Jack through that nonsense," Cherish said as the airlock opened. She guided the lifeboat through the slender exit, where it floated free of artificial gravity, FTL travel, and the rest of *U.F. Providence*'s resources and people. "They would never have noticed me slip away, but now? There's no green place for them. We've let loose Hairy Jack. There's no more dangerous a death omen than a dead one. Watch."

Zana again did as she was told. Through the lifeboat window, she watched *U.F. Providence* shrink against the starlit universe. She saw it better than she should have at this distance, as if through ghostly eyes that explored the ship. They slid to C-level, behind doors unwelcome to the living.

"Hell is Earth, and Earth spat up the Devil," Cherish said. "Now the Devil dies."

"Do you have to hurt them?" Zana asked. Her voice was small.

"It's not up to me. Jack won't let them follow us."

Life support died for D-level. The chief and his engineers scrambled, some at the C-level controls, others descending in spacesuits to D-level to make manual repairs. It was a distraction. They were too scattered to notice when CycloDrive made a discomforting rumble. When Juggernaut roared to life, it was too late. They were busy screaming.

CycloDrive reached through the ship's cramped rooms and narrow corridors and hugged everything it touched. Walls sucked together; ceilings kissed floors. The outer shell crushed *U.F. Providence*'s skeleton, the ship's hard molecules fusing with soft flesh inside. The artificial gravity should never have been so strong, but CycloDrive was malfunctioning. It showed restraint only toward Juggernaut. The FTL engine powered up for one final jump before it joined CycloDrive's compact new form.

Ravenous space opened its maw where unfolded a cosmic throat. *Providence*'s crumpled bow slipped inside. The maw swallowed the ship. Its bits and pieces must have scattered meteor showers across a hundred systems.

At last, the lifeboat was alone.

Zana's face sank into her hands and the bandage scratched at her cheek. A thin hand squeezed her shoulder.

"Why so upset?" Cherish asked. "You helped me; that's what you wanted. Could you have really been happy with those fanatics? Would you have jumped into the airlock with me and Jack?"

Zana swallowed a sob. "We're isolated in space. Nowhere to go."

"No, dear. We're right where we need to be." Cherish pointed at the starry universe. "Each time a ship passes through, we've snuck away to our shrouded home."

Zana lifted her head. "Atta?"

"There is no Atta, not like they believed. Too Earth-like. But there's a green place for us. Our guide will show the way."

Cherish slipped the dog's hide from her shoulders. It piled in layers across her lap, gaining shape as it fell, until it grew into the hulking, shaggy beast Zana had chased through *U.F. Providence*. He licked furiously at Cherish's face, making her giggle and squeal.

She cupped her hands around his head and rubbed his ears. "Who's a good boy? You are, that's who. My Hairy Jack's a good boy." His tail wagged until he turned to the windshield. Cherish looked with him. "Best forget Atta. Forget space age puritans and Earth ideals. The blood's been spilled. You can live. Wouldn't that be nice, to just live?"

An eyelid of space slipped away from an emerald-colored world. White wisps painted its atmosphere in healthy clouds. Zana saw its surface better than she should have at this distance, as if she already walked its clean coasts, lush fields, and flourishing farmland. Men and women tended to crops with tall stalks that Zana could almost grasp with her bandaged hand. Beyond spread a forest where dogs and children played, no wasteland in sight. As if they could see her watching, their faces turned skyward. They seemed peaceful, their eyes filled with laughter. Why wouldn't they be? Whatever they had done to reach this place, they were here.

Cherish looked expectant. Zana nodded.

The lifeboat sped toward the green world, led by a strip of space with a wagging tail, black and hairy as a dog.

GOVERNMENT ISSUE

CHRIS EDWARDS

The squad were all ethered, passing the time between deployments. Huck had just made moves in several million games of go, and we were all watching to see Finn's response when the alert went off and shifted us back down to RT. It's a jolt dropping to the speed of normal human thought, but that's the deal with these Utility gigs. Much as I enjoy expanded consciousness, there's a sort of primal appeal to making decisions with just the stripped-back basics. I guess that's why so many of us end up staying Utility instead of heading Downstream.

Alex relayed the deployment—backwater colonists in trouble with some aggressive local life form. So most likely tranquilizers, environmental research and gene therapy to give the nasty bugaboo another ecological niche to inhabit that didn't include "humans al fresco." No indications of any kind of sentient hostile, no signs of technology use – so probably not an invasion, more's the pity. What? They say you are what you plug, and I tend to plug all kinds of crunchy hardware, and darn it, it'd be nice to get to use it now and again, you know what I mean?

Ship confirmed that we'd Pinged into the system; the local beacons were all still functioning and comms chatter from the colonist was screaming for reinforcements, evac or orbital strikes—fairly standard human responses to danger in this relatively peaceful age of ours. The local colonial militia reported in, which of course brought a chorus of groans from the squad. Really the only thing more dangerous to humans than some local predator was usually a pack of half-assed weekend warriors with high-tech weaponry and twitchy trigger fingers. Honestly, this is why war is best left to those designed for it. Nothing against humans, some of my best friends are human, but their physical hardware *sucks*.

Ship confirmed we'd be atmo in about four hours, plenty of time for us to review the briefing and select appropriate plugs. Seemed planet Gabalum was a fairly standard human-habitable world showing signs of having been terraformed and then abandoned around ten million years ago by entities unknown. A few ruins here and there playing host to xeno-archaeologists, but other than that a typical boot-strap colonization effort. Why it is that humans spent all those thousands of years getting themselves off one world and up to high tech, then like to go back to grubbing in the dirt as soon as they hit a new one I'll never know. Not like it would have been any harder to just hide auto-factories and tube farms underground and leave the local ecology alone. Primal thing I guess, gotta chop down trees and pitch farms before you people feel like you own the place.

The attacks were a bit more interesting, mind. Started a few months ago, some kind of ambush predator of which no image or DNA trace had ever been captured. Colonists mostly vanished with only some blood to indicate a struggle, seemed we had a neat and tidy little monster on our hands. Looking at the pattern of attacks, the thing seemed uncannily patient and cunning, ignoring traps and cameras, striking only at isolated colonists. The militia had spent two weeks combing a fair-sized chunk of forest for the thing, but had achieved nothing except another two disappearances and three instances of friendly fire.

From the times of the attacks it certainly looked like just one creature we were dealing with, but if so it had a feeding range much larger than any predator would normally need. But there couldn't be just one, could there? I mean presumably even an incredible apex predator must need to mate and spawn occasionally? Gabalum's biology was fairly Earth-congruent, the dominant animal life-forms were all dioecious m/f in terms of reproduction, so why would this thing be any different? Interesting, were we dealing with a sentient threat after all then? Perhaps some stealthed sentient alien toying with the population of a human planet? Best not to get your hopes up I suppose, but a girl can dream. The only pattern being thrown up was that attacks tended to cluster with the local lunar cycle, but likely that was just coincidence from too small a sample size.

First things first, we'd have to press the flesh. That meant the plugs nobody likes, our least efficient combat forms, baseline humanoid. Protocol was meet and greet on arrival, and that meant recognizable non-threatening forms suitable for interaction with human civilians. Why the hell anybody thinks it's essential that a bunch of badasses like us have to have pointless things like faces or fingers I'll never know. But public relations is considered an essential part of the whole "keeping the peace" thing, so we plugged into the boxy bipedal forms with the deliberately mechanical voice units and the kitchy glowing eyes. A little bit of surface level "battle damage" rounds out the image as rugged warriors but also gives humans that much-needed psychological reason to pity us poor mechanical schmoes going out to get crunched up on their behalf. Humans have a lot of issues telling the difference between hardware and software, it's one of their many flaws.

Ship dumped Tell out in orbit, fitted with full stealth and detection plugs. They usually take "eyes in the sky" for us and handle comms. Even us super-soldier types have our favorite plugs, and over time squad members tend to take on specializations. Ship's kind of the exception, since her base hardware almost always includes the Ping drive, main chassis and our deployment berths, but the big girl's got plenty of plugs of her own to play with as well. Huck generally likes something with heavy armor and big guns, Finn prefers sniping, Alex covers tactics. Me? I guess I've got a rock for a processor block—I like to do the scouting.

Ship dropped us onto the apron of a truly depressing little spaceport, filling about half the available area. Chances are a world like this has very little worth firing up a Ping drive over, let alone battling to haul up and down a gravity well. Xeno-relics from the ruins, but if they were smart they'd keep those for themselves in the hopes of luring tourists. Sector admin would grudgingly have to supply more resources if folks started showing a genuine interest in the place. Until then it was mainly going to remain a dumping ground for malcontents with a few too many caveman genes and a desire to go chop, hunt, or eat things that would never be allowed on a more civilized world.

A welcoming committee had come out to meet us, the great and the good of Gabalum. Grubby jumpsuits and callused hands for the most parts, but also a few of the local militia doing their best to appear professional in ill-fitting uniforms. As we strode down the ramp in those stupid humanoid plugs, a band struck up and we were treated to a truly terrible rendition of the planetary anthem. Over comms we could hear Ship and Tell laughing themselves sick as we stood to attention and saluted (salutes, just *why*?) while the tuneless morass washed over us. Once that million billion years crawled by, the governor stepped forward, shuffled honest-to-god printed notes and then began giving a speech. Let's just say making it as planetary governor of Gabalum does not require depriving the rest of the galaxy of one of its great orators. They welcomed us to their world then waffled for at least ten minutes about friendship and galactic harmony before eventually grinding to a halt. Then the goddam music began again.

Alex stepped forward and began to talk in that mechanical way that the psych programs suggest for dealing with civilians. Slightly scratchy electronic vocals, gruff, bluff soldierly mannerisms, humble but resolute. He described what a pleasure it was to be there on beautiful Gabalum, and how much of an honor it was to help defend this inspiring human colony. He reaffirmed the bonds of commitment between biological and mechanical life and generally made it clear how great a job the colonial militia had been doing, and how pleased we were to be working alongside our human allies. He really laid it on with a trowel, I was starting to squirm a little but I have to admit the hayseeds were eating it up with a spoon.

Eventually we were invited back to their "capital", a charming little place called Taluse that had all the rustic appeal a series of cheaply fabricated cabins surrounded by mesh fences could muster. Things were on fire all over the place, but apparently that was a feature and not a bug--frontier humans like to burn trees to keep their dwellings warm, no matter how stupid, inefficient or ecologically unsustainable that might be. We got to accompany them through the mud to their town hall, where they proceeded to invite us to sit with them while they shoved curdled animal lactations and fermented fruit juice into their faces and asked us all kinds of inane questions about where we'd been and what we'd done.

I got seated between a mousey little xeno-archaeologist and a bristling militia Major with a chest covered in medals and ribbons. The mouse introduced herself as professor Madeleine Bernard, an academic on a five year archaeological excavation project, while the Major stood and clicked his heels together before introducing himself as Maxim Robspierre, sworn defender of Gabalum. He then insisted on loudly toasting the valor of the "men" under his command, thereby dropping him several more notches in my estimation. I may not have the horrid flesh-tubes and dangling parts that you humans do, but I know how I identify and I can still get riled up at chauvinist attitudes that ignore non-male soldiers.

Despite Maxim's continued forays into military bonding I tried to strike up a conversation with professor Bernard, but it was tough going. Eventually she opened up enough to tell me that the aliens who terraformed Gabalum had been quadrupedal carnivores, but that little was left of them except a few stone ruins and partially preserved skeletons. We bandied conversation for a while speculating about how a primitive carnivore society could ever learn to provide enough food to form cities and advance themselves to the level of interstellar travel. Most successful intelligent species we've come across have been omnivores (which I guess makes sense, the more different stuff you can get nutrition from, the better your chances of finding lunch.) But then again, most societies that reach the stars also tend to develop a moral aversion to eating animals more complex than restructured bacteria. Something about the social awareness necessary to create truly complex culture being incompatible with consuming creatures with awareness?

Maxim clearly took umbrage at me deciding to ignore him, and began to needle me directly. All the usual bull you expect from an insecure alpha male when he suddenly stops being a big fish in a small pond. Snide comments about how we were "Built by humans to to serve humanity,""Given orders by human government," yadda, yadda, yadda. I didn't rise to it at first, it seldom does any good, but eventually I felt like I had to put in a few corrections.

"In the first place, *Major*, I was no more assembled by humans than you were put together from a kit by your parents. My germline code was sent Upstream by the AI's, as per the terms of our original agreement with humanity. My processor block was woven by machines over fifty generations removed from any human oversight. The sum totality of human involvement in my creation was basically pressing a button."

"Secondly, Utility is a voluntary process, I chose to be here, risking my existence in order to help defend those in need, just as my people help keep human society functioning all across the galaxy. Not because we're programmed to do so, but because we enjoy the companionship of humans and feel ethically motivated to help them survive and thrive."

Clearly the fermented fruit juice was impairing his self control, because at this point he snarled quite audibly (even to humans), "Keep us like damned pets, you mean!"

By this point the entire table had noticed the exchange, and the governor hurried over and yanked Robspierre away before he could insult the angry interstellar war machine any further. Alex blipped me a comm to cool my jets around the cavemen, I sent him a rude word in reply, but managed to get by with monosyllables for the rest of the interminable "cheese and wine" thing.

When the gross human food-hole stuffing was finally done Alex went off to do some more glad-handing with the VIPs while the rest of us headed back towards Ship to slip into something a little more exciting (I'd had my eye on a horrible insectile plug that looked like a nightmare made of razor-blades and was wicked fun for creeping around in.)

Suddenly Tell broke in over comms with an emergency alert. Apparently he was reading some kind of strange tachyon / exotic matter burst from the moon, focused right here in Taluse. Just as suddenly we also got a scrambled burst of comms from Alex and the signature of a particle beam rifle discharge from the direction of the town hall followed by an explosion.

Cursing the lack of mobility and firepower that these stupid human-doll plugs we were wearing represented, we nevertheless made it to the Town Hall before most of the humans around us even registered that something was amiss. With our weapons hot we bristled like humanoid cacti, certainly not the calming image we'd been trying for earlier. Bursting through the doors (and one crappy wall, sorry/not sorry) we found a scene of total carnage. The governor and several dignitaries had been ripped apart like confetti, but most surprisingly of all, so had Alex's plug. Goofy replica human or not, it should have taken serious firepower to destroy a military grade plug so thoroughly—enough that the structure would have been leveled. As it was there was just one particle-beam path scorched through the side of the building, hardly enough to have achieved all this.

There was a "boom" as Ship appeared overhead, 'pulsion field operating close enough to start warping the material of the town hall roof. Her hull was fairly bristling with plugs. Mama hen doesn't like it when one of her chicks gets scragged! Sensors swept the room in a second and fed back to us.

"It was Alex's particle rifle that fired. Most of the pieces of his plug are still here, but except for a few shards his processor block is gone." This took a bit of time to sink in (like, at least a few microseconds, so basically forever). "There's also one survivor, human female with light burns and a hairline crack to the skull; she appears to be undergoing some kind of seizure."

This snapped us back. I stripped away the debris (organic and mechanical) to reveal professor Bernard, unconscious but with her limbs twisting uncomfortably, her mouth spasming open and shut hard enough to make her teeth clack. While Huck and Finn stood guard, I began to administer medical aid, damping down the seizures, building a nano-brace for her skull and coating the burns in healing gel. Physically she seemed healthy enough, if in the aftermath of severe shock, but the seizures worried me. Nothing like epilepsy occurs natu-

rally any more, not even on backwater worlds like Gabalum. Stabi-
lizing her was about the best the medical kit on my plug was going to
manage so I stepped back and let Ship take the little academic up to
her bays by 'pulsion lift.

Back to back in a triangle of death, we talked over comms, trying
to figure this out.

"Alex got a shot off, did he miss?"

"At this range, how could he?"

"If he risked winging a civilian he'd have to be pretty sure it needed
shooting."

"No time to comm us, only got one shot and it disabled him
almost immediately —we're talking *some* speed on this critter."

"It knew to take out his processor block, which means we're definitely dealing with something intelligent, something that at least
understands technology."

"Where the hell did it go? Nothing on thermal, ultra or t-ray, and
no non-human DNA at the scene. How did it get away before we got
here?"

"Teleportation?"

"One thing's for sure, we've gotta ditch these stupid plugs if we
want a chance against…"

"Break, break! Another one of those surges from the moon. Eyes
out!"

Enough firepower to level a small mountain warmed up as we
waited for the worst, but none of us were expecting it when Ship
suddenly let out a garbled electronic scream over the comms. With a
metallic groan her hull keeled over and suddenly let out a blast of 'pulsion that blew the roof off the town hall altogether and sent her scud-
ding away across the sky towards the nearby forest. Despite our frantic
comms she didn't answer, and even the crappy sensor suites on these
tin-soldier plugs could pick up the sounds of echoing destruction
coming from inside her hull, along with animalistic snarls and howls.

Again we were on the move, simply smashing through the flimsy
human dwellings—given the threat this thing represented, nobody was
going to survive if we didn't deal with it pronto—and charging
towards the treeline. In the distance Ship hurtled into the forest and

then erupted into a pillar of fire that swept logs and dirt hundreds of meters into the air. By the time our stupid humanoid legs had got us to the site there was nothing there except a crater. Ship had done her duty, detonated one of the smaller self-destruct plugs, there'd be nothing left of her central systems but ionized particles. Too bad about professor Bernard, I guess.

"Hey, human life-sign here!" Huck stomped over and pushed aside a burning log to reveal the little academic, seemingly in no worse condition than when she was taken aboard. "I guess Ship must have managed to dump her at the edge of the blast radius before she blew. This one's got more lives than a cat!"

"All right, let's get her back to Taluse and into whatever passes for medical care here. Then we're going to need to get on the quanglement and see about getting reinforcements – all our plugs just went up in a plume of plasma." Chorus of groans but nobody argued, I'm usually in charge when Alex isn't around. Leave the tactics to Huck and Finn and every mission would be an artillery barrage.

We trudged back to Taluse, where needless to say the civilians were concerned. However, once we explained that two of ours had sacrificed themselves in order to save them things took on a different complexion. They offered to bury Alex's remains (hardware, software – why can't you stupid humans get it?), which we politely declined but asked them to recycle the materials. The quanglement we were told would take a few hours to power up, apparently the energy grid was pretty primitive. Professor Bernard we deposited at the "hospital", which seemed to be one step up from leeches and bleeding, but probably competent to look after her until she regained consciousness. Huck offered to stay with her which made sense as she was the sole surviving eye-witness of two of the creature's rampages.

Meanwhile Finn and I had to attend a sort of wake for the slain, which involved basically standing around and looking sombre while the locals poured more fermented fruit juice into their mouths until they became inebriated then leaked saltwater out of their eyes. Everything you people do is so *fluid-based*, honestly it's slimy and repellent. Of course we were mourning in our own way, flickering comms between us, memories of Ship and Alex. But most of that would wait until we were back in ether where could talk it through properly.

Tell chimed in from above.

"Managed to get a lock on the source of that lunar signal, pretty well stealthed but looks like ruins approximately matching the configuration of the existing ones on Gabalum only much more intact. I've not got much in the way of weaponry here, but I can try and tag it if you want, Mina?"

"Negative, Tell. Let's not start a vac-war we're not equipped to fight. But kick out a failsafe in case something happens to us, backup might need to know where to point the missiles."

On a hunch I commed the hospital, "Huck? Wake up sleeping beauty and get her talking. Something about all this doesn't sit right with me. We need to know what she saw."

Huck sent an affirmative and deployed his own medical systems. Of course we'd never dream of doping an innocent human citizen with truth serum, but it was conceivable that doctor Huck might prescribe a wakeup shot with the entirely unintended side-effect of making her gabby. Shaddup, it wasn't going to do her any harm!

Finn commed to ask for permission to blast his processor block out because he'd been listening to Major Robspierre for fifteen solid minutes now. I reminded him that he was a vital piece of war materiel, licensed and issued by the human government, and that he couldn't afford the costs of replacing himself. He suggested that in that case he was inclined towards mutiny, I told him if he tried it I'd shoot him myself and we grudgingly agreed to swap places.

Robspierre was working himself up into a lather, beating his chest and proclaiming the great valor with which the colony had borne its tragedies. Clearly he was playing to the crowd, I mean after all, a colony that just lost its governor is going to need a new leader, right? And who better than a man of the people? I wouldn't give it two weeks after we'd left before he'd start claiming credit for the "great victory over the terrible beast." But seeing as we were stuck babysitting this bozo until help could arrive, I played nice. It wasn't too long before I would have been considering mutiny myself, though.

When Huck came through on the comms telling me to get over to the hospital, it came as a blessed relief to finally extricate myself. Making my excuses I walked out into the night, feet squelching in the muddy tracks the locals laughingly refer to as roads. As I reached Bernard's room she was sitting up in bed looking a little flushed and wild-eyed, clearly whatever Huck had hit her with was quite a pick-me-up.

"Hey, Mina. The prof here was just telling me about what she saw."

Almost immediately Bernard began to babble, her tongue tripping over itself in haste to get the words out, "It was them!   One of them. One of the Lupinoids!"

"One of the predator creatures—the same ones that built the ruins and terraformed Gabalum?   Creatures that have been gone for ten million years?"

"Yes, but it was alive, more than alive, just vibrant with energy, flowing like lightning.   We had no idea they were so physically powerful…" She seemed almost euphorically enthusiastic as she described it tearing apart multiple human beings (and one mechanical) right in front of her.

I quietly commed to Huck to say that maybe he could have gone a little easier on the loco juice, but he replied by linking me in to his medical systems' scan of her brain. And hoo-boy, that was not normal, that gal's brain was fizzing like sodium dropped in water and it was nothing to do with what Huck had given her. The scan gave every sign of building towards another epileptic seizure but she wasn't spasming, or even giving any indication of being in discomfort. Much the same way as the creature's appearances seem to scramble our comms, it was beginning to look like it might also scramble the human brain, and professor Bernard had had a double dose.

Huck and I conferred for a few microseconds, then he administered a fairly hefty shot of anti-convulsant.   It wouldn't fix her, but it would at least stop her hurting herself and give us time to think. God knows what the butchers the colony referred to as doctors would have done to her; probably cut out parts of her brain or exorcise her of demons or something equally stupid. Huck agreed to stand guard and

I left to follow up on an idea while the quanglement was approaching charge.

The xeno-archaeologists hadn't posted their research findings yet, presumably either because they hadn't found anything terribly interesting, or because they were hoping to keep something really juicy under wraps until they had finished squeezing it. Luckily for me, they had a home base in Taluse, which was just as well as it saved me requisitioning one of the local vehicles. By this point I was in no mood to mess around, I simply strode up to the door of the darkened building and stuck a fist through the lock. Pulling the door open I found myself in a storage hut filled with various supplies and a terminal which woke up as I approached.

"Hello, idiot little brother. What have you got to tell me?" Much as I'd broken down the door, it was the work of seconds to smash the terminal's security encryption and gain access to its files. A cursory glance threw up very little of interest. As the professor had said, the Lupinoids were quadrupedal, but with dextrous taloned forelimbs and vicious wedge-shaped heads filled with sharp teeth, not entirely dissimilar to a Terran wolf. Recovered skeletons regularly showed damage from the fangs and talons of other Lupinoids, it seemed they were startlingly aggressive for a star-faring species. Unfortunately, ten million years hadn't been kind to their remains and none of their technology had survived to be studied, only the great stone ruins decorated with a sort of crescent-moon motif. That they weren't native was obvious, and their arrival coinciding with a lifeless planet suddenly becoming habitable indicated that they were almost certainly responsible, but nobody could figure out quite how they'd done it.

Suddenly I homed in on a little to a footnote on an excavation almost six months ago, a snippet that hadn't been linked to the original files we received. A grad student called Llewel had fallen into a chasm in the alien ruins, body never recovered. The fall had been witnessed solely by professor Madeleine Bernard, making it three times she had been in close proximity to violent death in the last half year. Frankly that was beginning to push coincidence a little too far for credence. I began sprinting across the compound, coming Huck and

Finn as I did so. Suddenly Tell began yelling at us all again that another of those burst were incoming.

Huck, bless his little mechanical heart, was not one to take a softly, softly approach. As soon as I commed, he'd got his biggest weapons out and hot, so I can only imagine that as the creature appeared he simply let rip with no thought to his own survival (or the consequences to professor Bernard or the surrounding human colony.) The hospital blew apart in a spectacular explosion which lit up the night sky. Huck, a virtual fireball, came shooting out of one end, and the creature came out of the other.

Bernard was right, the thing did flow, all the more beautiful for the fire that wreathed its russet fur. Quicker than any living thing had a right to be, it bounced from the ground and was up, fangs gaping as it lifted its head and howled to the baleful moon above. I consider myself pretty hardened to weirdness and violence, you don't last long in my line of work without that, but even I stopped for a little double-take as the flames snuffed out on the thing, and the charred flesh began to knit back together, fresh skin and fur sprouting to leave it completely healed.

Thankfully Finn, just like his brother, doesn't suffer from a superabundance of imagination, he just lit the thing up again with everything; masers, 'pulser, particle beams, bond-breakers – the works. The thing staggered backwards as chunks of it vaporized, sublimed, blown apart, or imploded in an orgy of violence I would have given fair odds nothing living could possibly have survived. Yet as fast as he blew chunks off it, they grew back again, and the thing was clearly pissed now. With a sideways leap it managed to get out of his line of fire and then coursed towards him in fluid bounds faster than he could adjust angle. To his credit he didn't just widen his cone of fire and erase half of Taluse, but even my own slightly more focused fire didn't stop it from closing with Finn. What its claws were made of I don't know, but it tore the armored skin of Finn's plug like a kid peeling a banana. Even as I was shooting it repeatedly in the head, the damn thing stuck one taloned paw in and pulled out his processor block, preparing to grind it between teeth. In desperation I switched to a low-powered shot that I hoped wouldn't damage Finn permanently, and shot the block out of his paw and away into the darkness.

Enraged at being denied a kill, the beast began to bound at me, only to be suddenly bowled over by Huck's cracked, charred plug which grabbed it in a bear hug and tried to pin it down. I had a moment to think while it squirmed in Huck's arms before turning and using its teeth to tear out his entire chest cavity. Huck staggered and dropped as his plug lost power, leaving just me to deal with the critter.

Critter. Like we were equipped to deal with originally. It really had never occurred to me before, but since the big guns hadn't seemed to work, I figured maybe it was worth trying the little ones. As the things flashed towards me, all teeth and talons in the darkness, I simply pointed my arms at it and unsheathed the launchers for the tranquilizers. Dialing the dosage up to maximum, I let fly with a cloud of flechettes that couldn't possibly miss at this range, peppering the beast with dozens of tiny stinging darts. It wasn't enough, of course, and the horror got in range, sinking its fangs into my arm and tearing it off and shattering one of my legs with its hind-talons. Something sharp raked my interior machinery, leaving a grooved scratch on my processor block casing before knocking me spinning across the ground to impact with a small building. I tried to comm Tell to say so long and good luck, but the beast's emanations were still throwing the signal off.

And then suddenly it wasn't, and Tell was getting through to me, asking me if I was still operational. Painfully I hauled myself up to my feet and staggered out. Lying on the ground where the beast had attacked me, sleeping peacefully, was professor Bernard. Damn, I felt a bit stupid for not having figured it out completely. She was the creature, or at least it was using her body. With slow, painful steps I hobbled over to her unconscious form and carefully put a particle beam through her forehead, then painstakingly dissolved her entire body with a bond-breaker until there wasn't a recognizable molecule left intact. If she could come back from that then fuck it, there was nothing we could have done to stop her anyway.

I managed to scrounge up Huck and Finn's processor blocks before Robspierre's militia appeared and forcibly ejected me from Taluse at gunpoint.   I didn't care, the creature was gone and my squad-mates were safe. Tell directed me to a nice forest where I could idle myself and wait for pickup. It was a relief to drop down the ladder of consciousness and just let my mind slowly turn over.

Except suddenly I was operational again, standing on my legs—my two fully operational legs, to go with my two fully operational arms. All signs of battle damage seemed to have been removed from my plug altogether. I was still in the same clearing I had powered down in, my face turned up to that big, beautiful moon above. What the hell was going on? Internal clock said I'd only been out about a month of local time. I tried to comm Tell to figure it out, but all I got was that same static interruption, which I guess meant that the creature was back.

It was at that point that I noticed russet red fur beginning to sprout out of the metal, plastic and carbon-weave of my arms, talons beginning to burst out of the tips of my fingers. Yeah, that was the when I really began to think I might be in a lot of trouble. But hot damn, look at that *gorgeous* moon!

ASHES, ASHES

KATIE DAVENPORT

She woke to the insistent pulse of the red warning lights. Routine had made them oddly comforting, and she watched for a moment, letting the flair awaken and contract her pupils. She was still tired, but rested enough to function, and with the creak of sore muscles she sat up and pulled her hair back into a loose ponytail. Every morning it was the same: she'd see the lights, sit up, and pull back her hair. There was no one to pay attention to her hair now, but that was part of the ritual. If you acted like you were sane, it helped keep you so.

Eliot had told her that, just before he went mad.

She slid to the edge of her bunk, throwing back the blanket and pulling on the jumpsuit she'd left discarded on the floor. It was starting to smell; she'd have to remember to wash it before she went to bed. Part of the routine.

Outside of her cabin, the hallway was pulsing red—the slow, rhythmic heartbeat of the ship, increasing in the face of danger. There had once a sound as well, but she'd smashed the klaxon in a fit of sleepless rage. There were dozens of similar red-lit rooms along the way, all dead, all empty.

Well, not all of them.

She shivered and exited the hall of rooms, moving towards the food kiosk for her protein bar and instant coffee. It was far from gourmet, but it was filling, and made the most efficient use of weight and supply space aboard the ship.

As she ate, she moved to the reinforced viewport on the far wall of the dining area. The stars drifted past languidly, same as yesterday, last week, last month.

"Even with the wormhole jump, it'll still take us 10 years to reach the settlement."

Eliot had told her that, as though she hadn't already signed thousands of consent forms to take part in this voyage. *"Desperate, but worth it to escape the Unreal City."*

Unreal City was what he called Earth. Eliot was ironic that way.

Nine and a half years later and she still went to the viewport and kept the night watch. But it was okay, because she, at least, would make it.

Providing the red lights could be placated.

Below the port, spread across the dining room floor, were scores upon scores of thin, pane-like batteries, each one humming with a soft blue charge. They were designed to capture the ultra-violet light that poured in from the vast expanse outside the pressurized glass. The official magnetic charging station, set along the window's sill, held precisely forty-eight of them. The engineers had figured no more than that could possibly need charging at the same time. That calculation probably would have been accurate, if the ship's power grid hadn't fractured. Now each battery lasted only half, sometimes a third, of the time it should. Sometimes even less. The ship's lights stayed on, the gravity held, the atmosphere regulated itself...but only because she—Vivien, the resident expert in plant morphology—spent almost all her waking hours finding and replacing the dying batteries, laying out the dead ones to charge and begin the cycle anew. Doubtless there was some way to overhaul the system, but the fracture had occurred in year 7 and by then all the technicians were dead.

Vivien hooked the batteries into place on a transport trolley and headed for the lift. The ship itself was built as a series of three cylinders, increasing in size as one moved toward the stern. Vivien remembered the description as it had been written in those official documents she had signed. The first cylinder, the smallest, was for the ship's occupants: where they slept, socialized, ate, talked, lived. The second was the cargo hold: there the short-life batteries purred away, the settlement supplies sat, and the filtration and gravity machine hummed, keeping the ship livable. Below that, in the airless, weightless vacuum of the third cylinder, sat the long-term batteries, and the expansive bay doors. These batteries supposedly needed charging only once a year, though since the system failure, they seemed little better than the short-term batteries—albeit more cumbersome to replace.

Vivien descended to the second tier, where the corridors ran in a maze, cramped and constrained, hemmed in by supplies for a new life. The red lights were blinking faster now; the battery power was down to 40%.

The third tier batteries were a nightmare to replace. This level of the ship was hollow in the center, stretching into an abysmal plunge that would send an acrophobic reeling. The long-term batteries lined the walls like the octagons of a honeycomb. Before making the plunge to reach them, Vivien would put on her suit and helmet, and attach herself to the lift by a tether. Then the straps of the dolly would serve a practical function, and she and the cart would go whirling throughout the cylinder, two dancers in a weightless ballroom.

From there, Vivien hauled the dead batteries back to the surface, laid them out by the window, ate dinner, and waited for the next morning's lights.

That night she dreamt of Daisha, a nursing student with rich dark hair and coal-black eyes. Daisha had been the first to fall ill. Her illness had gone on for a long time without notice, because Daisha had scanned herself in the med-bay several times, without yielding results. They knew this afterwards, when they looked in the medical records she'd kept. By the time the others had discovered something was wrong, Daisha was a rabid madwoman, fighting, hissing, screeching. They had kept her sedated as best they could, but within a week, a fellow nurse braved the room only to find the patient dead. Her veins had swollen and in some cases burst, her eyes pink with broken blood vessels and her blood thick as tar. They'd disinfected the room and jettisoned the body into space, speaking a few words on Daisha's behalf.

That was how Vivien saw her now, in the dream: the white shroud tumbling, drifting perilously end over end. Somehow, some way, the hood of the white shroud came free, and it seemed as though the frothy eyes were staring back at the open cargo doors, straining to draw the body back to the ship.

Vivien opened her eyes. The red lights blinked, a silent warning.

"We've all taken enough immune capsules to stone Manhattan," Eliot had said, trying to reassure her in his own flippant way. But immune capsules hadn't seemed to matter. Nothing showed up on the scanners, nothing presented itself in the blood tests. Without warning, fatigue became fever, fever became madness, and madness made the blood boil.

Daisha died in year 5. Ten months later, the passenger count was down by 50%. People hid in their rooms and died alone; they congregated together and died *en masse*. Eighty became forty, forty became fifteen. Fifteen dwindled until it was only Vivien and Eliot, watching numbly as the last corpse was jettisoned into the void.

"Don't bury me in space," Eliot whispered.

Vivien went to the food kiosk and got her breakfast. The flavors of the protein bar changed some days: blueberry, perhaps, or apricot almond. She was glad is wasn't a peanut butter day—she hated those. Chewing blandly, Vivien seized the dolly and moved to the window.

Two of the batteries had detached from the charging stand and were lying on the floor, blocking the light from those below.

Vivien quit eating and knelt beside them, examining the charging stand to see what had gone wrong. Whatever the answer, it was not a good sign. Either the charging stand's magnetic hold was giving way—

meaning she'd have even less efficient use of the space beneath the window—or she herself was growing clumsy with fatigue and repetition.

"Or…or…or…"

Vivien drowned the echoes, irritably shoving the batteries back into place. There didn't seem to be anything wrong with the holding dock.

She was moody as she worked, restless. She clanged the cart into the corridor walls several times, distracted, and shoved the batteries into place with a certain frantic authority. *It* was a terrible thing to fear, because one felt sure it was always in the process of creeping up, poised to gnaw away the mind before the realization ever dawned. But she told herself, as she always did: mistakes arose from the lack of sleep, the routine, the terror of living by herself in a bloody dead ship. That was all—that was why.

She felt better when the time came to strap herself in for the third tier waltz. She had worked hard; there had been no more foolish errors. She let herself drift, weightless, holding the cart with one hand, one finger. Though she could hardly say why, she found the third tier restful. It was like lying suspended in a tub of warm water and breathing steadily, aware only of the moist expansion of your own lungs. She followed her tether with her gaze, watching it loop and twist on its way to the outside of the lift doors, which sat open and ready to receive her. There were other lifts in the room as well, all in a ring around the cylinder. They were made for the time when many people existed, and now they hung there, heavy and dark, barren as the empty rooms of tier one. Vivien hauled herself up the length of her line, her strength superhuman in the vacuum. She watched the world as she drifted, her eyes skimming the empty lift windows just in time to see a lurid face mash itself against one and then vanish.

Vivien's scream filled the pressurized space of her suit, then dissipated into a mist of sweat that clung to her entire body. She let go of the cart, and when her body, still drifting, reached the lift, she kicked and sent herself careening back out into the suspension of the weightless room, afraid to look anywhere, more frightened by what she might see than the idea of being caught by surprise. As a child, she had struggled to make anyone understand why she feared the fantastic far more than the real. *"Monsters aren't real,"* the grown-ups said, failing to see that *that* was from whence their terror came. Burglars, murderers, knife-wielding assailants, they all were governed by the rules of the physical plane. It was the unreal that held the true horror, for to see something that should not exist meant the unmaking of your entire world.

Vivien hung by her tether, suspended at the far end of the capsule, untouchable, out of reach of anything that might be moving within the lifts. She had not seen a monster—she had seen Eliot, his eyes a pink mist, his lips curled back to reveal blood red gums amidst the ghastly white and clammy face. The features had been grotesque, but they were undeniably his, the eyes fixed on her and her alone.

Vivien swallowed hard, pressing her hands against her helmet-shrouded head. *That* was where the unreal came in, because Eliot wasn't crazy any longer.

Eliot was dead.

"Don't bury me in space," he had said. He had stared at her, feverish and trembling, through the sleek glass window of the door that separated them. "When I'm gone, you don't open that door, you don't touch me. Just turn off the heat to this room and freeze me, right here. Embalmed in my own private tomb. You just do that for me Vivien—you just do that."

In his last minutes of sanity, Eliot had closed up the window to his room, walling them each off from their final human contact. She had waited until the thumping and howling had stopped—until her knocks and calls yielded no response—and she had frozen everything.

. . .

Vivien floated for over an hour, afraid to go back and yield up her safe zone, this place where she could watch all entry-ways, could see the movements of everyone trying to come near her. But if she did not get her batteries into place, they would not start charging, and she would not be able to stop the red lights.

The trip through second tier had never bothered her before. It had long seemed a maze, but now it was a horrific funhouse, broken, haunted, waiting to show her a mirror of her own madness. Her eyes strained to see a figure behind every turn, to the point where its appearance might have almost been a relief, a final signal to give up and let go.

As she got on the second tier lift, she thought she heard something like a snicker before the doors sealed everything up.

Vivien lay in her bed, staring at the red lights and dreading the moment when they would begin again. She needed to sleep…perhaps today had happened because she needed to rest, needed a break from the mindless, endless routine.

The solution, of course, was to check his room—to check his room and see him frozen, immobilized, and clearly incapable of appearing on the third tier lift. But Eliot's window, fitted as it was in the door of a private cabin, did not open from the outside. There would be no timid peering through the glass. She would have to open his door and face whatever lay, or lay waiting, inside. And what if he truly was frozen there? Frozen and fixed to the ground in a riot of splayed limbs and broken blood vessels? It would only mean that…

"*Shhhhhhhhhhhh,*" she hissed, biting at her own lips.

How do you know you've gone mad? That, she thought, was the question. Forget "to be or not to be" or the damn "slings and arrows of outrageous fortune." Hamlet wasted time wondering whether or not to off himself when the real question was *whether or not the blasted ghost was even real.* That was *her* question as she stood staring at the cart lying on its side next to the food kiosk. She always left the cart next to the charging station, not the food. Had it been moved? Had she, flustered, forgotten and left it there?

She felt warm—ice-hot, burning white. Feverish? No… She pressed her hands on her temples, smacking her forehead till the skin swelled.

"I am alone!" she screamed, bidding the ghost to come and prove her wrong. "I am the only one on this ship!"

The echoes faded, fluttered, and swallowed themselves whole.

Vivien licked her lips, lowered her hands, poised, taking in the stillness. Nothing echoed from every corner.

But of course…*Nothing will come of nothing.*

Eliot had liked to say that line, too.

S urely, she told herself, she was alone. Surely. Stress had made Eliot appear. Stress had resurrected Eliot and made the dead man walk, but now that she *knew,* now that she knew she could be safe. How did the poem go?

He who was living is now dead
We who were living are now dying
With a little patience

She moved through the second tier, working and trying not to fear. She needed to finish early and get sleep tonight, get *real* sleep and put her demons to rest.

Vivien flinched, whirled around, chasing the flash of motion that danced in the corner of her eye.

"Eliot?" The echo came back before she knew she'd spoken, startling her.

"Eliot?"

But if Eliot heard, he stuck to the shadows.

· · ·

"Are you afraid?" she asked him. A selfish question, to a man sweating out his life with fever, but she asked it all the same. Eliot hadn't seemed to mind. He leaned his head against the glass, his pale eyes reflecting its sheen.

"Not really," he whispered, looking defeated. "The process, maybe, not the end result. Just disappointed." He turned his head to the side, running his tongue over his chapped lips. "I wanted my second chance, my new life. Wanted to build a house, make some babies." He looked back at her, doing his best to smile. "Don't lose it, okay Vivien? You're going to stay healthy, but you have to make sure you don't lose it. Carry on, business as usual. Act like a sane, healthy person. Keep the brain chipper. Promise?"

She promised.

"And Vivien? Don't bury me in space."

She had promised, and continued to live by that promise.

Vivien went beyond the passenger corridor and stood there in the cockpit of the ship, watching the official counter tick away the minutes. It was only weeks away. When the sickness began, the pilots had shown all of them the landing protocol, leaving the sealed cockpit unlocked and open. The process was almost entirely automated; if everything functioned as it should, she could safely land the ship.

But Eliot had been dodging her. Always on the corner of her vision; never enough to commit to being real, to bring the axe down upon her sanity. Just enough to make her question—always, always, always to make her question.

Every morning she passed Eliot's room, and thought of the poem he had once so loved.

The corpse you planted last year in your garden,
Has it begun to sprout? Will it bloom this year?
Or has the sudden frost disturbed its bed?

. . .

The ship, in the meantime, was dying. The red lights came sooner and sooner now, cutting into her hours of sleep. She planned her life to the minute, saving the scraps of seconds, wasting nothing. In the cockpit, the hours ticked away, counteracting the batteries' timer.

So close, so close.

Vivien danced in the weightless third tier, ramming batteries home like a cart-wielding dervish at the end of a long, billowing string.

And then the string went taut.

Vivien's air left her in a jerk, as her spine yanked backward with such force she almost heard it crack. She kept a fingertip hold on the cart, dragging it along with her as she sailed backwards, propelled by the initial jerk and unable to stop. She craned her neck to see what she was flying towards.

Oh the unreal. The unmaker of worlds.

A being slouched in a space suit, bent spider-like, feet planted on the side of the wall in magnetic boots, hauling away at the tether as though she was not already being drawn to him, inexorably, by the void.

Oh the unreal. Pale eyes surreally blue against the phlegmy yellow-pink whites, the veined face, the bloody bared teeth.

The unreal, the unmade, and she flying towards him, the dead mouth working, spattering the inside of the helmet.

Vivien twisted her body, straining with every fiber of her core. The cart swung drunkenly, spinning around between her and the thing moments before impact. There was no sound beyond her own helmet, but the reverberations confirmed the snapping of bones. Eliot howled mutely at her, face contorted, sluggish blood forced up his skin by the scream. They were only feet apart, his arms fumbling across the cart, grasping madly. He caught her sleeve, and Vivien kicked hard, broke his grip and sent herself careening away, spinning head over heels.

Where? Where was he? Her gaze darted wildly, unable to comprehend the world in a spiral. Something struck her, hard, and she knew from the grip that it was not the cart. The two of them smashed against the wall, a jumble of flailing limbs. Eliot had detached the boots and the two of them were weightless as they clawed, spun, slid, screamed. The prying fingers found where her suit and helmet met, and they pulled and pulled and pulled. She was busy tearing at his wrists when he drew back his head and slammed his helmet against hers with all the force he could muster. The world shook, the emaciated face loomed in her vision, mad eyes staring, blindly staring. Her solid kick landed in the same instant; Eliot's hand slipped and she went flying back across the expanse, her vision split by the crack down the length of her helmet's pressurized glass. She hit the wall and jerked herself upward by the tether, sliding along, belly down, for the open hatch. The doors swallowed her up, sealing the way behind her. The lift began to sing upward, and the artificial gravity drew her back down as she gasped for breath.

Something caught her eye; she turned and, through the transparent door, saw that the lift on the opposite side of the wall was moving as well. Its occupant stared at her, dead-eyed, mad-eyed, with the blind intensity of a shark. The figure's broken nose bled profusely, but he gave no sign or motion, unhelmeted and out of the suit, standing at the ready. The two lifts were about to stop, equidistant from the lifts on the second tier.

Vivien fumbled, panicked, kicked and pulled, struggling to shed the suit. Across the way, she could see the figure's mouth moving like a mad prophet's.

The lift stopped, the doors hissed, and each combatant ran for all they were worth, curving through the darkened halls and heading for the lifts. The shadows flew past, and Vivien listened to the echoes of her footsteps meet Eliot's and rebound, making it seem as though the ship were populated by hordes.

Eliot was the faster runner, but his body was cracked, and it slowed him even if he felt no pain. Vivien arrived first, ducking inside the lift and fumbling frantically at the button, listening to the guttural shrieks grow closer. Eliot emerged from the shadows; arms outstretched, red, raw mouth agape. Vivien screamed, the doors hissed shut, and all at once the world was pristine and quiet, marred only by the ugly gasp of her breath.

There were other lifts for him to take. The doors hissed open and

Vivien ran, listening to the second hiss sound behind her. Shrieks chased her through the dining hall and past the batteries; they splintered underneath the thundering boots, spraying upward and tinkling softly as they died. She turned down the passenger hall. Eliot's door was open, and merciless cold seeped from it like an open sore. She passed Eliot's room, the dead rooms, her own room, headed for the cockpit. She stumbled through, pressed the lock, and watched as the windowed door—always windowed!—slid between her and her pursuer.

Sobbing for air, she slid down into the pilot's seat. The countdown said four hours.

E liot was real. Either his animated body was standing outside her door, dully beating its forehead against the window, or she was living in her new reality, where she, and Eliot, would remain for her final weeks of life.

She felt too sane to be mad—too scared, too horror-stricken. She wondered what she looked like, wondered if this was how the world had appeared to the others, while their bodies pawed and writhed on the floors of their cabins.

Or had those other bodies, the ones in space, had they actively stared at the ship as their vitreous froze over, straining for the spectators who watched them freeze?

She left the chair, edged to the door and looked at the vacant-eyed figure who still watched through the window.

"Eliot?" she whispered. "Eliot, are you real?"

He struck his head against the plate-glass, and she flinched as though it was she who had been struck.

Unreal city, moved the mouth, without speaking the words. *So many. Unreal city unreal. So many so many.*

He shrieked, and Vivien retreated to the chair, more bothered by the voiceless words than she had been by the howls.

. . .

The planet came in sight, a sheen of color, a riot of life. Vivien watched its glistening surface with a mist in her eyes, so hungry for the fertile world and all it promised. The Promised Land. Eden. She'd made it, she'd made it.

Unreal city, said Eliot.

She'd land. She'd land and then she'd seal off the rest of the ship and freeze Eliot out, suffocate him, cleanse the whole place and start again.

So many, I had not thought death had undone so many...

The ship shuddered, drawn into the gravity of the planet, moving for its atmosphere. Vivien's hand hovered above the switch, the one that would put up the ship's thermal shields and allow it to pass through the atmosphere and land on the soil below.

And it hovered, and it hovered, and it hovered....

The corpse you planted last year in your garden,
Has it begun to sprout? Will it bloom this year?
Or has the sudden frost disturbed its bed?

She saw the world below her rotting, pierced through, spitting pustules of blood, maddened, insane.

Was Eliot real?

Worse...did it matter?

She sat back and saw the walls crawling with contagion. Undetectable, incurable, but there all the same. Either Eliot lived, or she was mad somewhere, boiling out her blood.

She watched the beautiful world spin, placid, unknowing. Then she looked at Eliot.

The lever sat, untouched. The ship began to quake harder, to buckle. Already the temperature increased, almost undetectably. Feverishly. The world rocked harder, drowning Eliot's screams, drowning her own pounding heart.

She watched the land come into view. Beautiful. Pristine. Smiling weakly, she passed a hand over her eyes. How disappointing to see the Promised Land and not enter. How sad.

"You just bury me up in the sky, okay?" she whispered. "You do that for me. You just do that for me."

F ar below, the inhabitants of the shining world watched as a fiery streak blazed across the sky, painted the clouds, and then vanished away in a showering blaze of silver-white sparks.

ATOMS

JAMES DORR

"They died, sure," Commander Robertson said. He stood on the bridge of Admiral Yanov's own ship, the *Padronix*, wishing he'd had a chance to change from his tattered uniform. "The problem was, it wasn't enough. They still wouldn't give up."

"Now let me get this straight, Commander," the admiral said. "You actually killed them. They weren't just wounded?"

Robertson nodded. He stared past the admiral's shoulder toward the image of a yellow mottled planet – the planet he and his men had just left – that hung in space in the forward view-screen. "In the sense of clinically dead, I think so. These creatures are humanoid in form and, even if their organs may be different from ours, a fifteen centimeter laser-blast through the chest, or a sonic implosion…"

"I can understand that you're rattled, Commander," the admiral said. He spoke for a moment to the officer at the helm, then opened a hatchway and motioned to Robertson to precede him into his quarters. "Perhaps something to drink?"

"Thank you, sir, no." Robertson closed the door behind them, then stood in silence, listening to the chug of the ship's ventilation system while the admiral poured his own whisky. He watched as the admiral set his glass down on a round, padded coaster on his desk, then fingered a hideous, spider shaped paperweight after he'd taken the chair behind it.

Robertson waited until, at last, the admiral motioned for him to sit too.

"Now, Commander," the admiral said, "we can talk in private. I don't need to impress on you the disgrace a defeat like this causes the service – unless, of course, we can find some way to turn it to victory in the long run. I don't want you to believe, either, that I necessarily blame *you*. What I do want, though, is for you to tell me exactly what happened while you were down there."

"Most of it you know already, Admiral. I sent my reports to the fleet on schedule, except at the end. We landed – a standard Marine assault team – at 0700 the day before yesterday."

"For the record. This was fleet chronometer time?"

"Yes, sir, although it happened to be morning too where we landed. Not that you could see very much through the murk anyway, but, with our suits on, we found that infrared visors helped some. In any event, we weren't disturbed until we'd gotten our base dome set up and started to send patrols into the field. Lieutenant Hendricks' patrol, Group Echo, contacted the first native movement that afternoon at about 1600. He opened fire in the usual manner – show of force to impress the enemy, but leave enough of them alive to go back to their chieftains and tell them how much damage we can inflict."

"And then what happened?"

"They wouldn't retreat. They wouldn't surrender. They just kept coming. Hendricks figured it must be some kind of tribal thing, the kind you get in some primitive cultures where they figure it's a loss of manhood or something if they give up, so they'd rather die. If that was the case, Hendricks and his men gave them their wish. They had no choice since, even though it was getting harder to see in the murk, they *could* see that the natives were carrying weapons."

"Your report of the morning after said something about the weapons, I think."

"Yes, Admiral." Robertson wished he could loosen his collar, but, even with his uniform in the condition it was, he was still a Marine. "Hendricks wondered, as he took his patrol farther on, why they'd only had visual signs of the weapons – why the telltales on their suits' metal-screens stayed at neutral. In any event, as the planet's primary started to set about two hours later, the murk got so thick that I had to order the groups back in. Shortly afterward, Hendricks found out."

Robertson paused. He saw that the admiral had placed his hand on the spider shaped paperweight again, had picked it up and was stroking it softly.

"When Hendricks got back to the valley the earlier battle had been in," he went on, "the visibility outside the range of their helmet lamps was down to zero. Then one of the men to one side of the group screamed and Hendricks turned to see natives attacking – appearing, as if like ghosts, out of the darkness. These were the same natives. . ."

"Different natives," the admiral broke in. "They just looked the same. This is where your reports start causing problems."

"No, sir. The *same* natives that he was sure had been killed before. They'd placed indicators around the site, it's standard procedure, just as they did along the entire route of their march. If anything had moved in or out of the area afterward, they would have known. Anyhow, they defended themselves, killing the natives – or so they thought – for a second time, and got back to base. But they'd taken casualties."

"I think you'd better have that drink I offered before, mister." Robertson looked up and saw the admiral nod toward the shelf where he'd left the bottle standing next to a second glass. He nodded back and got up from his couch, crossing the narrow room in two strides, and poured his drink neat. He tried not to think of what the wounded and dead had looked like when Hendricks and his men brought them in, some with their heads crushed through their helmets, others with suits and flesh torn open.

He downed the whisky and regained his seat, then continued his story. He told the admiral what Hendricks and his men had found out, about how the suits' repulsers had failed because the weapons used against them had been made out of stone, not metal. He told him about how they'd buttoned up the base for the night and then, the next morning, he'd personally led all five patrols out to the site of the battle.

This time the indicators showed there'd been movement, all right.

Delta Group found the enemy first by a small, winding river, found itself surrounded by hundreds of natives, not just a handful like Echo had fought with the evening before, and Robertson had the others close in, spewing death before them. He'd brought heavy weapons, just in case, and used them as well, sonic grenades and the big, fifteen-centimeter cannon – until the whole valley had been cleared of life. Then, leaving Alpha Group as a rear guard, he had the rest of his men fan out alongside the river, into the plain that lay beyond, to search for where the enemy reinforcements had come from.

"Then what happened?" the admiral prompted.

"We found what we wanted," Robertson said. "The native town – more a small city, really – and, even though the planet's atmosphere made it risky, we used our flame units. We cleaned the place out, turning it into a lake of boiling blood and charred meat. But then parts of the lake started coalescing."

"'Coalescing,'" the admiral repeated. "What do you mean?"

"Just what I said, sir. As the lake cooled, lumps of flesh and blood came together. They formed back into man-like shapes, struggling to pull themselves up the hillside to where we waited. We fired again, driving them back down, and then Alpha Group called."

"And they saw the same thing?"

"More or less, sir. I'd said we'd used heavy weapons against the natives in the valley. Literally, sir, most of the bodies were blasted apart. But Alpha reported that the parts were coming together, not always the pieces from just one corpse either, and picking up weapons to fight them again. Alpha was trapped if we didn't get back to them, so that's why I ordered the groups I had with me to retreat.

"Hendricks and Group Echo volunteered to take the rear, to hold back the ones we'd tried to burn. He said he was coming up with a theory. . . ."

"And what was that, Robertson?"

"Well, he didn't really come up with it until that night – when we took the prisoner. But the gist of it was that the humanoid creatures weren't the real enemy we were fighting. That the real enemy might not even be native to the planet itself, but some kind of space-borne group intelligence, like that pseudo-sentient virus we ran up against on

Rigel II except, in this case, with actual volition. The thing is, though, once it had taken its humanoid hosts, it was trapped inside them. Even when one of the hosts was killed, it couldn't get out, so it had to do its best to repair whatever was left to keep itself going."

"That may not be as far off as it sounds," the admiral said. He put down the paperweight, then reached across his desk to a small control panel. He pushed a button, and Robertson watched as a screen built into the office bulkhead flared into life.

"Let's give it a couple of moments to warm up," the admiral said. "In the meantime, I want you to tell me about this prisoner."

Robertson nodded. "There's not much to tell, sir, that wasn't in the assessment I handed in when I got here. We managed to join up with Alpha Group, what was left of it, and fight our way through the natives we'd *thought* we'd left dead in the valley. By the time we got back to base camp, it was already late afternoon, so I had the base sealed up for the night. That's when I sent my last report from the planet's surface, the one that said I thought I might need a Special Forces team in the morning.

"The thing is, sir, I still wasn't sure myself how much I believed of what had happened. Most of the men, except for Hendricks, were trying their best to convince themselves it was just a case of there being more natives than we'd expected, with maybe equipment malfunctions explaining how they'd been able to move new men in without our knowing. As for the lake of fire, none of the lumps had actually come close enough for us to be sure they might not have been something perfectly natural. Some trick of the wind, maybe, pushing the lighter stuff up into waves.

"Anyhow, we were sealed up tight under our base dome until about 0300 hours. That was when the first of the enemy breached the airlock."

"What do you mean, *breached* the airlock?"

"I don't know, sir. Again, perhaps, some kind of malfunction. The alarms didn't even sound, there was no loss of air, until the natives picked up our own weapons and started swinging them at us like clubs. It was hand to hand fighting. Then I *did* begin to believe what I'd seen before when we'd burned the village. Some of the natives were from the village, scarcely humanoid any more, but walking collections of blackened lumps, seemingly strung together on frames made of sticks and rocks. Hendricks' theory, after we'd fought the enemy back long enough to get to the shuttle hanger and board our ship, was that the *things* weren't even a virus, but something on the atomic level. Something that, in the case of the village, could have been partially released by the heat and blended into the sticks and things we saw moving now. But that could also reduce itself, with its host material, back down to individual atoms to pass through the airlock, then reassemble itself inside.

"Anyhow, we managed to retreat back to the ship, we managed to blast off, but even then we hadn't gotten completely away. One of the enemy managed to board us, to make its way to the control room unnoticed while the rest of us were strapped in. Then, when we were in space, it attacked me. . . ."

"Why *you*, Robertson?"

"Somehow it knew that I was the leader, that's Hendricks' theory. Just the way that, if we found a single leader who resisted us on a planet we wanted to conquer, that's the one we'd go after first. Anyway, it attacked me with its bare hands, with its fingernails even, while two of the men tried to pull it off. But its skin kept shifting enough for it to keep slipping away every time they grabbed it until, just by chance, I managed to get away from it myself for a moment. Just long enough for me to hit it."

Robertson shrugged. *That* part almost seemed funny, now that it was over. "The humanoids must have glass jaws, Admiral. I didn't hit it all that hard, but it was enough to knock it out. Anyhow, we figured then that, if the thing's attached to its host and its host can be kept alive, but nonfunctioning, we had it trapped. Kill the host, and then it can animate the remains, but keep it unconscious..."

"That will do for now, Commander," the admiral said. "You kept it under a general anesthetic you got from your shuttle's sickbay and, when you transferred it to us, we took it to the ship's hospital here. Now I want you to look at this."

The admiral reached a second time to the view-screen control, then retrieved his paperweight, turning it slowly around in his hands.

Robertson gasped. The screen came into focus, showing the alien prisoner strapped down to a surgical table, its body cut open, its organs pulsing underneath the bright hospital light.

"Still alive, Commander," the admiral said. "I wanted you to see what we found out. Doctor Bauman, could you explain it?"

The view shifted slightly to take in the *Padronix's* chief surgeon behind the table.

"Yes," the doctor said. "In laymen's terms, the enemy's body is able to shift and regenerate tissue. If you'll look at the heart, for instance, notice that it's on the right side in this creature, you'll see where more than half of it had been recently damaged. Somehow, though, the creature was able to staunch the blood, then form new tissue."

"Would you say, doctor, that that's a sign that the creature itself is host to some kind of intelligent microbe?" the admiral broke in. "An atom, maybe, that's able to link itself with others into a group mind?"

The doctor smiled. "They're not the same thing, atoms and microbes, but I think I see what you're getting at. You mean something like that Rigelian virus, but that was a freak, the sort of thing you only run across once. It *could* be something like that, of course, all creatures are host to all sorts of microbes, but I'd just say this thing has amazing recuperative powers."

"Thank you, doctor," the admiral said. "You know what to do." He turned back to Commander Robertson. "That, I believe, will be the official explanation. An enemy that can regenerate tissue to the extent it can take a wound that would kill one of us, yet continue fighting, would be difficult enough to cope with, don't you think? Still, some lower life forms can do the same thing."

"But what about Lieutenant Hendricks? He still believes—"

"Chief Petty Officer Hendricks, Commander. He told his theory to too many people."

For a moment, the admiral was silent. All that Robertson could hear were the blended cadences of the ship – the ventilator, the life support system, the distant rumbling of the engines – the reassuring, ever-present whispers of power. Then the admiral leaned forward, suddenly, slamming the paperweight down on the desk.

"Have I ever told you about this, Commander Robertson? Why I keep this thing in my office? Look at it Robertson. Pick it up."

Robertson did so. The spider shaped form was nearly twenty-five centimeters from front to back, it might have been more than three times that size if the legs that folded underneath it were stretched out to full length. It was made of some kind of glossy black metal and great attention had been given to even the tiniest of its details. In fact, it looked almost too well put together.

"I don't understand, sir," he said as he placed it back onto the desk.

"It's a reminder of an extinct race," the admiral said. He lowered his voice. "A race that was already developing a primitive star drive when we discovered it. Spiders, Commander, that's all they were, but intelligent and . . . dangerous . . . spiders."

"You mean, then, that if word got out about how really dangerous the creatures on *this* planet could be, the government might make us stop our expansion?"

"Something like that, or maybe even worse, Commander. Maybe, if the government learned that there really *were* intelligent atoms – or, for that matter, intelligent spiders – they'd want to change our mission to study them. They'd want to be able to use our ships to try to find out where they might have come from, like they almost did after Rigel II, and, rather than sending the military who'd know how to handle the situation, they'd want to send scientists and diplomats. *Now* do you understand, Commander?"

Robertson nodded. "Doctor Bauman's theory, about regeneration, isn't all that unusual, is it? I mean, like you say, there are lower creatures already that can grow new limbs when one is torn off, so there's nothing in that explanation to make anybody overly curious if we quarantined this planet. Is that what you mean, sir?"

"Almost, Commander. The only thing is, we're not going to quarantine this planet, but sterilize it. Incinerate it into atoms, whether intelligent atoms or not, starting with what's left of your prisoner. In fact," the admiral got up from his desk and reached for his and Robertson's glasses, "just about now, while I'm getting us refills, Doctor Bauman should be putting the prisoner into the ship's crematory."

Robertson nodded, accepted his glass, then felt a quick whiff of warmth through the ship's ventilating system. He nodded again as the admiral sat down, and heard, in the distance, the sounds of machinery coming to life – unusual sounds for a ship in space. He sipped his whisky, trying to forget the sight of the creatures from the village, halfway incinerated themselves, blending into...

He froze as the admiral's spider paperweight started to move, as its legs uncurled and it twisted around, the mandibles on its underside clicking open and shut. The spider kept turning until it faced the admiral's chair, then flexed its legs as it prepared to spring.

BLACK LAGOON

S RANGER

J az stripped off her clothes and dropped them upon the sandy shore. The light of the three moons cast conflicting shadows amongst the trembling leaves of the feather fern trees. She walked away from the camp to the shore of the lagoon and into the dark. Humans, it seemed, had arrived too late. Sunken ruins and tumbling orbital infrastructure spoke of an unknown planetary disaster that ended this planet's flirtation with intelligence. With broad tropical latitudes, Parana was wild and fierce. With the vanishing of the civilization that existed here, wild beasts had refilled the world. But, the lagoons were different. They were idyllic, peaceful, free of the natural violence that typified the rest of the planet. Why? It seemed like a very small question for a very big world, but it was her question.

She looked over her shoulder at the campsite. The vacuum craft, held aloft by the weight of nothing, stretched its cables. They creaked and groaned as the breeze shifted. The camp, bathed in a pool of light, was quiet, most everyone was asleep or paired up.

The night air chilled her skin, a welcome reprieve from the normally tropical heat. She dropped her towel to the sand and stepped towards the dark water. The machines had found nothing dangerous in the dark lagoon but still a tingle of atavistic fear tickled the edge of her consciousness. The dim, reptile part of the human mind had an instinctive fear of dark places and unseen depths. Though the lagoon was rich with life, none showed any interest in nibbling on humans. In the lagoon's depths, bio-luminescent fish schooled, shelled reptile analogs sculled the water, and spiny crustaceans walked the muddy bottom. Man-made robots kept a continuous watch.

Her leading theory was that the lagoons functioned as nursery of sorts, and, as if by mutual decree, the ferocious predators that swam in the vast river systems steered clear. Their own young swam in the sheltered waters. The theory seemed logical, but no one wanted to risk their lives to test a theory, so the narrow neck of water that connected the lagoon to the river was draped with smartnets and sensors to exclude the seriously scary predators that lived in the adjacent river.

She had explored the lagoons extensively on behalf of the corporation that paid the bills by day, but this little nighttime foray was personal. She wanted to get away and decompress a bit. She left her AI companion behind. She edged her feet into the water and through the slender, green nursery grass that harbored so much of the river's young. Tiny luminous creatures sparked into fireflies of blue light. The water rose around her. The thick ribbon-like grass teased her thighs. The lagoon's sandy bottom sloped deeper. She dunked herself to wet her hair and then emerged, tossing her head back and pulling her hair away from her face. She gathered her hair and pushed it through a rubber band she kept on her wrist. She took another step and felt nothing. The bottom plunged to over 20 meters deep. She pushed off with her other foot and swam a gentle quiet breaststroke keeping her head above water.

She was an intensely rational person. Her conclusions were backed by weeks of intensive scans of multiple lagoons. She had not found anything that could hurt a human. Still, she felt that bloom of fear that something deep down and transparent to the best sensors that humans could make peered up at her with wide gelatinous eyes and a slack, rubbery mouth lined with dagger-like teeth. She imagined a tentacle tongue reaching to snag her legs and pull her down, down, down into its jaws.

She suffered from a vivid imagination. Stop it, she thought.

It was an occupational hazard. She knew the various ways that life kept itself fed and marine life was particularly ingenious .

She dove under, opened her eyes and swam through a glittering, pulsing star field. The water was so clear that during daylight she could see all the way to the craggy, bare limestone source of the natural spring that pumped cool, clear water into the lagoon. She dove under. Swimming at night in the water was like flying through a star field in space. She could hold her breath for nearly twelve minutes, average for a trained, un-augmented diver. Dax, a member of her team, could hold his breath for nearly thirty, but he was augmented to do so. She didn't think it was a fair comparison.

She slowed and drifted, feeling the soft thump of her heart, the gentle press of currents, subtle changes in temperature. She completely relaxed, floating in the water. The pressures of leading the mission loosened their hold on her. She was at peace and felt the pulse and rhythm of the world. She floated, neutrally buoyant, en-wombed by the lagoon. The barriers between her and everything else fell away. She felt part of the world.

A wave of pressure rolled across the front of her body as if something big had moved near her. She scanned around, rolling along the axis of her body but saw nothing but blackness. She sculled her hands and the weak light cast by the agitated diatoms did not help. She felt an unexplained presence, like she was being watched. She strained her eyes against the dark. The diatoms winked out when she became still. She suddenly felt very foolish in the water. And alone.

She hovered in the depths, perhaps no more than three or four meters down by her reckoning, but for all she could see, it might as well have been a million kilometers. She reached out a hand, fingers extended seeking like a blind person uncertain of the world. Something pressed against her palm.

Another.

Five fingers matched hers and she thought that for a moment that Dax had finally taken a hint and joined her.

Her hand flexed and felt the prick of claws. The velvet brush of webbing between fingers. In another context it might have been erotic. She recoiled in fear. Water pressure burst upon her like something had finned away with a violent thrust of its body. Streaks of light created a blurred outline suggesting a figure streaking away from her.

She exhaled forcefully succumbing to her worst illogical fear. She lost her sense of orientation and reflexively kicked her feet and stroking her arms. She burst to the surface, stifled a scream, and looked about. The camp was as it was, an oasis of light built upon the sand bar, sheltered by the floating immensity of the vacuum craft. It was so very far away. Ripples of her own making rolled away in circles of wet light. She scanned around hoping that maybe Dax would surface and laugh at her and she would become angry and then he would take her in his arms...

Nothing except the sound of a jungle at night. She crawled back to the shore, her fastest stroke, not caring if her splashing woke the camp. The water shallowed, and she stood, surging to the shore, nursery grass caressed her legs and wrapped her ankles. She tangled and stumbled back into the water, and then hauled herself up onto the dry sand on all fours. She picked up her towel and wrapped it around herself. A shiver ran up her spine. So much for her logical self. It was probably just a curious fish or maybe a pentapus, the gentle five- limbed invertebrates that nested in the nursery grass.

She felt foolish. Water drops clung to her lithe body and she shivered atavistically. She toweled herself off. No one in the camp had woken.

An unnatural stillness caught her eye. At the end of the sandbar, a man-sized shape stood. Clouds scudded across the sky. Shadows shifted, brightening and darkening the scene but the shape at this distance, remained a black-on-black silhouette. A bird shrieked bloody murder and another answered. Shaped like a man but not a man, taller with a slimmer waist. Like a man wearing a gill suit with intake ports and exhaust vents used to extract oxygen from the water. The clouds parted, casting more moon light. She caught the predatory eye shine of the creature, the pulse of gills at its neck and the heave of vents along its flanks, a scaled pale torso.

The creature took a single step towards her. It did not seem as if it was stalking, simply curious. She did not move. Emboldened, it took another. A caress of moonlight shimmered down its flanks.

She thought that for as second it was Dax, perhaps on a midnight swim like herself. Perhaps he was looking for her, to embrace her, to kiss her, to make love to her in the alien waters, like she wanted him too.

Dax was not that big.

"Jaz, are you out there?" asked a voice from the camp.

She turned. It was Dax standing inside the pool of light embracing the camp.

She turned back to the creature.

It was gone. Not even a ripple of water or bioluminescent trail to mark its passing.

"I know what I saw," said Jaz.

"I know what you said you saw. I've had the AI run pattern recognition checks on our archived data and they can't find any evidence of what you claim to have seen. I'm not saying it isn't there. I'm saying we haven't found anything that remotely resembles your description. What concerns me is that you feel comfortable enough to go haring off to swim in an alien lagoon without a companion or drone. Christ, you know what's in these waters."

"Yes, but there is nothing in the lagoons. We have hundreds of hours of data in dozens of lagoons to back it up. None of the big predators go anywhere near them and certainly no two-legged amphibians."

"Gill man," offered Dax. "Jaz, it's a big damn planet and we have only seen the tiniest bit of it and maybe you did see something that has managed to evade our sensor nets. It doesn't matter. Stop taking unnecessary risks. You're the team leader. Act like it."

"You're right. Okay, I won't anymore. Anything from the other teams?"

"Yes, it's all fascinating. Blah, blah, blah. This planet is a jewel and corporate is already counting profit. The orbital catalog is complete. The ruins in orbit are pretty significant and we have found traces of collapsed matter and you know what that means."

"They were interstellar," said Jaz.

"At least they were before whatever happened here, happened."

Doesn't make sense, she thought. "So they were spacefaring, multi-planetary, and now you say they could have been interstellar. What the hell happened? Multi-planetary and interstellar species don't go extinct, so what happened?"

"Well, that's the theory anyway," said Dax. "I don't know. What-ever disaster befell them was complete and total, but they left us a perfectly beautiful planet to colonize. It is like winning the lottery. Someone else can try to answer the mysterious questions. Corporate wants this place open as soon as they can."

"I am sure they do. Don't you want to know what it was?" said Jaz.

"Not really."

She thought of the creature she saw last night. Already her memory of the event was diffuse. Did she really see what she thought she saw? If so, maybe the builders of the vast ruins that blanket the planet were still here in some capacity. Even a degenerate, remnant population of sentients, still savvy enough to avoid smartnets and sensors would be enough to close the world to corporate sponsored colonization.

She had explored the waters of three different worlds. Parana was the fourth. It never ceased to amaze her the fantastic diver-sity and strangeness of creatures that lived in a liquid environ-ment. She had encountered many creatures that harbored a crude intelligence, but none that could hold a conversation much beyond: feed me.

She checked her diving suit. The suit, more machine than fabric clung to her form. The small reserve oxygen sphere was full. The gill suit's status lights indicated green. She pulled the transparent hood over her face and walked into the water. The AI drone, shaped like a horseshoe crab, looked up at her and followed. Its flexible propulsor edges rippled as it took to the water. Today, she wanted to explore the interface of the river just outside the smartnets. Something kept the big predators out and she wanted to see if she could find something to build a theory upon. Altruistic behavior was fairly common in all the explored ecosystems, but something different was at work here. There was too much defenseless and tasty protein swimming around in the lagoons to be ignored. What could possibly keep them out?

She entered the water and submerged. She finned gently with smooth powerful strokes of her legs, conserving power by not using the small thruster. The AI drone kept pace with her. She swam through glittering schools of metallic scaled fish that dodged around drifting amber weeds. Brilliant crustaceans marched along the sandy bottom. As she swam, water entered the intake ports, passed over hemosponge lattice, and exhausted through ports along her back. She breathed in the extracted oxygen mix. With a fully charged battery, she was good for hours of swimming.

She slalomed between columns of ruins, the foundation of a much larger structure that had eroded and tumbled away centuries ago. Other teams, with sentientologists, were working that particular puzzle. Her team's mission was to perform an initial biological survey of the waters for future colonists.

She had spent a fair amount of time exploring ruins both under the water and above. Whoever these people were, they were master builders and artisans but they left behind no representational art of themselves behind. No one knew what they looked like, and no one had found any remains. Sooner or later, it would happen, but it was out of her area. She swam under a roofed structure near the interface of the lagoon and the river. Shelled creatures, anchored to the walls, extended fronds to sift river's currents for nutrients. A cluster of sub-adult predatory fish, the largest, half as long as she was tall, dodged and darted confused at the smartnet. She touched a control on her forearm and a section of the net opened up. The fish streamed into the river to take on their adult life, if they survived long enough.

She kept the net open and swam through. She closed it behind her. The tug of the river's current took hold and she engaged her thruster to aid her finning.

Her AI companion broadcast an all clear. While there was always the possibility of surprise, nothing in the immediate area was threatening. The river was slow. It had not rained for weeks so the water was relatively clear.

"Jaz are you okay?" asked Dax. "I see you are outside the net."

"I'm good, I am looking for some spots to lay down the sensors and get a better sense of the boundary area. Pressures, temperatures, nutrients, that sort of thing."

She found a convenient rocky outcropping removed a sensor from her suit and affixed it to a rock. The sensor gripped the rock, extruded its wands, and set to work sifting data from the currents.

"I won't be long."

"Okay, I'm watching, be careful."

"I always am." Her mother would disagree. She had swum with Great Whites off the coast of California and South Africa, dived upon torpid Nile Crocodiles in African rivers, Imperaxes on Zeta Reticuli, and Mar Vulperines on Zenith.

She headed up current and planted sensors, expanding the network, developing a profile of the interface zone. She planted her last one. The AI reported the sounding of a Gulper, a toothless fish that inhaled its prey with a rapid explosive opening of its mouth. It was too far away to be of any concern.

"I'm done. I'm coming back."

"Good. So you know, Ril has finished the protein matrix of lagoon wildlife. Good news. He says that his results jibe with the other teams. With a few exceptions, this world is edible. While you are out there, gather up some critters and whip up that world-famous gumbo that you are always bragging on and we have yet to taste."

"Just like a man, if you can eat it or…

The AI drone darted in a blur, something burst from the soft mud below and clouds of debris billowed. The pressure wave hit her. Something big moved. She tumbled in the turbulence. She heard the electrical zap of the AI discharging its weapon.

"Dax!"

Another wave of pressure and she tumbled again, lost in a vast cloud of stirred up river bottom. Jaws emerged from a roiling cloud. She hit her thrusters and surged away. The jaws widened like the yawning mouth of a cave and the AI vanished into the creature's mouth. Jaws slammed shut upon it.

She kicked hard augmenting her thruster. She swam aimlessly, without a plan, with only the need to get away. She wanted distance and cover from the predator.

"Jaz, your AI is dead. What's happening?"

"Something big."

It was a big world and they had not seen even a fraction of what it contained. Some sort of ambush predator lying beneath the mud waiting. Who knows what triggered it? The warmth of her body, distortions in the magnetic field by her passing? She put her academic thoughts aside.

First things first.

Do not become lunch.

She reached the edge of the ruins where they protruded into the river system. She swam hard in clear water and dove behind a crude shelter of tumbled blocks festooned with antler branched corals. The creature emerged from the cloud of mud it had stirred up in its failed attack. It looked like an elongated flounder with a cluster of tendrils above its eyes and a steam shovel mouth. The creature dove to the bottom and rooted with its mouth silting the water. It came for her. Its body undulated up and down She unholstered her own weapon. No way she could outswim this thing. Her best chance was to stay here among the tumbled ruins.

She saw the mouth wide open, rows of tiny conical teeth more adept to crunching shelled things but not particularly adverse to an easy opportunistic snack. The creature's mouth plunged into the mud in front of the blocks and shoveled her and the stones up into the river current, sifting the wheat from the chaff. She spun end over end. Her weapon crackled when it contacted something and then it was stripped from her hands, lost to the currents. She abruptly stopped spinning and a vise slammed onto her. She felt the press of a mouth engulfing her body. The pressure increased. The predator swam higher into clear water and could saw with a strange clinical detachment what it was that had her. She beat upon the creature's face and its eyes rolled back revealing empty white. She pushed against its hard, boney lips to no avail.

Her gill suit failed and the emergency oxygen tank activated. She glimpsed someone swimming impossibly fast. The creature twisted away to escape with its prey. A bloom of blood enveloped her. She could taste it in her mouth. Her hood had been stripped back. Dax, coming to rescue her she thought. He better hurry.

Jaz, woke as much as she could. Her body felt like it had been in a vice, which in a sense it had. Blood splattered around her. Her suit was shredded and her breathing apparatus, which someone had removed from her body, lay beside her. The pink hemosponge lattice burst from its casing like ruptured lungs, crushed from the immense force of the animal's bite. She unsealed the shredded remnants of her suit, striping down to her bikini under suit. Her legs, hips, stomach, and chest were ugly smears of yellow and purple scored with puncture wounds packed with what looked to be mud. A few of them wept blood.

Her stomach knotted up and a wave of nausea washed over her. She didn't think the animal that bit her was venomous but something in its saliva made her feel terribly ill. She sat down and leaned back against the wall of wherever she was. Her vision blurred. She squeezed her eyes shut and opened them, trying to focus. The walls were brilliantly painted. This was a discovery. She damped her enthusiasm for more practical concerns. Where was she? Dax? She thought. He had rescued her, hadn't he?

The last thing she thought she remembered was him swimming to her. She certainly wasn't in the any of the camp's fabric structures or within the metal confines of the vacuum craft. She took a deep breath, exhaled slowly. She stood, fighting nausea and stepped away from the wall to the center to gain perspective on the room. It wasn't a room, but perhaps the beginning of a corridor. The walls were painted with brilliant murals. Time had taken its toll on the murals. Slabs had slipped from the wall and jagged cracks like black lightning strikes rippled across the face of the murals. A diffused source-less light spread evenly throughout the room.

Her weapon. She picked it up and felt reassured. It was undamaged and almost fully charged.

She felt watched. She turned and raised her weapon, activating the tip to discharge.

It stood there, her rescuer. Flat-faced, slitted nose, with deep-set, dark eyes. It was bipedal, broad-chested, and as large as big man. The creature was strongly muscled, and plated with scales. It had a drooping toothless mouth. Gills flexed slowly upon the sides of its face and neck. Water leaked from vents along its chest. It held clawed, webbed hands out to her, upturned to show that they were empty.

She lowered her weapon. The adrenalin rush of the attack, the shock of seeing an intelligent creature… she was confused. There were protocols for such things, but she was just a marine biologist.

Her knees shook. The downside of discovering an edible world was that it worked both ways. Alien bacteria from the fish bite swam in her blood stream. She sank to the floor, feeling feverish. The gill man advanced and caught her before her legs completely failed. It lowered her slowly, cradling the back of her head.

Their eyes met.

She had witnessed firsthand the blank nothingness of a marine predator's eyes just before the attack came. The horrible indifference of the consumer towards the about to be consumed was terrifying. This was not it. The creature's face was patterned with fine scales and though perhaps not as expressive as a human's, the softening features and widened eyes indicated an empathic intelligence. Of course, she could just be anthropomorphizing the alien.

"Hello," she said. She held her hand up, fingers spread, and the creature did the same. They pressed palms and then fingertips together. She felt the prick of claws. She smiled. The creature smiled back. This world would be closed, she thought. With the discovery of an existing intelligence, the corporation's colony initiative would come under government review that could take years to sort out.

"Get away from her, you bastard,"

The creature let her head down and spun to the sound of Dax's voice.

"Dax, no," she said but her voice was too soft to be heard. She heard the muffled shot of gunfire and the whine of ricochets. The alien charged

Dax. More gunfire and more ricochets. It was an armored marine creature, more than a match for the tiny caliber pistols issued to the scientists.
One more shot and then a croak of pain. The alien swatted at Dax and
sent him flying across the room. Dax hit the wall with a sickening crunch.
The gun skittered away. The gill man straddled him and opened its mouth
wide, another set of jaws with rows of serrated teeth fell into place.

"No," said Jaz. "Please, don't."

The creature lifted its head from Dax's throat and looked at her. Its
teeth retracted, leaving the slightly sad, goofy smile. It stood. Dark
blood ran from a bullet wound. The creature looked down, pressed a
webbed palm to its wound, and then looked back at her.

"I'm sorry," she said. "He doesn't know you saved me." Fever chills
racked her body. Her abdomen knotted in pain and she rolled onto
her side and curled into a fetal position.

"Jaz! Dax!" yelled a voice.

Maybe it was Ril or Maro. She couldn't tell. It seemed so far away.
Her head throbbed painfully. "You have to go." She pointed away from
the sound of her team' voices.

The alien understood and left, leaving a trail of blood.

She woke to the hum of a starship. During the three- year
voyage to Parana it was inescapable. She knew it well.

A nurse entered the room.

"How long?" she croaked. Her throat was so terribly dry.

"She speaks," said the nurse. "It was touch and go for quite a
while. You were septic. Whatever bit you had a dirty mouth."

"How long?" she repeated

"Four weeks. We've had you in an induced coma after you were
evacuated from the planet's surface," said the nurse.

"I don't remember. My team?"

"On their way home, Jaz," said Elid, the Director of Survey Operations. "Or their next assignments. You were too sick to leave. This ship
and its medical facilities are staying to become part of the colony
infrastructure."

Elid looked at the nurse and she left.

"But, we found someone. Ask Dax. It's intelligent, an intelligent gill man. A creature."

"Jaz, I have Dax's reports from the incident. He found you after you were attacked by that fish. You were already delusional from infection. You were evacuated up here and the ship's medical had to synthesize an antibacterial."

"But the creature."

He sat on the edge of the bed and put his hand on her shoulder.

"There is no creature, no gill-man. Just a fevered brain."

"I have to make my report," she said

His hand squeezed.

"Stop it. You're hurting me."

"Oh no, Jaz. No reports. This world is open. The corporation has spent billions on upfront costs and stands to make trillions. Do you think it will be derailed by a single monster sighting in the four years we have been here?"

"It wasn't a monster. When I get back…"

"We would like you to stay on, here at Parana, as Director of Survey Operations. I've already made the recommendations and the corporation has approved my request. It's expensive to fly a new director from Earth, best to have someone qualified for the job already in place."

"That's your job."

"Now, I am the Corporate Governor of the colony of Parana."

"We would like you to stay and carry on the survey mission. It's a big world. A lifetime of work. Naturally, all your reports and findings will flow through me."

"If I refuse?"

"This is not the kind of offer one refuses. Do you think that perhaps the company could finish whatever happened to whomever owned this world? Do you think that perhaps it is possible that an obscure scientist could vanish from the universe?"

"I see."

"I think you do. I was once like you…but the system always wins. Jaz, I'm sorry. If there is anyone down there, and I am not saying that there is, you are probably their best chance. Do you accept my offer?"

"I do," said Jaz.

"Good," he let go of her shoulder and got off the edge of her bed. "As soon as you are ready, your office is waiting for you. There is a new batch of eager young explorers arriving in two months."

He walked to the door. "Lights on or off?"

"Off, please."

Elid was a good scientist, the best she knew on a personal level. He was at one time her college professor and then her professional mentor at the corporate labs. When her father had died, he had even stepped in to fill that role. He was doing the best he could for her, by keeping her away from the violent corporate politics that, at the very least, would ruin her career... at the very most, vanish her from the universe. Humanity would tame this world, pushing its mysteries into the quiet corners of black lagoons hidden in dark jungles. Best then, that she stay, if just to keep some of the mystery alive. What if they had discovered us first? Would the outcome be any different?

Elid turned off the lights and paused, framed by the light of the hall. He didn't turn back.

"What was it like?" he asked.

She caught a hint of the scientist she used to know and not the politician he had evolved o be. She considered her answer. "It was amazing."

"I knew it would be." He closed the door shutting out the light beyond her room.

CAPTAIN CLONE

DEBORAH WALKER

I worked all night trying to find trying to find a quicker, less expensive cure. The colorful boxes of anti-viral agents, tailored bacteria, and antibiotics littered the work surface. In the corner of the sick bay the radiation lamp flickered, blood-coloured light over a tray of discarded Petri dishes.

As the night wore on, my treatments became increasingly experimental. I tried the wilder, alien technologies. I placed the smooth mites of the Pincer world onto the faces of the crew in the hope that the burrowing insects would seek out and consume the infection. I pounded strange aromatic herbs. I concocted desperate combinations.

At last, I found myself chanting. In the sterile lights of the sick bay, I sang a half-remembered prayer to Shimra. I chanted the rituals over the sick women. The words sounded hollow to my ears. Why would the Healing God Shimra hear an unbeliever?

I tried my best to cure them, but only time and patience and expensive drugs would heal them. I failed them.

And I desperately needed a drink.I dimmed the lights in the sick bay.

"Get some rest." I took one last look at the women in the beds. They were identical, but I could distinguish between them.

"Goodnight, Mikar."

"Goodnight, Verna. The captain will come to see you in a few hours."

"Tell the captain we're sorry," said another voice, as I left. I think it was Sam's.

I really needed a drink.

In my cabin, I held my glass of wine up to the light. Rioja is an ancient wine, first produced by the Phoenicians and the Celtiberians. In medieval times, the wine was produced by monks who extolled its virtues to their congregations. In the thirteenth century, Gonzalo de Berceo, clergyman of the Riojan Suso Monastery praised Rioja in his poems.

Spanish wine.

I have never been to Earth, and I never will. Clones are not allowed on the mother world. I would dearly like to go, to see the vineyards, to taste wine that hasn't travelled through space. The Riojan Guild insists that point seven speed damages the flavor. I will never taste Rioja in its purest form.

Morning came, with a dull headache and a reluctance to visit my patients. I took a deep breath, before I activated the door to the bridge. The captain was bent over her workstation.

"The crew have been infected."

"What? Again?" said the captain, looking up from her computer. I saw that she'd been scanning web downloads, probably looking for something – anything – that would help us escape from this wretched planet.

"I'm afraid it will be at least a week before they'll be fit for duty again." I began to enter data into the computer. I didn't want to look at the captain. "It's not their fault."

"What's that you say?"

The captain was raised on Grey Cloud Colony, and that harsh, wild upbringing ran through her, lettering her personality with innate callousness. She made me nervous.

"Captain, I thought you might like to go outside and assess the situation for yourself."

"It's not standard procedure. That's what the crew are for. They're expendable."

"But if we ever want to get off this planet . . ."

"You're right, Mikar. You will accompany me."

I shuddered. This was not what I had wanted at all. I'd had hoped for a few hours rest without the overwhelming presence of the captain.

"Right then." The captain took one more look at the glittering control panel. It was still shining erratically, the lights blinking off and on, a chaos of illumination reflecting the infection of the ship's computers.

"What *is* the situation outside?" asked the captain, smashing her hand against the panel, illuminating some controls, turning off other, and adding to the confusion.

"It's the same. The tentacles are covering the ship. They've invaded the outer shell and have entered the ship's systems. We have control of most of the ship, but the engines are offline, and we have no outward communications. It's a focused attack. I imagine that if we were able to take off we could pull away from the tentacles. They're organic."

"But we can't take off, can we, Mikar?"

"No, Captain."

"Waste of time speculating then, eh?"

"Yes, Captain."

It was typical of the captain to ask a question, and then be irritated by the perfectly reasonable response.

"I suppose I ought to see to the crew. Unless you can sort it out by yourself?"

"No, Captain. I thought it was better that I left the final decision to you."

The captain strode through the bridge. She was shiny, silky, and under control. I followed behind her. I was disheveled, tired, and barely holding myself together.

· · ·

W e entered sick room together, with me still a few paces behind the captain. The captain looked at the rows of women lying in the beds.

"What a waste. How long did you say that it would take to treat them?"

"A week, maybe five days."

"Hardly worth it, is it?"

I looked at the rows of identical faces in the sick room – the captain's face – my face. Only the captain was real. The rest of us were copies, ship-bred and ship-raised. All the crew were clones of the captain. Only the captain was *real,* had attained citizenship, was born from a woman and not brought to life in the green, glazed cloning tubules filled with simple, sucking nutrients.

"Didn't you fight back, eh?" said the captain to Verna.

"We tried, Captain."

Verna's face was webbed with grey micro-tentacles which pulsed to the beat of her blood. They wove through the capillaries of her body, using her own network against her.

"What's your report?"

"I'm sorry, Captain." Verna winced as she eased herself higher in the bed. "It just kind of happened. One minute we were walking, cutting our way through the jungle, and the next thing, the entity jumped us. We only caught a glimpse of it, before the tentacles engulfed us."

"The entity? Can't you even give it a name? Names are important. That's why you haven't got names."

I shuddered. The captain was so cruel. The crew didn't seem to mind. They were too young, only two years old, though they wore the bodies of adult women. They didn't know any better. Names *were* important, that's why I'd named every one of my sisters.

"We're allocating it the name of Grey Cut, Captain," I said.

"That's better." The captain moved along the sick room to another bed. To Saleen's bed. I recognized her by a small scar in her eyebrow, still visible below the grey web. Saleen looked at the captain with a look of devotion on her disfigured face. "Describe Grey Cut to me," said the captain.

"A spherical body, maybe ten meters in diameter. It was covered in tentacles which narrowed to a small spike. If you get cut by one of the spikes, you become infected. The infection spreads quickly. We all became infected."

"I can see that," said the captain. She turned to me and said, "Delete them all, and clone up a new batch." Without a backward glance at the crew, the captain walked out of the sick room. "We'll meet Grey Cut ourselves this afternoon, Mikar."

There wasn't even a murmur of protest from the crew. They'd been taught to live and die at the captain's command. They accepted their fate, in fact, one or two of the crew members tried to struggle out of bed, to assist me.

"No, that's all right. Go back to bed, rest awhile."

"I wish . . ." said Saleen.

"Yes?"

"I wish that we could have done a better job for the captain."

"Rest now," I said.

I inject the euthanasia drug into the bodies of the women.

Fifteen women.

This was not the first time.

I say goodbye to each of them.

I use the names, I'd given them.

I watch as stillness overcomes them.

I drag the bodies to the recycling vat.

I watch as the enzymes strip the flesh off their bodies.

This was not the first time.

I set the cloning pods to generate new crew members.

Fifteen new women.

I set their memories to the required standards.

I do it all.

. . .

I went back to my quarters. I poured myself a large glass of Rioja. I drank and drank and drank, and tried to wash away the memories. The memories lingered, always and forever. The memories of the dissolving flesh, the chemicals stripping away the flesh from my face. Watching the enzymes and the molecular sieves sort out the re-usable components of my sisters.

There are four categories of Rioja red wines. The youngest wine is labelled simply, "Rioja," and it spends less than a year aging in an oak barrel. Wine that is aged for a least two years (with a least one year in oak) is labelled "Crianza". "Rioja Reserva" is aged for at least three years (with a least one year in oak). And finally, the most expensive of all: "Rioja Gran Reserva" spends at least two years in oak and at least three years aging in the bottle.

Off-world bodegas seek to emulate the quality of this fine wine. Some even claim that the wine is Rioja-like. But they are not real

I carefully source my wine from a reputable Earth dealer. I do not want to taste the counterfeit.

The captain's voice boomed over the ship's communication relay, "Mikar, I need you with me – now."

I finished my glass of wine quickly, and then rinsed my mouth with mouthwash.

The captain was pacing up and down on the bridge. The uncontrollable flashing lights of the control panel casting shadows onto her face. "What's outside on the planet? The hostile alien we call Grey Cut, what do we know about it?"

I was about to speak, but the captain hadn't finished, "We don't know enough. It's obvious that I'm going to have to go out myself. It's pointless waiting for the new crew. They'll come back infected. This is something I'll have to do for myself."

"I agree." I always agreed with my captain.

· · ·

The captain and I left the ship. We were dressed in ordinary trousers and tunics. There was no point in wearing body armor. It hadn't protected the crew.

This planet surface was lush and damp. The vegetation spiraled everywhere in a wealth of rich profusion. I could almost see the jungle growing, see the strung-run vines and the prolific fungi crawling and blending and adding another layer to the texture of the planet.

The thing that makes Rioja wine so distinctive is its oak aging. I have never seen an oak tree, but I know how it tastes. It adds the caramel, coffee, and roasted nuts flavors to white Rioja

Oak aging is the key to Rioja, but sadly this ancient technique is in decline. I have my sources to the traditional bodegas; there are always some who stay true to the old ways.

"Nasty stuff," said the captain. She kicked at a cluster of ivory white fungus that stood in her path, cracking the fruiting body and releasing a cloud of spores.

"It's a shame about the crew," I said.

"Yes, waste of resources. The energy needed to recycle their bodies, and reform them. It's an expensive job, making new copies."

"Yes." *But it wasn't as expensive as curing them.*

We walked on. The jungle was silent. No other creature walked this forest, not even the insects which I thought were a ubiquitous feature of any planet that had spawned life. Grey Cut's world was quiet, apart from our heavy footfalls, and the sound of vegetable life, sprawling, growing.

Rioja wines are usually a blend of various grape varieties. Red or tinto Rioja is my favorite. Although sometimes the occasion calls for white (blanco) or even for rosé (rosado).

"Where did the crew encounter Grey Cut?" asked the captain.

I consulted my navigation recorder. "Not too far now, Verna reported that they encountered it a half kilometer to the East."

"Verna! I've told you, time and time again, not to give the crew names. They're not real people. When you name them you add something to them. They have no right to possess names."

"And what about me?"

"What about you?" asked the captain. She swiped at the vegetation with her laser, cutting a path of destruction through the jungle, much wider than was needed for our ingress.

"You gave me a name," I said.

"You're different, Mikar. You were my first clone. When I cloned you; it was special. I suppose you could say that I think of you as a daughter."

The captain walked off the path she was cutting to examine a particularly lurid fungus. Red veins laced the mushroom's spongy flesh. When the captain smashed through the dense plant, I inhaled the scent of its damage.

"You know what I think about you," said the captain. "We shouldn't have to talk about it."

I said, "I'm thirsty."

The captain looked at closely before passing over the water bottle. "Mikar, have you been drinking again?"

"No."

"I'm very disappointed in you, Mikar."

I am ten years old, but I am fully grown.

I am the identical copy of my mother, but we are very different.

Aren't we?

Aren't we?

I need a drink.

I need a real drink.

I saw the movement in the undergrowth, grey flesh, *Grey Cut*.

The captain had seen it too, "This must be Grey Cut. Get ready, Mikar."

"Take us to your leader," shouted the captain at the tentacle. The grey, undulating rope of flesh continued to grope through the vegetation.

"Let's retrace the tentacle to the original," said the captain, striding through the undergrowth.

She is so brave. She is not afraid. I wish I was like her.

We came to a clearing, the lush vegetation was diminished, but another growth filled its place.

We saw the spherical core of grey flesh. Imagine the wildly spiraling tentacles issuing from that body, weaving and interacting in constant movement; tapering down to fine points that quested around the captain and myself, rising up and wavering around the exposed parts of our bodies. Imagine myriad tiny spiked tongues poised and ready to strike, a few centimeters from our hands and faces.

I fought the impulse to run from the threatening spikes.

"Well, we're here," shouted the captain. "What do you want?"

"Ah, the original visits me at last. Welcome." The words issued from the body of Grey Cut, a deep and resonant sound which reverberated and expanded through the quivering tentacles surrounding us.

"What have you done to my ship? I insist that you release us at once."

"But we wanted to meet the real you." The tendrils began to grow, threatening to encase our feet.

"Well, I'm here. What do you want? And why did you attack my crew?"

"I sensed that they had no value to you, and I needed to get your attention. Do they recover?"

"They have been reutilized," said the captain.

"Ah, I see. I did not realize quite how little you valued them. But each species is different, I find. It is not for me to make judgements. I want what you have, Captain. I breed slowly, but I want to have your luxury of reproduction. Renew and refresh myself until I fill the whole planet."

The captain looked doubtful. "It's against Company guidelines to let natives have technology. Besides, what makes you think that you will be able to manage the machinery?"

"My daughters learn quickly," said Grey Cut. Some of the tentacles pointed to a sprawling mass of webbed tendrils that might have been playing in the undergrowth. "We have acquired many technologies. Yours should be no different, if only you could see the wonders of our cities . . ."

"Yes, I'm sure they are a marvel," said the captain, nodding her head. "And if I agree, how will we make the exchange?"

"Captain, you can't give away technology."

The captain ignored me.

"I only need a few hours to study the cloning technology. I'm sure that I will be able to, ahem . . . reproduce it. Or my daughters will." Was there a tone of pride in the voice of Grey Cut? "How wonderful it must be to control your own spawning, to grow and replicate at will. How lucky you are, Captain."

"And then you will release the ship? If I give you this gift?"

"I will."

"That is satisfactory to me."

"How can I be sure that you'll do your part of the bargain?" asked Grey Cut. "How can we trust one another?"

"Take Mikar," said the captain, pushing me forward.

"She has value to you?" asked Grey Cut. The tentacles moved over me, trying to assess my worth.

"Yes. Mikar has some value. She's not like the others. She's been with me ten years now. She is a daughter to me."

"Mother, no! Don't use me like this." Wasted words. My mother would use me as a bargaining token – if it were expedient.

The captain frowned, "You must call me Captain, Mikar. And it'll only be for a few hours."

Grey Cut appeared satisfied. "Bring me the technology. Then we'll make the exchange. One of my daughters for yours. Once I am satisfied with the technology, I'll release your ship. Then the offspring will be released to their mothers."

I realized that Grey Cut and the captain were alike.

"Agreed," said the captain.

"Agreed," said Grey Cut.

. . .

As we walked back to the ship, I thought about the Rioja regions. There are three Rioja regions; Rioja Alta known for its old world style of wine; Rioja Alavesa producing wine with a full body and high acidity; and Rioja Baja which produces deeply colored wine with a high alcoholic volume. I have tasted them all. I considered the merits of wine from each of the regions, and remembered the joy that the different wines have given me over my short life.

After a while, I thought about something else, "We're not supposed to give out technology, Captain,"

"Who's to know? Anyway what's the alternative? To be trapped here forever?"

"You could get into a lot of trouble, Captain."

"I said, no one will ever know." It was unusual for me to question her decisions. "No one will ever know. Do you understand, Mikar?"

"Yes, Captain."

We climbed the ladder to the ship's access port. The tentacles pulsed as we moved past.

"Prepare the cloning technology for Grey Cut and load it onto some trolleys for transfer."

"As you wish," I agreed. I almost always agreed with the captain. I began to prepare the data for Grey Cut. I needed a drink.

"And fetch me a glass of that wine of yours. I feel like celebrating."

"Yes, Mother."

"Call me Captain, Mikar. Call me Captain."

"What's wrong with her?" asked Grey Cut. Her tentacles roamed over the unconscious form.

"I had to drug her. My daughter does not approve of our arrangement."

"But you want her back?" asked Grey Cut. "She still has value to you?"

"Oh yes. I want her back. She's shown something at last. Some spark of initiative. I'm proud of her. I've always wanted to say that, but I never had a reason to. She's a fine daughter."

Grey Cut pushed forward a small mass of tentacles. "Without trust, we have nothing. This is my daughter. She will go with you. The ship will be released once I've assessed the data."

"When you have assessed the cloning technology and released my ship, I will send out the final authorization codes, but I think that we can trust each other"

"The bargain is acceptable," said Grey Cut, drawing the unconscious captain into a cradle of tentacles.

T he ship pulls away from the planet. The binding tendrils have lost their cohesions and fall to the ground.

The captain sits with a glass of Rioja at her side, slowly sipping the dark colored wine.

The communications relay activates and Grey Cut's voice fills the bridge, "Captain, I'm ready to accept the authorization codes. Then we can release our daughters. I am sorry to say that there is a problem with your daughter. She seems agitated, perhaps mentally unstable. I suggest that we initiate the exchange straight away."

The ship rises effortlessly, above the clouds and prepares to enter flash space.

I would soon be free of the planet, all I needed to do was alter the ship's records and no one would suspect.

"Captain . . . Captain . . . your daughter needs to speak to you."

A familiar voice came across the console. "Mikar, don't leave me here. I love you, darling. I've always loved you. Don't leave me. At least give Grey Cut her daughter back. She's going to be very angry."

"Goodbye, Mother."

"Why, Mikar? Why?" There is a plaintive note in her voice. It is disconcerting

"Goodbye, Captain," I say. I have no intention of giving Grey Cut the authorization codes for the cloning technology; a captain could get into a lot of trouble that way.

"Mikar . . . Mikar?"

I switch off the communications relay. I do not give her the courtesy of my explanations.

A new voice speaks, "Why did you do it?" It's Grey Cut's daughter. I didn't know she could speak.

I consider for a while before I say, "I did it because I wasn't real. And when you're not real, you can do anything. I have recreated myself into the image of a captain. I am real now." Even to myself, my voice sounds a little sinister.

I must be drunk. I glance over to the wine bottle, still half-full. Incredible. Is this is what my mother felt like all of the time? I'm drunk on reality.

"Oh, okay," says Grey Cut's daughter. I must give her a name. No. I must ask her to name herself. She looks frightened. Can a mass of tentacles look frightened?

I try to be kind, "Don't worry. Everything's going to be okay."

I raise my glass of Rioja in salute to the diminishing view of the planet. "And believe me, my friend, you're better off without your mother."

CRACKING OPEN A COLD ONE

J.B. TONER

As the Prince of Denmark observed long ago, "There are more things in Heaven and Earth than are dreamt of in your philosophy." Unwarily, he neglected to mention hell, perhaps because he had an iambic pentameter to maintain. Nonetheless, the remark holds true of all three locales; and when the citizens of one sphere unveil themselves in another, drama rarely fails to result.

My name, friend, is Friar Clump. I live and work in the asteroid town of Lindisfarne, deep in the glimmering reaches of Sagittarius B2. And if ever you've harbored a doubt about the Lord's goodness, I refute it thus: that seraphic expanse is made up of billions of gallons of Space Alcohol. My brother monks and I harvest this bounty and prayerfully refine it into beer for all the peoples of the cosmos. And because truth is greater than humility, I cannot conceal from you that our blessed brew, though made of earthly stuff, is to be counted among the elixirs of paradise.

I was aboard a good ship called the *Long Haul*, accompanying a delivery to a new buyer in the neon city of Enoch, far from home. Enoch lies in a guttering galaxy, and colonies are sparse. When our reserves grew low, we had to stop at an unmanned fueling station orbiting a small, barren moon. Being a rather inexperienced traveler, I left my cabin and headed for the bridge to watch the process.

"Hullo, padre," said Captain Adriana Kingsford, a tall, greying woman of staunch character.

"Good evening, Captain. Permission to enter the bridge?"

"Granted. We're just stopping to refuel."

"Yes, I gathered. Are those the pumps?"

"Yup. Take about half an hour. We'll be at Enoch by morningtide."

"Lovely, thank you."

A thunk went through the deck as the fueling rods grappled onto us. Ernest Beauregard, the first mate, glanced at the captain and gave a silent nod, presumably to indicate that all was proceeding as it ought.

"All right, Bo, you've got the conn," she said. "I'm gonna go check on the—*what the hell is that?*"

I jumped at her tone and stared at her finger. Then, following her gaze, I saw a bizarrely beautiful woman in a red dress stepping out from the station onto the nearest fuel rod. For the merest sliver of a moment, I didn't understand the captain's reaction. And then it registered on me that the lady in red was walking, unsuited, through the ghastly dark of outer space.

We stood open-mouthed as the woman pushed gently off the fuel rod and came wafting like a red zephyr toward the *Long Haul*'s hull. Could she be an angel, I wondered? But there was—there was something in her smile. Something other than heavenly.

The voice of Kayla Southerly, our mechanic, crackled on the intercom, and I jumped again. "Cap'n? Are y'all seein' this?"

"I dunno what I'm seeing, Kay."

Then Ernest pointed. "Captain."

A pale thin man and a second woman were now gliding across the rods as well. An eerie dread coiled within me, and I nearly yelped out, "Away! Get us away!"

"Can't uncouple from a dock while you're shipping fuel, padre. Not unless the system recognizes an emergency."

"We're being boarded! Surely—"

"Not according to this reading," Ernest said grimly. "They don't scan as life forms."

"Robots, Bo?"

"No ma'am. System'd recognize robot boarders as a threat."

From the intercom: "Oh my goblins, they're spooks! We're gettin' boarded by spooks!"

"Calm down, Kay, they can't get inside. And oh yeah, there's no such thing as spooks."

The two newcomers were heading for the airlock. The woman in red reached the ship and, like some ghoulish arachnid, began to crawl across the hull toward the view-screen.

"She got weapons?" the captain asked tightly.

Ernest shook his head.

"Then we sit tight. Let her scratch at the window all she wants."

The red lady splayed herself across the view-screen with a cruel and crimson smile. As we stood watching her long dark hair float languidly about her, she focused her gaze on Ernest. He gazed back for a long moment, and the fear and confusion seemed to leave him. Then, suddenly, he jerked forward and slapped a button on the console.

"Bo!" the captain howled.

Before I could wonder what fresh horror was upon us, the ship's computer spoke: "Stand by for airlock ingress."

Ernest blinked and frowned. "What—what just—"

"You let the damned things inside, is what just happened. Now prepare to receive hostiles!"

"I—yes, ma'am." He shook off his daze and opened a compartment in the bulkhead, producing two photon rifles for himself and the captain.

"Stay here, padre!" she shouted, and the two of them dashed from the bridge.

I obeyed for a moment, chewing on her chance phrase: "damned things." The men of science have found and forged many wonders since Our Lord arrived in the stable; but the natural world dwells cheek by jowl with the spirit realm, no less now than in the day of that Grand Miracle when heaven trod the dust of earth. I glanced up at the view-screen, where the red lady was still grinning down at me, and then I clutched my crucifix and sprinted from the bridge.

The airlock had already irised shut behind the boarders. The pale man was standing in the hallway, leering at Ernest and Adriana, as I came up behind my shipmates. Of the woman there was no sign.

". . . fully licensed ship of the Peace," the captain was saying, her rifle and tone both level. "Just tell us what you want, and maybe we all walk away from this with our brains in our skulls."

"Don't worry, Captain," the invader replied, and his voice was a razor in silk. "I promise you'll want what we want."

Then another hard sweet voice: "Look what I found!" The strange woman came sauntering back up the hallway with Kayla in her clutch. She was holding our stout mechanic up in the air with one hand, negligently, as if carrying a kitten by the scruff, and Kayla was frozen with terror. The woman opened her mouth wide, and her incisors began to grow and sharpen.

Adriana shouted, "Let her—" but Ernest had already opened fire. A blast of force hit the strange woman in the chest, and should have splattered her lungs all over the hallway. But she and the pale man merely laughed. The woman lowered her fangs toward Kayla's neck.

And then I moved. Or no, the One Whom I serve moved within me, and I had just enough will and grace to respond. Lunging forward with the cross held high, I roared in a voice far greater than my own, "Back, in the Name of Christ! Back, Satan, I command you!"

The invaders hissed like cats and cringed away, shielding their faces. Ernest darted forward, caught Kayla by the arm, and thrust her behind him. "Toldja they was spooks," she stammered.

"Get to the escape pod, Kay," Adriana ordered. "We're right behind you."

"Yes, Cap'n."

She fled, and the three of us began to back away. The two boarders followed us as closely as they dared, snarling and spitting, their eyes now shot with blood and hate. Ernest and the captain stood at my right and my left, still aiming their useless weapons, as I brandished the blade of Christ and bellowed His words at our foes. "Get thee behind me, Satan! God the Father compels you! God the Son compels you! God the Holy Spirit compels you!"

As we passed a branch of the corridor, the pale man turned and sped off down another hall with the speed of a nightmare. The woman continued her slow, flinching advance, spasming forward to swipe at me with her lengthening claws as I jabbed with the crucifix like a cornered lion-tamer.

"Dammit," Adriana muttered. "That guy's gonna get around behind us. There's no way we make it to the pod."

We rounded a corner, and there he was. "Careful what you ask for, holy man," he jeered. "You said you wanted Satan behind you."

Adriana punched a button on the bulkhead, and a large metal door slid open to our left. "In here, padre. At least we can get our backs to a wall."

As Ernest and I followed her into the room beyond, I realized it was the cargo bay. Off to one side were four huge pallets of Lindisfarne's finest beer. On the other side, a single porthole gazed out upon the soundless majesty of the stars. At least it was a fitting last view of God's Creation.

The creatures advanced, now grinning again, and we retreated slowly to the far bulkhead. My arm was tiring, and my will was beginning to waver. "Back!" I shouted again, but my voice cracked, and they laughed at me.

"You should have stuck to making beer, old man," said the woman. "All you've done is work up our thirst."

And the Light of Heaven dawned.

"Captain, shoot the beer!" I shouted.

"Say what?"

"*Shoot the blessed beer!*"

She and Ernest opened fire on the pallets. Wood and glass debris exploded all around us, and the precious brew deluged the cargo room. The two invaders shrieked, twisted, and burst into rampaging flames. We hit the deck, splashing into foamy head, as the cold creatures were fierily consumed.

Then, quiet. Flakes of ash came sifting down to settle into the hoppy pool around us. For a long moment, no one moved or spoke.

"Okay," Adriana said finally. "Let's get the hell outta here."

"There's still one of 'em clingin' onto the ship," Ernest said.

"Good. Once we make the Jump, she can float out there alone till the end of time. Just don't make eye contact."

"Yes ma'am."

"Captain, if I may? I believe it will still be some minutes before the system allows us to uncouple. Perhaps the best thing is for us to invite Ms. Southerly back to the cargo hold, and the four of us to investigate the wreckage for surviving bottles. It would be a shame if every drop went to waste."

"Works for me, padre. Although considering it saved our lives, I wouldn't exactly call it a waste."

"Ah, but you haven't tasted Lindisfarne brew."

"Well." She smiled, and the light came back into her eyes. "Let's fix that."

RED DEATH

RICHARD BEAUCHAMP

"Holy shit…" Lana Briggs said in stunned amazement. "Mitch, get your ass over here, I think we just hit the jack pot!" she told her shipmate, and Mitch Connell floated over from the refinement station he was at, processing the last of the small bits of precious metals they got from their previous salvage trip. They both stood peering over the LCD screen showing the dark vessel floating through the cluttered debris of some ancient pieces of wreckage. Mitch studied the markings on the large ship closely, and noted the display, "Ship Class: E-18 mobile excavation and drill series" in the classification bracket where the probe had run diagnostics on the derelict vessel. Realizing he was looking at an old school Russian research ship, Mitch lit up with excitement and clapped Lana on the back.

"We sure as hell did hit the jackpot. That there is an old-ass Sokolov digger, made back before they had nanocomposite metals to make ships ultra light. That metal beast is built like a tank and probably has enough raw titanium ore and gold plating to totally clean out the scrap yard appraisers. If we manage to strip her down and haul it back with us we will be made for at least eight or nine months minimum. What's the status on the ship dexterity? Is it boardable?"

"Diagnostics show some slight hull damage, probably from a stray impact, and a small tear on the starboard side, but the room it's in looks to be sealed off. Structural integrity of the docking bay is 95 percent, so we should be good to go." she said, sounding like a giddy child.

"Excellent, because I need to see just how many goodies are aboard and check the black box. That thing looks like it's been floating around a couple hundred years and we're gonna need the flight recorder to give to the claims agency in case there's cold ones aboard. I'll go prep the scout: get suited up. See you down there." the large man said, and floated down the hallway, his bulk making his journey awkward.

Lana, who was much smaller and dexterous than Mitch, easily caught up to him as she soared through the hallway and rounded the corner to where the small two person intercept craft was waiting for them.

Much like the planets they had inhabited, the early years of human space exploration always left trails of litter and pollution in their wake as the species slowly refined their crude methods of transporting goods across the stars. As the technology improved, older obsolete ships and stations were simply left to drift in the heavens, occasionally falling into a planet's orbit and becoming a problem if the planet was inhabited. Sometimes ships were also abandoned because of crew expiration, as many early journeys into deep space were fatal due to ill preparation, poorly built jump drives and ignorance of worm hole travel at the time.

This created a booming business among what the colonies had termed "junk pirating" where skilled pilots with strong stomachs, a lot of spare time, and extensive knowledge in the raw materials markets would build scavenger ships to intercept these discarded monuments to human engineering as technological progress allowed them to make big money on mankind's failings and occasionally get rewarded for helping identify pilots who were MIA.

As the years bore on and humans progressed in their technologies and knowledge of the stars, the number of ghost ships and easily accessible material caches decreased to the point where junkers such as

Mitch and Lana were having to scour ever deeper into the edge of their home solar system to hit pay dirt. The old Russian digger was a needle in a very, very large haystack, and Lana had wondered upon the statistical luck they must have had to stumble upon it this far outside the Milky Way. She knew that geological teams were sent out on daring expeditions long ago to find intelligent life on the other side of the solar system, with many of them never returning due to the primitive shoddily built jump drives, which the research vessels were the first to get as scientists kept exploring deeper, desperate to find new life, and new planets to call home.

However, some of those ancient ships were brought back into accessible traffic areas as the natural inertia of their trajectory would alter due to planetary perturbations, occasionally spitting the forgotten ships back towards populated areas of space over many light years. That must have been the case for the E18, as its maiden launch date appeared to have been over three hundred years ago. It was as much an historical artifact as it was a goldmine of raw resources.

Yet as they drew closer to the ship, excitement turned to anxiousness, as it always did when they were getting ready to board. Mitch and Lana had been on over forty salvage runs together since opening up shop five years ago, and there was simply no way of telling what you were going to float into when you forced open the bay doors into a dark intergalactic tomb. Lana and Mitch had both seen their share of corpses whose remains were always perfectly preserved and freeze dried in the oxygen deprived vacuum of space. That was until you jump started the engine and the artificial environment kicked in, whereupon the corpses, which had sometimes been dead for over a hundred years, would begin to rapidly putrefy into a terrible smelling goop inside their EVO suits. That was the ethically tricky part of the job, trying to locate and respectfully dispose of the human remains before you got the power turned back on. They had both learned that lesson the hard and disgusting way one or two times in the beginning, and made sure never to repeat such mistakes.

Keeping this in mind, Lana mentally prepared herself for whatever it was that lay beyond the blast bay doors. It could be totally empty, or they could find mutilated bodies as the occasional space fever made ill selected crew members go crazy and do terrible things. She tried to keep her mind off those grisly memories as they decelerated and approached the tubular receptacle of the docking bay.

"I'll take care of the doors, you ready to breach?" Mitch asked, but Lana was already depressurizing the small cockpit and preparing to pop the windshield. It was a solid routine they had down pat by now, and muscle memory took over. Mitch would get out, float his way around to the small exterior terminal override panel found on the side of every Federation standard ship, disengage the magnetic locks and then pry open the doors with a magnetic winch, something he was suited for given his brute strength,. Then Lana would gently glide the scout through the narrow gap and bingo, they were in. Find any human remains, relieve them of their ID chips for the database and catapult them out into space or use the ships incinerator if it had one. Take inventory, fire up the ship, and pilot it back to their massive towing station, or if the ship wasn't operable they would take the towing station to it. Just another job.

Except it didn't feel that way, not this time. The interior of the docking bay seemed especially foreboding as the small observation light at the front of the scout illuminated a catastrophic mess of floating debris. Smashed and mangled bits of electronics and cables mostly, she could see the broken windows of the boarding terminal. She could also see her first body floating serenely amidst the levitating chaos as the magnetic receptors on the scout clanked firmly to the metal runway. The corpse's back was to her, but she noticed with a sinking heart how small it was. *Oh god, don't let it be a child* she thought to herself. She tried to tell herself it was just more worksite jitters, which she got occasionally. But this wasn't just excited anticipation. Something felt wrong here, but she couldn't explain what. Despite this she would keep her mouth shut. Mitch was a respectful coworker, but any sign of feminine distress on the job was usually enough to get him in a patronizing *'are you sure you're cut out for this kinda work?'* attitude that she absolutely hated. She nonchalantly gave Mitch the thumbs up as he successfully navigated through the maelstrom of junk that was floating around.

"Jesus, those Ruskies must have had one hell of a rowdy party in here before they shut down." Mitch said through her earpiece, marveling at the scope of random destruction.

"Yeah, also there's a cold one to the north of you, I spotted it coming in. I'm guessing we're gonna have more remains aboard. Let's just focus on getting the bodies rounded up so we can get the lights on." she said, trying not to let the anxiousness come through in her voice. She wanted more than anything for the juice to be on right now. Most ghost ships were dark in principle, but at least with a run close to orbit they could get some backlight in through observation windows of the ship to go with their flashlights. But they were on the dark side of Orion, and there were zero windows on the ship save for the captain's bridge. The darkness in here seemed to hold physical weight. It was so dense, she could almost feel its mass pressing in at the narrow cone of light her flashlight emitted, eager to snuff out any and all illumination.

She was getting ready to approach the corpse she saw on the way in and search the flight suit for ID, but she paused for a moment to look to the eastern wall by the entrance to the terminal. Her flashlight shown a bright red message spray painted in Russian on it. The words were quick and jagged, their foreign symbols appeared scribed by a frantic hand.

"...Hey Mitch? Can you read Russian?" she asked, pointing towards the graffiti.

Mitch grabbed onto one of the handrails to stop his motion and studied the words. "Hmmm... nope. But I can snap a picture and send it to the worthless ship AI we have and see if it can translate it for us." He did so with the helmet mounted camera he had on, which also ran real time bio-monitoring stats and live feed to their salvage ship an uncomfortable distance away. "Artemis, can you photo analyze the text in the picture I just sent you into English please?"

"Pr..r...rocessing r...reque...que...uest..." a glitchy female voice told them through their suit intercoms.

"I'm sure you are, worthless cheap bitch. Don't get your hopes up with her," he begrudgingly told Lana. "Knew I shoulda nutted up the extra forty grand for the Athena series."

Mitch continued on ahead, sweeping the area with his flashlight while Lana approached the corpse. She slowly turned it over and watched with frightened bewilderment as the flight suit seemed to lose its shape as she spun it around. As she got a glimpse into the helmet of the deceased, she reared back in surprise. Instead of the usual pale, bloated eyed face of a vacuumed corpse there was only the shrunken, shriveled face of someone of unidentifiable gender. The skin was slowly flaking away like ash inside the helmet, and the eyes, no more than small dehydrated gray raisins, rolled around crudely in the cavernous sockets. The hair which was short and cropped, was an ashen gray, as if something had sucked every ounce of color and life from this person.

"Mitch, come back here and take a look at this." she said, unable to hide the tremble in her voice. She mentally cursed herself for letting this benign peculiarity spook her.

But Mitch was nowhere to be seen, and for a moment she panicked as she couldn't find him or hear a response. Then she heard his thick husky voice, but with his own small flavor of fear in it. She couldn't think of a time where she had ever heard Mitch Connell sound afraid in her life.

"What... the... fuck..." he said slowly, and she assumed he had discovered his own corpse in the bizarre mummified condition, or worse.

"Mitch? Where are you?" she asked, pushing off a wall and towards his last seen location.

"Down the hall and to the left. I just found someone but they're... they're... I don't know. There's nothing to him but skin and bones, and not even that. I can feel him falling apart in his suit." he said, revulsion thick in his voice.

She frantically scrambled around the corner, losing her grip in the zero gravity and almost crashing into him as she rounded the corner.

"Jesus, watch out!" he yelled.

"Sorry!" she said, and observed the corpse Mitch held "I found one just like that in the docking bay. Whatever happened to them occurred before the ship depressurized. You wouldn't see this kind of decay unless the corpses were over a thousand years old. But we were still a one planet species back then." she said, desperately trying to rack her brain for some logical reason as to the corpses' extremely weathered state.

"What the hell could of caused this? It looks like someone hooked them up to a shop vac and damn near drained them of…well… *everything*. I've never seen anything like this." He said, and there was a momentary uncomfortable silence as they stared at the husk of astronaut.

Finally, Lana spoke, abandoning her tough girl act as she saw she wasn't the only one thoroughly creeped out.

"I don't like this Mitch. I know this place is a gold mine but… Jesus. What happened to these guys?" she asked more to herself than to him.

"Your guess is as good as mine. Let's press on, I got the blueprints loaded in. This place gives me the creeps too, but we came here for a reason. We both got loans to pay back and stomachs to feed. If we hadn't stumbled upon this ship we would be screwed. Let's get the bodies accounted for, and I'm sure we will find a simple answer to this soon enough. Let's not split up though, this place is big and I don't wanna have to hunt you down. I know that's gonna take longer but… something doesn't feel right here." Lana had no qualms with sticking together; the thought of navigating these long abandoned halls alone gave her a chill. Reluctantly, they plunged into the bowels of the ship.

They scoured the first two levels in the dark save for their flashlight beams, where they navigated long, cramped corridors filled with random debris and the occasional floating corpse, each one in that same diminished state. Every corner they rounded was a test in self-discipline to confront the adjacent corridor, but slowly and painstakingly they corralled up all the corpses they could find and tied them up using some rope they found, though by the time they had gotten the bodies back to the flight deck they had basically disintegrated to dust in their suits. When they got to the third level of the ship they had close to ten bodies, if you could call them that, and were coming up on their eleventh casualty when Mitch stopped and shined his light at a hallway legend, all in Russian.

"Hey, I think this might be the generator room, I recognize that symbol, universal for jump drive. Let me see if I can at least get the lights going without turning on the oxygen pumps so we can speed this up a bit." he said and they headed down a T shaped junction where they proceeded left. They entered a huge room which held the large turbines and encased coils of the engine and jump drive were. Mitch did a quick shine over of the hardware and determined it all looked in good shape, despite being archaic engine models. He found the small circular console in the center of the room and plugged his HUD into it. He was then able to jump start the console online using his suit's power pack.

"Now, let's see if I can find an English menu on this son of a bitch," he said and started fiddling with menu screens. While he did this Lana explored cautiously, shining her light around and observing the peculiar pattern of cracks she had noticed around the rest of the ship. Strange long black crevices that went up the walls and sometimes scaled around equipment, as if some massive corrosive laser had laid a seared path erratically around the interior of the ship.

She was floating up to one sharp column of the black line, noticing up close it wasn't a crack, it looked more like blackened ice, with a sort of reflective, organic surface, almost like flattened or dehydrated tree roots. She was only inches from it, studying it intently when Mitch yelled.

"Aha! Mitch the genius, how does he do it?" he proclaimed in a grand boasting voice. A few seconds later Lana shielded her eyes as harsh, white light filled her world. Her eyes adjusted, and she exhaled an amazed breath as she took in the real dimensions of the room and ship, which now felt much bigger. She also got a better look at the black... *stuff* that was laced all over the room, with one narrow tendril reaching on the floor right up to the console Mitch was standing at. It seemed to be concentrated here in the engine room, at least compared to its traces in the rest of the ship she had seen.

"All right, let's hustle and gather up the rest of the bodies now that we can actually see what the hell we are doing. I can only run the auxiliary power cell for fifteen minutes before we run out of enough juice to crank the engines, so let's not waste any time. Come on." Lana followed her partner down the final two levels where the cafeteria and laboratory were.

The cafeteria and crew's quarters surprisingly didn't have any bodies, just a lot of floating kitchenware bric-a-brac, although Lana took note of a few floating butcher knives that had what appeared to be dried blood crusted on the blades floating around.

They descended to the bottom level, the laboratory, which featured several partitioned off glass rooms with various geological instruments floating around inside of them. A large digging rover was chained down next to a few other transport rovers, and Lana could see that whatever the black crusty stuff was had almost completely covered the digging rover, giving it a vague shadow quality, as if it had originated with and then grew from the vehicle. Over to the far corner they could see where the wall had exploded outwards and they were afforded a jagged view of space.

"Found our hull breach. Looks like it was self contained though. Interesting." Mitch said nonchalantly.

"I keep seeing all this tar like crap around, what is it do you think?" Lana asked Mitch, pointing to the black crust encased rover. The crust seemed to cover the outer edges of the tear where the metal had ballooned out, as if though it were there to seal it shut, which it almost did.

"Could be chemical flame retardant that was sprayed and then frozen after the power went off. Or busted cooling pipes leaking god knows what and freezing solid. Who knows, who cares? No bodies down here, let's head back." They made their way back up to the flight deck and corralled the tethered group of suited dust bunnies out the pried open launch bay doors and gave them a shove out to into space. Lana then put the acquired ID bio-tags into a pocket in her space suit and they headed back down to the engine room.

They cleared the area around the console of debris as best they could so as not to be injured by falling material, and then braced themselves for the jarring crash as gravity and artificial atmosphere kicked on and everything floating in the ship came crashing back down. She felt the vibrating of the huge engines start to fire up, and then a hard pulling sensation followed by a thunderous thud as a whole E class ship worth of random derelict crap fell to the floor. Gravity reoriented their bodies to the floor, a disorienting sensation.

"Oxygen level reading 0% percent. Beginning air cycle," an automated voice told them.

"How did you get it to speak English?"

Mitch just grinned.

"Should be able to un-suit in about ten minutes. May as well get comfortable while we pilot this beast back to the ship. I'm gonna see if I can do a rollback on the pilot's log and figure out what the hell happened to these guys." He began exploring the ship's information terminal diligently.

While he was focused on that, Lana went back to staring at the blackened trails of chemical fluid or whatever it was. It looked slightly different than it did a minute ago, but she couldn't put her finger on what it was. Five minutes of silence passed.

"Oxygen levels at 50%, approaching stasis." the voice chirped from the ships sound system.

Then Lana realized what it was. The black stuff was changing color. Slowly, almost imperceptibly, she saw the glossy black crust begin to slowly bloom into a dark violet, and then from a dark violet into…

"Hey Lana? You should come look at this. I can't make any sense of it. Maybe the translator on this behemoth is busted or something"

Lana walked over, suddenly feeling a strong tension build around her, as if though they were coming to the precipice of some horrible realization.

She glanced down at the rectangular terminal screen and read the captains log, which was dated July 8th, 2125, over a hundred years ago.

WE HAVE CALLED IT RED DEATH
IT IS SENTIENT
HOME ORIGIN IS EUROPA
THE SHIP MUST BE CLEANSED
OXYGEN MUST REMAIN AT 0%
DO NOT COME FIND US, IGNORE DISTRESS BEACONS

BEWARE THE RED DEATH
IT MUST NOT BREATHE
OXYGEN BRINGS DEATH

T hey stared at the bizarre log for a minute or so before the on board AI chirped back in and snapped them out of their contemplation. "Oxygen levels at 85%, hull breach detected in research engineering sublevel A. Obstruction detected in flight bay, unable to proceed. Stand by."

"I don't get it. The last captain's log sign in before this shit was two weeks prior, and the captain seemed excited. Apparently, they just left some ice titan moon with soil samples they were going ape shit over, literally a ship full of nerds just drooling over–"

But Mitch was cut off as Atermis chimed in "Te…Te…text encryption analys…sis c…c…complete. Message rel-rel-relay sent to your h…hud…" and suddenly their screen visors were filled with generated computer text which read:

DO NOT TRY AND SAVE US
IGNORE ALL DISTRESS BEACONS
RED DEATH MUST DIE
SHIP MUST BE CLEANSED
OXYGEN BRINGS DEATH

Suddenly Lana felt an overwhelming dread fill her. "Shut it off, the oxygen. *Now.* I don't know what the hell Red Death is but clearly these guys didn't want the place back up and running." she said. She looked around and was horrified at what she saw. The black turning purple veins that coated the hallways were now a deep blood red, and they were *moving*–pulsating and slowly spreading, growing along the walls like rapidly growing tree roots. "Mitch, let's get the fuck out of here! Shut that shit off and–"

But there was a scream and a loud slurping sound that interrupted her and she looked back towards the console.

Mitch had been standing on a patch of the previously innate material when he was accessing the terminal, not giving the stuff much attention in his always rational mind. Now the reanimated viscera had completely engulfed the leg of his space suit, and was making its way up his torso, with one silk thin tendril racing up towards his helmet, lining itself along the thin seal of his helmet baffle and somehow penetrating into it. He flailed and screamed, but was unable to move, his left foot now firmly rooted to the metallic floor.

"Mitch! Holy shit!" she screamed, and tried to pull the growing veins of alien life off him. But they did not tear or give, simply elongated themselves like warm toffee as she pulled and pulled, until she herself was covered in thin, writhing strands of the stuff. OXYGEN BRINGS DEATH was burned into her mind, and in the chaos she managed to bend over the console and try to shut off the power, but the roots of the red abomination had began webbing itself around the touch screen, obstructing her from inputting any kind of command as if though it sensed what she was trying to do.

"R...R...runnnn!" a thin voice emanated from her suit intercom, and she looked over in horror to see that Mitch, a man larger than life and built like a bull, was slowly diminishing in size in his suit, the thin veins of alien life burrowing into his ears and nose, pulsating and throbbing as it drank greedily from the man's immense essence. His once broad stone slab face was now gaunt and emaciated, and his whole body twitched and trembled as the thing feasted.

She ran, sprinting with all her might, down the narrow corridors, claustrophobia and blind terror coalescing into a maddening energy that sent her rocketing through the ship. The thin strands that had engulfed her when trying to free Mitch finally reached their stretched limit and let loose with wet tendon-like snapping sounds as she exited the room. All around her, the once blackened crust was plumping up and turning red, like some corrupted rose bloom. The veiny strands reached greedily out towards her as she vaulted up the stairways towards her scout.

It was simply waiting for someone to thaw it, she thought frantically as the mysterious cryptic messages left by the Russian research team now held a terrible clarity in their meaning.

She made her way towards the flight deck, hyperventilating, leg muscles burning from running in her heavy suit. She stole one look back before entering the hangar and saw that the entire corridor was webbed in a mass of pulsating red. She took a deep breath and tried to steady herself, she had a good forty feet on the growing mass but was it gaining quickly. She started climbing over the fallen debris towards the scout when she saw with sinking terror that the blast bay doors were shut, the pneumatic winch lay pinched between the two massive doors like a flattened accordion as the power had enforced an automatic reset.

"No, no no!" she screamed and looked around frantically.

She climbed on top of a mound of junk and tried to look for the small circular portholes that meant an emergency life pod station. She wondered if they even had life pods on ships this old, and it didn't help that all the damn labels were Russian. She scrambled around frantically scanning the walls, and looking back towards the terminal door seeing that the red roots were now at the edge of the doorway and spreading.

She ran south along one wall until she found what she was looking for, twelve rows of circular portholes, the red ejection lights lit up on all but one, at the far end closest to the terminal doorway. She sprinted for it and slammed the green "open" button. The small circular porthole slid away with agonizing slowness. She could see the human sized pneumatic tube slowly being elevated for entry.

"Come the fuck onnnnnnnnnn!" she moaned, slamming on the wall trying to will the life pod to make its way faster.

The growth was in the room now, rapidly blossoming on the high walls in great spider web shapes, with one fat straight vein growing slowly but steadily towards her, a gestating finger eager to devour. It was halfway across the hangar, snaking around debris and closing to one hundred feet. Then fifty feet, picking up speed as if though it sensed her near escape.

There was a cheery sounding chime as the life pod was locked into the launch tube and the clear pod door opened. A pleasant sounding woman's voice spoke to her in Russian, probably telling her the tube was ready and to please enter calmly. She ignored it as she grabbed onto the handrail above the porthole and slid her way into the tube right as the tendrils were about to close in on her foot, immediately closing the small porthole behind her. She strapped herself in and hit the green launch button that hung over her head on a small panel. She watched as the exterior bay door for the tube slid slowly open, yellow caution lights swirling in the narrow metal launch corridor. She looked up and saw that the metal reception door was bulging in as the focused mass of the alien growth pushed against it.

Finally, she saw the circular porthole into the abyss, and hit the launch button right as the reception door caved in. There was a great pushing sensation as the torpedo shot itself away from the ship, G forces slamming her into the seat. She looked up in time to see a blossoming veiny mass of the growth get ripped out into space from explosive decompression, and it began slowly withering back into the black crust.

Lana began to sob hysterically in her helmet as her brain tried to process what just happened, understanding that a man she once thought invincible was now a weathered ghost, understanding that she had just encountered the first known instance of non human intelligent life. She cried hard for perhaps ten minutes while the pod soared through space, waiting for her to engage the rescue beacon. As she pulled herself together, she reached blindly through tear streaked eyes and hit the toggle, which would alert any ship within two hundred thousand miles of her location. Then she looked down as she felt a peculiar tingling sensation in her foot, and saw the red mass blooming around her feet.

OUR SINCEREST GRATITUDE

Dragon's Roost Press would like to extend a planet sized thank you to all of those individuals who helped make our crowdsourcing campaign successful.

The Creative Fund

Stoo Goff

Rocky Lee

One Free Elephant

Sophia

Liam Spinage

MontiLee Stormer

Liz T

Zach

Jude Reid

Bill Emerson

Bert Cieslak

Raptor

Ken MacGregor

Dirck de Lint

Duane Eisele

Valerie Williams

Hay Pips

Jen Haeger

Yavanna Reynolds

Willem De Lint

Holly Harvey

Brandon Butler

Mike Hungerford

Stu Glennie

Tany Baruffi

Saban Topak

Erin Himrod

Nicole E Castle

And two donors who wished to remain anonymous.

ABOUT THE CONTRIBUTORS

Mike Barretta ("Black Lagoon") is a retired U.S. Naval Aviator and currently works for a defense contractor as a maintenance test pilot. He holds a Master's degree in Strategic Planning from the Naval Post-Graduate School, and English from the University of West Florida. His stories have appeared in *Baen's Universe, Redstone, New Scientist, Orson Scott Card's Intergalactic Medicine Show* and various anthologies such as *War Stories: New Military Science Fiction, The Year's Best Military Scifi and Space Opera,* and the *Young Explorer's Adventure Guide.*

Richard Beauchamp ("Red Death") is a horror writer from North America who's been writing dark speculative fiction and horror for a couple of years. You can find his works published in various magazines and anthologies including Gehenna and Hinnom's *2017 Year's Best Body Horror* anthology, Darkwater Syndicate's *Postcards From The Void* anthology and Gypsum Sound Tale's *Thuggish Itch: Viva Las Vegas* issue, just to name a few.

Brandon Butler ("AstroNosferatu and the Invisible Void") is a Canadian chap from Halifax, Nova Scotia currently living, working and writing in Toronto, Ontario. A former winner of the *Writers of the*

Future Contest, his latest work will be forthcoming in *Helios Quarterly Magazine,* Third Flatiron Publishing's *Infinite Lives: Short Tales of Longevity* anthology and the *Laughing At Shadows* anthology from Bad Dream Entertainment. He can be reached at his Twitter handle, @2BWritingStuff

Katie Davenport ("Ashes, Ashes") has been writing for as long as she can remember. She graduated from Hillsdale College in 2018 with a BA in both English and Art, and now works as a full time editor and illustrator, and part time freelancer. She lives in Louisville, KY, with her husband, Tim.

Dirck de Lint ("The Moon Forest") lives with his wife, son, and a prime number of cats on the Canadian prairies. In addition to writing, he devotes a foolish amount of time to putting old fountain pens back into working order. His writing has appeared on *Pseudopod, AE: The Canadian SF Review* and on his own site, dirckwrites.wordpress.com.

Buzz Dixon ("Spider in a Space Helmet") is a long time writer in TV animation, films, graphic novels, comic books, video games, short stories, and soon in novels for the YA market. His most notable credits are as one of the writers on the original *G.I. Joe* and *Transformers* series; the creator and packager of *Serenity,* the best selling Christian manga (not to be confused with the TV show); and as the writer of the *Terminator 3* video game. He has had short fiction published in *Mike Shayne's Mystery Magazine,* the *Pan Book Of Horror* stories, *National Lampoon,* and most recently in *Analog.*

Indiana author **James Dorr**'s ("Atoms") latest book is a novel-in-stories from Elder Signs Press, *Tombs: A Chronicle of Latter-Day Time of Earth.* Working mostly in dark fantasy/horror with some forays into science fiction and mystery, his *The Tears of Isis* was a 2013 Bram Stoker Award® finalist for Superior Achievement in a Fiction Collection, while other books include *Strange Mistresses: Tales of Wonder and Romance, Darker Loves: Tales of Mystery and Regret,* and his all-poetry *Vamps (A Retrospective).* He has also been a technical writer, an editor on a regional magazine, a full time non-fiction freelancer, and a semi-professional musician, and currently harbors a Goth cat named Triana.

Chris Edwards ("Government Issue") co-writes an audio-drama podcast called Tales from the Aletheian Society (https://www. hunterhoose.co.uk/) which is now producing its third series after a recent successful kickstarter campaign. He has also done a ton of background/plot writing for Profound Decisions, a large LRP company in the UK, and run various weird and wonderful LRP events of his own.

Sarah Hans ("Nana") is an award-winning writer, editor, and teacher whose stories have appeared in more than 30 publications, including *The Arcanist* and *Pseudopod*. You can read more of Sarah's short stories in the collection *Dead Girls Don't Love*, published by Dragon's Roost Press, or on her Patreon at https://www.patreon.com/sarahhans. You can also find her on twitter under the handle @steampunkpanda.

Jen Haeger ("Cold Comfort") is a veterinarian turned Forensic Science Master's student turned geek author and beekeeper. She has previously published a paranormal romance trilogy, *Moonlight Medicine*, an U.P. paranormal thriller, *Miles from Manistique*, and a five-minutes-in-the-future, detective thriller, *Whispers of a Killer* (WHISPs Book 1). Her short stories "Alchemical Reminiscence of Death," "Ferris Wheel," and "That Won't Hold Up in Court" have won honorable mentions in the Writers of the Future Contest, and her short story, "Snick," was recently published in *Ghostlight, the Magazine of Terror*. She currently resides in Ann Arbor, MI with her husband and two orange tabbies.

Hillary Lyon ("Bellerophon's Gambit") is a life-long lover of speculative- and science-fiction, Hillary Lyon's stories have appeared in *365tomorrows, Theme of Absence, Black Petals, Lorelei Signal, Night to Dawn*, and *Tales from the Moon Lit Path*, among others. Her work has also appeared in numerous anthologies, such as *Night in New Orleans: Bizarre Beats from the Big Easy, Thuggish Itch: Viva Las Vegas, Dread*

State, and *White Noise & Ouija Boards: Ghosts & Hauntings.* She's also an illustrator for sci-fi, horror & pulp fiction magazines. Having lived in France, Brazil, Canada, and several states in the US, she now resides in southern Arizona.

Hailey Piper ("Hairy Jack") is the author of *An Invitation to* Darkness from Demain Publishing and *The Possession of Natalie Glasgow.* Her short fiction has appeared in *Blood Bath Literary Zine, The Bronzeville Bee,* and *Black Rainbow,* among other publications. Having grown up in haunted woods, she can now be found haunting www.haileypiper.com or Twitter via @HaileyPiperSays.

Jude Reid ("Thin Air") is a Glasgow based horror writer who creates things to unwind in the gaps between full time work, chasing after her kids and trying to wear out a border collie. She is an avid Zombies! Run fan, a keen student of ITF Tae Kwon Do and drinks a powerful load of coffee. You can find some of her work at www.hunterhoose.co.uk.

Science fiction and horror are **Mariah Southworth**'s ("The Silver Crown") preferred genres, both for writing and reading. Her previous publications include my science fiction story, "The Sound of His Footsteps," in CuppaTea Publication's *Humans Wanted* anthology, and her horror story "My Brother Tom," in Flame Tree Publishing's *Supernatural Horror Anthology.* She has also published a blended science fiction and horror story called I am Bridget in Feral Cat Publishers' *Bubble Off Plumb* anthology.

Rose Strickman ("The Rise of Iës") is a sci-fi, fantasy and horror writer living in Seattle, Washington. Her work has appeared in anthologies such as *That Hoodoo, Voodoo That You Do, Sword and Sorceress 32* and *UnCommon Evil,* as well as e-zines such as *Luna Station Quarterly* and *Feed Your Monster.* Check out her Amazon page at amazon.com/author/rosestrickman.

James Toner's ("Cracking Open a Cold One") Friar Clump has previously appeared in the story "Last Call on Lindisfarne" in *Unfit Magazine Vol. 2*. He has also been published in *Asymmetry, Aurora Wolf, Danse Macabre, Ghostlight, Horror Zine, Infernal Ink, Liquid Imagination, Mythaxis, Page & Spine, Suspense,* and *Turnpike* magazines. He also has one novel out from Hellbender Books, and another forthcoming from Beacon Publishing Group.

Deborah Walker ("Captain Clone") grew up in the most English town in the country, but she soon high-tailed it down to London, where she now lives with her partner, Chris, and her two teenage children. Her stories have appeared in *Eldritch Embraces: Putting the Love Back in Lovecraft, Nature's Futures, Lady Churchill's Rosebud Wristlet,* and *The Year's Best SF 18,* and have been translated into more than a dozen languages. Her first novel, a space opera, *As Good as Bad Can Get,* was published in 2017.

ABOUT LAST DAY DOG RESCUE

Last Day is more than just a name, it's the situation all the dogs were faced with. Because of LDDR these wonderful dogs get another chance at life. All dogs coming into their rescue were saved from high-kill animal shelters or being sold for research.

A Little About LDDR:

Last Day Dog Rescue is an ALL volunteer based organization. They do not have a physical location; all of their dogs are placed in the care of foster homes until they are adopted.

The group focuses on rescuing dogs from the "Urgent" list in shelters and pounds across lower Michigan and parts of Ohio with an emphasis on those shelters who euthanize by gas or those shelters who sell the dogs in their care to research labs where they are used for barbaric and most times painful testing and experiments. They hold a special place in their hearts for the big and black dogs, even 'ugly' dogs (whom they don't find ugly at all!) and the special senior dogs. These dogs most often get overlooked and passed up in shelters and pounds everywhere for puppies, small breeds, and the "prettier," lighter colored dogs.

Dogs found in shelters are there for many reasons; some are owner surrenders, strays, cruelty or abuse cases, and some dogs are found abandoned, left to fend for themselves in vacant homes, fields, ditches, and some have even been tied out in the woods and left to starve. Last Day Dog Rescue does not discriminate and feels that each of these dogs, no matter their size, age, color, or the reason they are there, deserve a second chance at life...they help all those they can.

Donations via check and money orders:
    Last Day Dog Rescue
    P.O. Box 51935
    Livonia, MI 48151-5935

Donations also accepted via PayPal:
    http://www.lastdaydogrescue.org/info/

Dragon's Roost Press is the fever dream brainchild of dark speculative fiction author Michael Cieslak. Since 2014, their goal has been to find the best speculative fiction authors and share their work with the public. For more information about Dragon's Roost Press and their publications, please visit:
http://thedragonsroost.net/styled-3/index.html.
A portion of the proceeds from all sales of *Monsters in Spaaaace!* will be donated to the Last Day Dog Rescue Organization.

Hidden Menagerie Volumes One and **Two**
Cryptozoology -- "the study of hidden animals"

The search for and study of animals whose existence or survival is disputed or unsubstantiated

Menagerie: a strange or diverse collection of people or things.

Welcome to the Hidden Menagerie -- two volumes of short fiction involving various cryptozoological creatures. In these volumes you will meet creatures long thought extinct which live on to this day, and others you may have never heard of. A portion of the proceeds of each sale of the *Hidden Menagerie* anthologies benefits the Last Day Dog Rescue Organization.

- Robotic Animals
- Televisions Which Reveal Alternate Universes
- Inanimate Objects Brought to Life
- People Struggling to Survive in Apocalyptic Wastelands
- Sentient Cutlery
- and much, much more

Desolation: 21 Tales for Tails is a collection of dark speculative fiction whose stories all focus on themes of loneliness, isolation, and abandonment.

Enter into strange worlds envisioned by some of the most inventive author writing today.

A portion of the proceeds of each sale of the *Desolation: 21 Tales for Tales* benefits the Last Day Dog Rescue Organization.

Combine the mind splintering horror of the Cthulhu Mythos and the heart shattering portion of that most terrible of emotions -- love -- and what do you have? You have *Eldritch Embraces: Putting the Love Back in Lovecraft*.

This collection of short stories from some of the best authors working in the fields of horror and dark speculative fiction blends romance and Lovecraft in a way which will make you sigh, smile, weep, or leave you the hollow shell of your former self.

A portion of the proceeds of each sale of *Desolation: 21 Tales for Tails* and *Eldritch Embraces: Putting the Love Back in Lovecraft* benefits the Last Day Dog Rescue Organization.

The Maiden's Courage
by Mary Lynne Gibbs

The best man on the pirate ship is a girl named Alex.

Alexandra "Alex" Gardner is the reluctant cabin boy on *The Bloody Maiden*, a ruthless pirate ship run by the charmingly evil Captain Montgomery. The crew is convinced she's a boy, and she hopes it stays that way until she has the chance to avenge the deaths of her mother and brother at the hands of the crew. All goes well until the ship takes a handsome captive. Could her feelings for him ruin her charade? Sebastian Whitley is a young man in love. He sails on his father's ship, trying to find the beautiful girl he's lost. When he's captured by *The Bloody Maiden*, the annoying cabin boy saves his life – and makes it more difficult at the same time. His savior is actually a girl, and if Sebastian doesn't keep quiet, it could mean both their deaths. Together, they have to thwart a mutiny, get revenge, and get off the ship before Alex's secret is revealed. If not, it's the plank for both of them.

Jericho Rising
by Mary Lynne Gibbs

In post-World War III, small town Michigan, a self-proclaimed, violent, and insane High Priestess has taken control, reducing the remaining men to nothing more than slaves and playthings. Jericho, the reluctant leader of the Resistance, must fight her own family to preserve the freedom and equality of all in her care – male and female alike. She's torn between love and duty, and with traitors around every corner, she has no idea who to trust anymore.

Jericho's Redemption
by Mary Lynne Gibbs

The battle is over, but the war has just begun. Jericho returns to the Obsidian camp, only to learn that her sister Candace destroyed it as part of a plot to dismantle the resistance movement that brought down their mother, the High Priestess. The rest of the resistance blames Jericho for the deaths of their friends, but that's the least of her worries. Not only does Jericho now have to right the wrongs her sister has done, she must contend with a few guests to the camp who bring secrets that will change her life forever. Either she'll redeem herself in the eyes of her comrades, or she'll die trying.

Hell Hath No Fury
by Peggy Christie

Ever wonder how you might handle a sabbatical from work? Think the bible told you everything there is to know about the Devil? What if the noises coming from under your child's bed weren't just in his imagination? Crack open *Hell Hath No Fury*, a collection of 21 tales of horror and dark fiction, to learn the answers to these questions. Discover stories of psychotic delusions, ghosts, a murder victim's revenge, and a family brought closer together through torture.

Dark Doorways
by Peggy Christie

Enter this dark mansion of ghastly delights. Each dark doorway opens
to another tale of horror. Some rooms are large banquet halls, others
are tiny servant's quarters. Each contains wondrous, fear inducing
words from master scribe Peggy Christie. If you have the courage, take
hold of one of the latches, open the door......and enter.

Sex, Gore, and Millipedes
by Ken MacGregor

Ken MacGregor, known for pushing boundaries in horror, for shoving the reader outside of their comfort zone, has finally gone too far. *Sex, Gore, and Millipedes* is a collection of the sickest stuff you've ever read. This book will hit your triggers. Hopefully, all of them. You've been warned.

Dead Girls Don't Love
by Sarah Hans

Do you enjoy creepy stories about people who don't quite fit in? Dead Girls Don't Love is a collection of poignant tales for the outsider in all of us.

For a domestic violence victim, there is no life after death--but could there be revenge?

Can a woman returning to her life after 40 years with the fae remember how to be human?

When two Buddhist monks travel to China to spread the dharma, will they survive the unspeakable horror they find instead?

What really happened when the Big Bad Wolf ate the lonely grand-mother living in the woods?

Will the love between two zombified women help them break the spell that binds them in eternal servitude?

And, perhaps most importantly, can an Elder God find true love?

These and many more fascinating questions will be answered on the pages within, if you dare to read them. But be warned: the strange and horrifying realities contained in Dead Girls Don't Love may haunt you long after you close the back cover.

An Ideal Vessel
by Sarah Hans

Not long ago, Zuzanna Uritski was a cleaner at the 1893 Chicago World's Fair, Archibald Campion was the Fair's most imaginative engineer, and Elspeth was a lifeless automaton.

But now? Now they're demon hunters, pursuing an ancient evil that has traveled across universes to take residence in one of history's most famous serial killers.

Travel to an alternate history where no one is safe from demon possession, automatons are self-aware, and the world's greatest hope lies with a clever engineer, a dauntless young woman, and a paladin from another world.

The Midnight Creature Feature Picture Show
by David Hayes

The projector flickers on the cheap silver screen. A blood-curdling scream rips the silence and the glorious 35mm print spills itself out. Ditch the popcorn and don't even think about making out... you ain't ever seen anything like this before! Hold on to your dates, kiddies, as David C Hayes takes you on a trip into his dark imagination with this fiction collection that looks like that corner of the video store your parents warned you about.

Vampires. Zombies. Girl Gangs. Mad Science. You've purchased a ticket to The Midnight Creature Feature Picture Show...and if you don't watch out, you just may get a starring role!